Acclaim for the Novels of Opal Carew

"A blazing-hot erotic romp . . . a must-read for lovers of erotic romance. A fabulously fun and stupendously steamy read for a cold winter's night. This one's so hot, you might need to wear oven mitts while you're reading it!" —*Romance Junkies*

4 stars! "Carew's devilish twists and turns keep the emotional pitch of the story moving from sad to suspenseful to sizzling to downright surprising in the end. . . . The plot moves swiftly and satisfyingly." —*RT BOOKreviews*

"Fresh, exciting, and extremely sexual, with characters you'll fall in love with. Absolutely fantastic!" —*Fresh Fiction*

"The constant and imaginative sexual situations keep the reader's interest along with likable characters with emotional depth. Be prepared for all manner of coupling, including groups, exhibitionism, voyeurism, and same-sex unions. . . . I recommend *Swing* for the adventuresome who don't mind singeing their senses." —*Regency Reader*

"Carew pulls off another scorcher . . . she knows how to write a love scene that takes her reader to dizzying heights of pleasure." —*My Romance Story*

"So much fun to read . . . The story line is fast-paced with wonderful humor." —*Genre Go Round Reviews*

"A great book . . . Ms. Carew has wonderful imagination." —*Night Owl Reviews*

"Opal Carew brings erotic romance to a whole new level . . . she writes a compelling romance and sets your senses on fire with her love scenes!" —*Reader to Reader*

Pleasure Bound

Opal Carew

St. Martin's Griffin

New York

PLEASURE BOUND. Copyright © 2010 by Elizabeth Batten-Carew. All rights reserved. Printed in the United States of America. For information, address St. Martin's Press, 175 Fifth Avenue, New York, N.Y. 10010.

www.stmartins.com

Library of Congress Cataloging-in-Publication Data

Carew, Opal.
    Pleasure bound / Opal Carew. — 1st ed.
        p. cm.
    ISBN 978-0-312-58015-5
    1. Bisexual men—Fiction.   2. Bisexuality—Fiction.   3. Triangles (Interpersonal relations)—Fiction.   4. Sexual dominance and submission—Fiction.   I. Title.
    PR9199.4.C367P54 2010
    813'.6—dc22

                                                            2010037248

First Edition: December 2010

10 9 8 7 6 5 4 3 2 1

To Mark,
Matt, and Jason,
with all
my love

Acknowledgments

As always, thanks to Rose and Emily, for your continued support and hard work. You both go above and beyond and I really appreciate it.

Thanks to Mark and Colette, for their insights, helpful comments, and encouragement.

I'd like to thank Tom, Vimala and Rita, and many other helpful folks at H. B. Fenn, for helping get the word out about my books. Thanks to Nathalie Atkinson at the *National Post,* for the great article about me. Loved it!

Pleasure Bound

One

Images of the sexy bad boy from the next cottage haunted Marie as she stepped outside onto the wooden deck and glanced across the tranquil lake. She took a deep breath of fresh country air as she walked down the stairs and headed toward the water. She wanted to sit on the beach and enjoy the sunrise in quiet solitude before other cottagers were up and about. Maybe take a refreshing dip in the calm water.

Of course, if she happened to run into the gorgeous guy from next door, that would be quite fine.

She liked his name. Zeke. It was different from the names of the other men she dated. Of course, Zeke was a *completely* different type of man. The men she dated were very nice. Dependable. Confident. Pleasant. Although she'd only spoken with Zeke briefly, and it had been friendly and pleasant, she could sense in him an aura of . . . danger. No, that wasn't quite right. She felt safe around him. Protected almost. It was more as if he would like to . . . dominate her.

That he would take control and totally master her. Which sent tingles through her.

It wasn't anything he'd said. In fact, it was probably more a matter of how she reacted to his extremely masculine presence. And a result of their first encounter.

Marie's friend Sylvia had invited her to the cottage for the Labor Day weekend. They'd arrived last night and had been enjoying a quiet evening under the stars roasting marshmallows and talking. As much as they could with a wild party going on at the next cottage, with its tough-looking crowd. Marie had never seen so many tattoos and body piercings in one group of people. As the evening progressed, the music had gotten louder and the partygoers more drunk. When tempers flared and a fight broke out, Zeke had shown up out of nowhere.

At first, Marie and Sylvia had thought Zeke was one of them, in his tight jeans and black T-shirt, a tattoo along his arm and the two spike piercings in his eyebrow, but he'd turned out to be more like a knight in shining armor. He'd settled them down, promising to bust their butts if they acted up again. He had an air of authority that they couldn't ignore.

Nor could she. A knight in shining armor was nice, and she was glad he'd been on hand, but the bad-boy aura was a total turn-on. He'd stopped by their cottage afterward to see if they were okay, explaining he was in the cottage two doors down. He'd come to the lake to enjoy some solitude. They'd invited him in for a drink and chatted for a half hour, then he'd headed out.

She sighed as she walked past a clump of bushes toward the secluded patch of beach Sylvia had shown her yesterday. Birds chirped in the trees, the water swished against the shore, and the haunting cry of a loon sounded in the distance.

Her beach towel draped over her shoulder, she slipped between the bushes to the quiet inlet . . . then stopped cold. A man was wading into the water. He had a large tattoo of a fierce-looking dragon arched along his back, another tattoo coiling along his arm and over his shoulder, and a black tribal band around the other bicep.

And . . . he was completely butt naked!

And a fine butt it was. She couldn't help watching the muscles ripple as he stepped forward. As if sensing her presence, he stopped and turned around. She felt her cheeks burning at having been caught ogling him, but he simply smiled, revealing beautiful white teeth. That square jaw and those rich olive green eyes . . . it was Zeke.

How could she not have recognized the golden serpentine body of a dragon tattooed along his upper arm and disappearing over his shoulder? Of course, she had been busy admiring those hard, tight buttocks.

The whole time they'd chatted at the cottage last night, Marie had wondered what the rest of that tattoo, which had disappeared under the sleeve of his T-shirt, looked like. In fact, she'd wondered what it would be like to see him naked, as well as what it would feel like to have his lips pressed hard to hers. Now, she knew. At least, the naked part.

As he watched her, his cock hardened and rose. Man, his butt was fine, but his cock was absolutely sensational! Enormous. She'd love to . . .

"Join me." His words, almost matter-of-fact, held a spine-tingling tone of authority.

Mesmerized, she dropped her towel and walked toward him. Tremors rippled across her flesh as she got closer. He held out his hand and she took it, then he tugged her toward him and drew her into his arms. She sucked in a breath as her bikini-clad body came in contact with his hard masculine body. Naked flesh to naked flesh. He smiled a devilish grin, then captured her lips.

His mouth, firm and confident, moved on hers with quiet authority. When his tongue brushed her lips she opened and he invaded her firmly and thoroughly. Breathless, she stepped back and stared at him in awe. He scooped her up and carried her into the water, his lips merging with hers again.

It was sweet heaven. He was so . . . masculine. So . . . powerful. Yet she felt totally safe with him.

The water caressed first her bottom, then more of her . . . cool . . . but she barely noticed. As he continued deeper, the water surrounding them, he released her legs and she curled around until she faced him, then she wrapped her legs around him. His hard cock nestled between them, pressing against her. Oh God, she wanted this man. She didn't care that they'd just met. That she never had sex with a man until at least five dates. She wanted him. Here and now. What was wrong with being a little wild and crazy every now and again? Why couldn't she do something totally out of character?

She reached down to her bikini bottom and untied the strings holding it together at the sides, then tugged the scrap of fabric away. He grinned at the obvious invitation. His fingers slid down her belly and found her wet passage, then glided inside. Oh God, his touch felt so good.

She wrapped her hand around his thick hard cock and stroked, then pressed it to her slit, sending her hormones spinning. His cock glided over her slick flesh but did not slide into her. Thank heavens, since she'd seemed to have lost her mind and thrown caution to the wind. His hard cock rubbed against her, stroking her clit, driving her wild.

"You are gorgeous and incredible." He nibbled her ear as his fingers found her clit and stroked. Wild pleasure throbbed through her.

His fingers slid inside her again, his thumb continuing to stroke her sensitive little button. His lips played against her neck as she gasped in pleasure over his shoulder. His thumb vibrated against her clit and a torrent of blissful energy surged through her. She moaned, clinging to him as the orgasm washed over her.

He captured her lips and kissed her soundly.

"Sweet thing, you are something else."

He carried her back to shore and lay her down on a towel stretched out on the sand. The seagulls cried and the songbirds chirped in the trees. He prowled over her and stripped off her bathing suit top. When he drew her hard, cold nipple into his mouth, she gasped. He sucked as his fingers toyed with her other nipple.

She ran her fingers through his black shoulder-length hair, enjoying the total decadence of the moment. The pleasure intensified, spiraling through her, sending her hormones churning.

"Oh God, take me," she pleaded.

He grinned, then she felt his hard, hot cock stroke along her slit again.

"Have any condoms?" he asked.

She shook her head. "No, but I'm on the Pill."

"I've been tested," he said. "What about you?"

She nodded.

He grinned and surged forward, impaling her with his

hot, hard shaft. His cockhead moved deeper inside her. On and on. Stretching her.

Once he was fully immersed, he lay for a moment, smiling at her.

"This is not the last time I want to do this, sweet thing. I promise you that."

Then he drew back, his wide cockhead dragging along the walls of her vagina in an intensely pleasurable stroke, then he drove deep again. She moaned. Oh God, she'd never had a man so deep inside her. She stroked her hands across his broad muscular shoulders as he drew out again, her gaze locked on his intense olive green eyes, then she clung to him as he thrust inside. Then he drew back and thrust deep again.

She couldn't believe this sexy, overwhelmingly masculine man was making love to her. Thrusting his big cock into her. She tightened around him, intensifying the pleasure of his thrusting. She moaned as waves of pleasure washed through her, then exploded in a vibrant, incredible orgasm.

He thrust hard again and groaned as he released inside her.

As she lay beneath him catching her breath, his big body covering hers, his big cock still fully embedded in her, she sighed. Following her instincts certainly had its rewards.

Today was the day.

Ty turned the key in the lock and opened the door. As soon as he stepped inside, he heard a thump in the kitchen followed by a series of smaller thumps as the little four-legged critter with pointed ears trotted toward him, its quizzical green gaze locked on Ty.

People always thought cats were such quiet creatures, but this little guy sounded like a small elephant, despite his sleek black form. Ty scooped up the animal and tucked its furry body against his chest while stroking under its chin and was rewarded with an agreeable rumbling. He'd never realized how much he liked hearing a cat purr. Or feeling one nudging its head against him, demanding attention.

"Hey, fur-ball. Do you miss Marie?"

The cat tipped its head in the way it did when it wanted Ty to scratch the side of its chin. Ty scratched the sweet spot as he walked into the kitchen.

"She'll be back tonight."

He placed the cat on the tile floor and retrieved the can opener from the drawer beside the sink, then opened the last can of food from the supply Marie had left on the granite counter. At the sound of the can opening, the cat rubbed against his legs, meowing loudly. Once Ty placed the bowl on the floor, the critter began eating noisily. He poured himself a glass of orange juice, then leaned against the counter and watched the cat devour its meal.

He'd never really liked cats before—too damned snooty—but then, he'd never really gotten to know a cat before.

And then there was its owner. *Marie.* From the first moment he'd met her six months ago, he'd known he was in love with her.

Problem was, she was already dating someone. Until a month ago.

When that idiot had walked out on her and broken her heart, Ty had been there. A shoulder to cry on. Every day for the past four weeks, he'd wanted to drag her into his arms and kiss her breathless, to show her exactly how he felt about her, but he hadn't. She'd needed a friend and that's what he'd been.

But now was the time to move forward. To tell her how he felt about her. Not completely, of course. She would probably run away screaming. With a woman like Marie, he needed to move slowly. He needed to be subtle. Tell her he was interested in her. Ask her out. Gently coax her into falling in love with him.

And keep the beast inside him in careful check.

Every time he closed his eyes, every time he thought about holding her in his arms, her warm curvy body nestled against his, his body reacted with a fierce passion. His groin flooded with heat and his cock grew as rigid as a nightstick. Next came images of her arms bound above her head, her ankles held wide apart, sending his senses whirling. He longed to tear off her clothes, then explore every silky inch of her well-proportioned body.

He trembled as the natural Dominant in him longed to command her to drop to her knees and free his cock, then draw it into her sweet mouth and suck it deep. To hear her call him *Master*. He almost groaned out loud at the thought.

But he wouldn't do that to Marie.

Five years ago, it would have been a different story. Although he'd left behind the young ruffian from the streets, he'd allowed himself to keep that side of his nature in the bedroom. Dominating his women. Capturing them. Binding them. *Mastering* them. Whatever it was that appealed to each woman. All role-playing, of course. And every woman left quite happy with the experience.

But after the incident with his *supposed* best friend, he'd decided to leave that part of his life behind. Too many links to people better forgotten.

At a sound from the hallway, he jerked around, then smiled as he saw a sleepy-looking Marie leaning against the door frame, her shiny brown hair deliciously mussed and her sky blue eyes only partially open. She wore an oversized yet very enticing T-shirt, which draped nicely over her sensational body, and revealed most of her long shapely legs. Clearly, she wore nothing underneath but a thong. Or maybe regular panties, but he preferred to believe it was a thong. Or nothing. All he really knew for sure was no bra. His gaze dropped to her puckering nipples and his heart rate doubled.

"Ty?"

He jerked his gaze back to her face. Luckily, she'd been yawning so she hadn't noticed his distraction.

"Here to feed the critter," he said.

She glanced at the fur-ball, still munching away at its dinner.

"Right." She crouched down and stroked the cat, who murmured then returned to eating. "How you doing, Jade?"

"Seems to be more impressed with the food than you."

"Yeah, we did the affection thing last night. Now everything's back to normal as far as she's concerned."

Marie grabbed the orange juice from the fridge and filled a small glass, then took a sip. She leaned back against the counter beside him.

"Why'd you and Sylvia decide to cut the weekend short?"

She shrugged. "I just felt like getting back."

Her evasive manner told him there was clearly more to it than that.

Whatever the reason, she was here now, and he was anxious to move forward with his plan to win her heart.

Two

"Marie, there's something I want to talk to you about," Ty said. "Do you want to go out and grab some breakfast? Or I could whip us up something here."

"Oh, uh . . ." She glanced toward the doorway. "It's not really a good time."

He grinned. "Why? You have someone in the bedroom?"

At the dark flush staining her cheeks, his gut clenched. Good God, she had a man in there?

"Thanks for feeding Jade while I was gone." She wouldn't meet his gaze as she headed for the doorway. "I'll talk to you later."

She disappeared down the hall. Back to her lover.

God damn it! He couldn't believe it. He'd waited too damn long!

Marie fled to her bedroom. Damn, what must Ty think of her? Jumping into bed with a guy she hardly knew. Bringing him back to her apartment to spend the night.

Ty was such a nice guy. He was probably shocked by her wild behavior. Not that he'd ever tell her that. He was a good friend. And sexy as all get-out. She'd often fantasized about sampling that hot body of his. In fact, daydreams had turned into hot erotic dreams where she'd woken up tangled in sweaty sheets tempted to bound down the hall and knock on his door with every intent of seducing him within an inch of his life.

Ever since she'd broken up with Everett, she'd hoped Ty would ask her out.

But he hadn't. And it was just as well. He was just like every other guy she'd ever dated. Pleasant. Caring. *Nice.* But after being with Zeke, she realized what she really wanted was hot, hard, and dominating. A real bad-boy type. Someone who could teach her what a bad girl she could be. Maybe even *punish* her for it. She slipped into the bedroom and closed the door.

"I was wondering where you'd gone."

At Zeke's sleep-raspy voice, she gazed at him. His whisker-roughened face and tousled dark hair made her want to climb right back into his arms. His lazy green eyes perused her body, singeing her nerve endings. Her nipples pushed forward and her insides ached with need.

"I heard someone in the kitchen," she said.

Suddenly alert, he pushed himself up in bed, ready to bound into action.

"Don't stress. It was just my neighbor coming in to feed my cat."

He relaxed, then smiled. "Ahhh, the little fur-ball."

"Her name's Jade."

"Noted." He patted the mattress beside him. "Now, how about you come back to bed."

11

She smiled impishly. "Oh, I don't know. I thought I'd get dressed and go out shopping."

"Oh, really?" He tossed the covers aside to display his muscular naked body, an impressive erection towering over his tight abs. "That's too bad. I have this little problem I was hoping you could help with."

Her gaze locked on his enormous, oh-so-hard cock. She wanted to touch it. To taste it. To glide down on it until it filled her so full she thought she'd burst.

Slowly, she strolled toward the bed. "What kind of problem?"

He grabbed her wrist and playfully tugged her toward him. She fell across his solid chest and his arm curled around her, holding her tight to his body. He kissed her, his firm lips mastering hers. Then he rolled her over. She lay with her back propped on the pillows as he prowled over her and captured her between his knees. She stroked the brightly colored, sexy dragon tattoo covering the left side of his chest.

"My cock wants to be somewhere soft and warm." He took her hand and kissed the palm. "Like in your hands." He kissed her lips again. "Or your mouth. Or . . ."

His eyes twinkled and her heart stammered. His fingers stroked down her stomach, glided between her legs, then straight into her slick opening.

". . . in your hot little pussy."

Her insides melted. He stroked a few times and intense need blazed through her. She wanted him to thrust into her right now.

He wrapped his hands around her hips and tugged her downward until she was flat on her back, then he impaled her with one stroke. She groaned at the exquisite sensation of his big cock driving into her.

Instead of pulling back and beginning a series of thrusts, he stayed put, deep inside her, and grinned.

"About this neighbor of yours . . . maybe we should invite her to join us." He kissed the soft skin under her chin, then nuzzled her neck. "I'd love to watch you go down on another sweet little pussy."

She quivered at the thought. He could be so wicked.

"My neighbor's a guy."

He raised an eyebrow. "Really? Even better. Let's get him in here. It would be sexy to watch him fuck you."

Her cheeks burned. "You're awful." She could almost believe he'd do it.

He pulled back and glided into her again.

"You wouldn't like that? Your handsome neighbor holding you? He is handsome, right?"

An image flashed through her mind. Of Ty's warm brown eyes. His straight sandy brown hair, which was a little long on top so it sometimes fell in spikes over his forehead. His square jaw and full, sexy lips that she always had to fight the urge to kiss.

She nodded, without thinking.

"His cock gliding into you. And me watching from the chair in the corner."

She shook her head. "You're a crazy man."

"Then I'd come up behind and . . ." He slid his hand under her body and stroked her buttocks, then glided along the path between them, then toyed with her opening. He teased it, then pressed his fingertip in a little. "I'd push in, too. Right here."

His finger went in a little deeper. She wriggled at the unaccustomed yet erotic invasion.

"Then you'd have two guys taking you . . . enjoying you."

His finger slipped free and he pulled back, then drove his cock into her again. "That's a pretty hot fantasy for most women."

She moaned at his words as much as at the feel of his cock gliding deep inside her.

He leaned in to her ear. "Think about it, Marie. Close your eyes and pretend your hot neighbor is thrusting into you right now."

Her eyelids fell closed and she couldn't help herself. *Ty's* arms were around her. *Ty's* cock gliding into her.

Zeke thrust deep and hard and she cried out.

"He's a good lover, isn't he? You love his cock thrusting into you." He kissed her neck. "And I love watching."

He thrust several more times and she moaned.

"What's his name?" Zeke asked.

"Ty."

He thrust again. "Say it again. Louder."

"Ty."

Zeke thrust again and again. "Keep saying it."

"Ty."

A hard thrust.

"Oh . . . Ty!"

Thoughts of Ty . . . snippets from her dreams . . . Ty making love to her . . . driving his cock into her. Excitement quivered through her.

"Think about me watching you, while this guy fucks you hard. Imagine me behind you, driving my cock into your tight little ass."

She sucked in a breath as his coarse words sent her imagination whirling. She could almost feel his cock pressing against her back opening, then pushing inside. As one cock drove into her vagina, the imaginary one drove into her from behind. Oh, she longed to feel that for real.

"Two cocks thrusting into you," Zeke murmured as he stroked her hair back. "Two men making love to you. You'd like that, wouldn't you."

She nodded, then moaned as his finger stroked her clit. Then a mind-shattering orgasm blasted through her and she wailed as she shot into ecstasy.

"Oh God, sweet thing, you are so hot!" He groaned then exploded within her.

Ty finished his juice, then stroked the fur-ball once and headed for the door.

"Ty."

He glanced toward the hallway. Had Marie called his name?

"Oh . . . Ty!"

Hell, she was in there making out with some other guy. His hands balled into fists. Yet, she called out Ty's name. Was it a slip on her part, or was the other guy named Ty, too?

Not likely. Ty grinned. So it looked like Marie had feelings for him. One thing was for sure, if it was a slip, this new romance of hers had probably just come to an abrupt end.

As Zeke held this über sexy woman close to him, he couldn't believe his luck. She was so hot, yet so incredibly sweet. Definitely not his usual kind of woman. But she brought out a protective side of him.

He wanted to keep her safe, but at the same time he wanted to push her to the limit. To command her and control her until she burst from the sheer pleasure of it. Because he could sense that she wanted to be Dominated. She'd probably love it if he tied her up until she was totally helpless, then manhandled every delectable inch of her incredibly sexy body. Or if he snapped a collar around her neck and commanded her to pleasure him completely.

He kissed her forehead as she snuggled her head against his chest, thinking about the pleasures he would introduce her to in the coming weeks. Because he had no intention of letting go of this woman.

Marie sighed as Zeke stroked her head. The curly hairs on his chest tickled her nose as she nuzzled her cheek against his solid, muscle-ridged flesh.

She had totally gotten into it when Zeke instructed—no, commanded—her to imagine Ty making love to her. Calling out Ty's name . . . thinking of his cock filling her . . . really made her feel like Ty was the one making love to her.

Even now, she longed for Ty's arms around her, even though she currently lay naked and wrapped around Zeke's hot, hard body.

Ty was solid and dependable. He was the kind of guy she usually dated. And he was super sexy and gorgeous. But Zeke was wild and sexy and crazy, in a good way. Exciting. And different. And maybe that's what she needed right now. Different. Ty was a safe choice, but probably not a good choice. After all, she'd always dated his type and the relationships always ended. After a few months, she always ended up feeling restless and eager to move on. Which meant his type probably wasn't the right type for her, and she didn't want to risk messing up a great friendship. Not that she really thought Zeke would lead to happily-ever-after, but he would help her break out of her rut and figure out what she really wanted in a man.

All she knew right now was that tame wasn't it. She wanted someone who would push her limits. Let her get a little wild and funky. From everything she knew about Ty, that wasn't him.

Marie grabbed her second earring and slid it into the hole in her ear, then raced toward the living room to answer the door. A second knock sounded. She glanced at the clock on the DVD player. Seven forty-four. She still had to finish putting on her makeup, make breakfast, and get out the door in time to catch her bus at eight thirty.

She peered out the peephole. Ty stood on the other side of the door.

She sucked in a breath as heat suffused her cheeks. What did he think of her after correctly guessing that she'd had a man in her bed yesterday morning? He knew she hadn't been dating anyone before the long weekend, thus the man in her bed was basically a stranger.

She pulled open the door.

"Good morning." She smiled.

He smiled at her. She couldn't help noticing how handsome he looked in his work clothes. His broad shoulders filled out his royal blue shirt quite nicely, and his dove gray dress pants accentuated his trim waist and long legs. No doubt, he would complete the outfit with a tie just before he left for his job as a software architect.

His sandy hair was neatly combed, but a spike or two already trailed down his forehead.

"Hi. I wasn't sure if you remembered that it's Tuesday, with the long weekend and all. Breakfast is almost ready."

"Oh . . . I didn't know you still wanted to do that, now that my course is over and all."

In July and August, she'd taken a sculpting class on Monday evenings which kept her out until eleven o'clock, which meant she got to bed an hour later than usual on a work night. Ty had offered to cook breakfast for her on Tuesdays to allow her to sleep an extra half hour. It had become a wonderful routine she'd looked forward to, both because of the great food—he was a sensational cook—and the great company.

"I like our Tuesday mornings. We don't have to give it up just because your course is over." He grinned. "And you can't abandon me this morning. I made a variation of your favorite, eggs Benedict, but I replaced the bacon with thin slices of smoked salmon. The recipe calls it Norwegian eggs. And I made the hollandaise sauce from scratch."

Her mouth watered. She loved anything with hollandaise sauce, and Ty's homemade sauce was to die for.

"You had me at 'breakfast is almost ready.'"

She followed him down the hall to his apartment. As always, his place was spotless. His brown leather couch and chair, solid dark oak furniture, and minimal use of bold artwork gave his apartment a masculine feel. She followed him into the dining room where the table was all set with his red and black mugs and cutlery.

A thermos jug of coffee sat on the middle of the table. He poured her a cup as she sat down. She added cream and stirred as he went into the kitchen, which was open to the dining room, and grabbed two English muffins from the toaster. He dropped them onto the two plates on the counter, then assembled the other ingredients. She watched in eager anticipation as he spooned the hollandaise sauce over the eggs, then returned to the table and placed the delectable meal in front of her.

"It looks amazing." She cut a piece and took a bite. The textures of the creamy sauce, smooth eggs, flaky salmon, and toasty bread combined in her mouth to produce a delightful sensation.

She swallowed and smiled. "You're an amazing cook."

He sipped his coffee and smiled. "I aim to please."

Soft rock music playing in the background and bright sunlight shining in the large window overlooking the city added to the pleasant ambiance.

"It looks like it's going to be a gorgeous day," she said.

"It's going up to seventy-eight today. Too bad the weekend's over." He took a sip of coffee. "Did you have a good time at the cottage?"

"Oh, yeah, it was fun."

He raised an eyebrow. "I bet. You met someone new, I take it."

She stopped cutting into her eggs and glanced at him. "Um, yeah, I did. He was at the next cottage. We . . . sort of hit it off."

"He must be pretty special. You broke your five-date rule."

Damn, she wished she'd never told him about that. When he'd helped her through her breakup with Everett, they'd shared tequila shots along with thoughts on romance. He had told her he hadn't dated for a while, that he was waiting for the right woman so he could settle into a stable long-term relationship. She had told him about her five-date rule. She'd also told him that she always dated Mr.-Nice-Guy types, but there never seemed to be any passion, and she found herself longing to move on and find a guy who sent her senses—and her heart—into overdrive.

He'd patted her hand and assured her that Mr. Right was out there for her. At the comforting warmth of his touch and his intense gaze boring into her, sending her senses spiraling, she'd searched those warm brown eyes of his, overwhelmed by an almost irresistible urge to kiss him. In fact, she'd been sure he'd wanted to kiss her, too, and she'd found herself leaning in close, waiting for him to capture her lips, her eyelids almost falling shut.

But he hadn't kissed her. He'd politely leaned back, as if not noticing her intent.

She'd almost made a total fool of herself.

"Yeah, well . . . sometimes rules are made to be broken. Especially when you meet a super hot guy at a friend's cottage, with only two days to make a move."

His eyebrows arched upward. "So you made a move on him?"

"Well, in a way. He was skinny-dipping and he . . . sort of caught me watching him."

It felt weird talking with him about this, but only because of that almost kiss. Before that had happened, they'd always talked with an easygoing openness. Sometimes they'd discussed what they found attractive in the opposite sex. Like one of the times they'd gone running together and she'd pointed out the guy with the nice tight set of buns running ahead of them.

He'd point out attractive women and what he liked about them, too. She'd been surprised at first. He didn't go for the blatantly sexy blonde who had crossed their path several times. He liked brunettes with slim figures and good muscle tone rather than bouncy and voluptuous women. In fact, women who looked a lot like Marie. She often wondered if he'd just been trying to build up her confidence. Since he'd come to know her, he'd picked up on her lack of confidence in her attractiveness.

Ty was such a nice guy. It would be just like him to do that.

"So you jumped his bones?" Ty asked, raising an eyebrow.

Despite Ty's teasing tone, Marie sensed an undercurrent she couldn't quite place.

"Do you disapprove?" she asked.

Three

Marie respected Ty and didn't want him to think badly of her, but what was done was done.

Ty's gaze locked on hers. "Of course not." He touched her cheek. The gentle brush of his fingertips sent ripples of awareness through her. "I would never disapprove of you . . . or anything you do."

Her pulse pounded in her ears and her breathing seemed slow and far away. All that existed for her at that moment were his warm brown eyes gazing into her soul. And his tender touch on her cheek.

Then he drew his hand away and everything returned to normal.

She drew in a deep breath.

Oh God, why did she have to feel this intense attraction for Ty? Another Mr. Nice Guy. If she got involved with him, it would only end like all her other relationships. Then this wonderful friendship they shared would also end, and she so didn't want that to happen.

Falling prey to her attraction to him would be exactly the wrong thing to do. Bad for her, and bad for him.

It might have been impetuous leaping into a relationship with Zeke . . . even worse allowing it to continue beyond a weekend fling . . . but she was glad she had. He was opening her up to a whole new world of sensuality and she wanted to embrace that exhilarating newness.

Since Mr. Nice Guys hadn't worked for her, maybe a bad boy like Zeke was exactly what she needed.

At lunch, Marie decided to get outside to enjoy the warm sunny day. She walked to the park near her office and sat on a bench by the river to eat her sandwich.

A cyclist rode by and she glanced across the glittering water. The bright sunshine, the clear blue sky, the leaves rustling in the trees, all reminded her of being at the cottage this past weekend. With Zeke.

Images of Zeke filled her mind. His devilish smile. The tattoo that trailed down his spine. The way his dark hair, a little too long on top, tended to trail over one eye, and how he often tossed it aside with a flick of his hand.

A child's laughter drew her attention back to the park and she smiled as she watched a toddler glide down a slide into his mother's arms at the nearby play structure. She wished she could sit here all day, but a quick glance at her watch told her it was time to return to the office.

She sat down at her desk and dropped her purse in her drawer, then glanced at her e-mail inbox. In the list of unread messages, she noticed one from dragon.zeke. Her heart fluttered as she clicked on the e-mail to open it.

Okay if I stop by tonight? We can do pizza.

She smiled. Zeke hadn't said anything about wanting to see her again when he'd left yesterday evening and a part of her had feared he'd just walked out of her life.

She noticed by the green dot beside his name that he was online now. She opened a chat window.

me: Pizza tonight would be great. What time?

She waited a moment, then the message "Dragon.Zeke is typing . . ." appeared in the chat box.

Dragon.Zeke: What time do you get home from work?
me: About 6.
Dragon.Zeke: Let's play it by ear.
me: Okay. See you tonight.

For the rest of the afternoon, she felt lighter than air. She'd be seeing Zeke again tonight!

Finally, five o'clock rolled around and she grabbed her purse and headed for the bus. She boarded the crowded bus and got off at her stop. About ten minutes later, she hurried into the lobby of her apartment building, then unlocked her mailbox and pulled out several letters. Mostly bills.

She summoned the elevator, wondering when Zeke would arrive. As the doors whooshed open, someone stepped up behind her and followed her into the elevator. She turned around and came face-to-face with Zeke.

"Oh, hello," she stammered. She pressed "17."

God, he looked *bad* . . . in a very good way. Torn blue jeans with a chain cascading from one belt loop to another, then hanging straight down, punctuated by a silver skull. A black muscle shirt exposed his bulging shoulder and arm muscles, as well as the delicious dragon tattoo on his upper arm. Not to mention the two metal spikes through his eyebrow.

He smiled seductively and winked, then leaned against the mirrored elevator wall. Another woman raced toward the closing doors and Marie pressed the Open button. The doors opened again. The woman stepped inside and nodded to Marie, then glanced at Zeke, her gaze shifting from his tattoos to the chain hanging at his hip. She stepped to the opposite corner, clearly uncomfortable with Zeke's presence, and pressed "3."

The doors closed and the elevator started upward. It stopped on the third floor and the woman disappeared. The door closed and the elevator continued upward.

Now she was alone in the small space with Zeke. Soon they'd be inside her apartment and he'd be touching her and . . . The vibration of the moving elevator matched the quivers inside her. Zeke pushed himself forward and pulled a key from his pocket, then unlocked a door on the control panel. He pushed a button and the elevator halted.

"What are you doing?" she asked, knowing damn well what he was doing.

He turned toward her, his eyes blazing with heat.

"I'm going to fuck you. Right here. Right now."

Goose bumps quivered along her flesh.

She licked her lips. "We . . . can't do that here."

He stepped toward her, and she stepped back until she was pressed into the corner, his hard muscular body against hers. He grasped her face in a gentle hold and stared into her eyes.

"We can and we will."

The authority in his voice sent thrilling excitement shuddering through her.

"Yes," she said.

"Yes, what?"

"I . . . uh . . ."

" 'Yes, Master' is the appropriate response."

Oh God. Her pulse quickened.

"Yes, *Master.*"

A slow smile spread across his face.

"That's more like it. Now open your blouse for me."

She hesitated as she glanced up at the corner of the elevator, wondering if there were security cameras.

"Now." His sharp tone sent her heart pounding in exhilaration.

She released the buttons. Quickly.

His gaze followed her fingers, watching the blouse part to reveal her breasts, encased in a simple white lace bra.

"Ah." He stroked his finger along the top edge of one lacy cup. "So virginal."

His finger dipped under the lace on one side and drew it downward, then tucked the fabric under her swelling breast. The nipple thrust forward. He stared at the dusky rosebud and smiled, then stroked his finger over it. She moaned at the exquisite sensation. He bared her other breast in a similar fashion, then cupped his hands under her aching mounds and stroked the nipples with his thumbs.

When she thought she couldn't stand the intense sensations rushing through her another moment, he leaned down and lapped at her hard nipple, then drew it into his mouth, and sucked hard. She gasped, clutching his head tight to her.

At the feel of his mouth on her other nipple, she threw her head back and moaned. He grasped her face, then captured her mouth, driving his tongue inside, pulsing against hers in a passionate dance.

"You are so damned sexy," he murmured, his voice hoarse.

He turned her around to face the mirrored wall. She sucked in a breath at the sight of her naked breasts, the dark rose nipples thrusting forward, reflected in the mirrored wall. He cupped her breasts in his big hands, then stroked them. Her nipples peaked into his palms and her vagina ached with need. His thumbs circled over her hard nubs again and a spike of pleasure jolted through her. Her vaginal muscles contracted.

As she watched, he drew her skirt upward, slowly, baring her thighs a little at a time, then he glided his hand up between them. She opened her legs, wanting to feel his touch higher. Her insides melted with need. She could feel the slickness between her legs.

He eased her back toward him and his leg pushed forward until her weight pressed against it, the heat of his hard muscular thigh burning through her. He kissed behind her ear and his warm breath whispered against her cheek.

"Stroke your breasts," he commanded.

Her hands glided up her ribs to her breasts, then she stroked over her hard tips with her fingers. She toyed with the hard nubs, stroking, then squeezing.

"Oh yeah." His olive green eyes blazed with heat as he watched her.

"Now turn around and suck my cock."

A shiver ran down her spine as she turned around and knelt before him, the bulge in his pants quite obvious, then tugged his zipper down. She reached inside his worn jeans and wrapped her fingers around his hot, hard cock.

She drew out his purple-veined shaft and licked the tip.

He sucked in a breath. "Do you like my cock in your hand?"

"Yes," she murmured. "Master," she added quickly.

"Good girl. Suck it deep."

She wrapped her lips around him, then drove forward, relaxing her throat and ignoring the gag reflex. She drew back and sucked, her cheeks hollowing, then she dove deep again.

"Oh God, you're good at that."

She bobbed forward and back while he stroked her shoulder-length hair from her face. She loved the feel of his big hard cock in her mouth, stroking her tongue, gliding into her throat. She paused for a moment, concentrating on his cockhead. Tightening her lips around him, she dragged her teeth lightly over the ridge of the corona, then swirled her tongue around the smooth surface. Then she dove deep again. Her fingers slid underneath and she cupped his balls, then stroked them gently.

"Stop," he commanded.

She drew away, releasing his hard shaft from her mouth, and stared up at him. He drew her upward, then pressed her against the wall. He tugged her skirt higher and pressed his knee between her legs. She opened her thighs and he stroked over her mound, then slid under the crotch of her panties, finding her slick opening. He grabbed her panties and tugged them down her legs, then off. He stood up and pressed his body tight to hers, his breath searing her.

"I'm going to fuck you now."

She nodded, hot need blazing through her.

He wrapped his hand around his cock and pressed the head to her opening, then he drove forward. She gasped at the exquisite invasion.

He grasped her thighs and lifted. She wrapped her legs around him, allowing his cock to press deeper.

"Oh God, fuck me, Master."

He drew back then thrust forward, back then forward. She clung to him as he drove into her again and again, his body compressing the air from her with each thrust. Enhancing the highly erotic experience.

He was fucking her in an elevator! How sexy was that!

Waves of intense pleasure flooded through her. She gasped as his hard cock drove into her again and again.

"I . . ."

He drove deep and she gasped again.

"I'm going to come."

He thrust harder.

"Do it, baby," he said. "Let me hear you come."

She moaned as the blissful pleasure erupted through her, her nerve endings exploding in ecstasy.

He groaned and tensed against her, then pulsed inside her.

She leaned against him, gasping for air. He kissed the top of her head, then drew back. His big cock slipped from inside her.

He grinned. "I bet you've worked up an appetite for that pizza."

She tugged down her skirt and he helped her fasten her blouse buttons before he returned to the control panel and pressed another button that started the elevator again.

"Where did you get the key?" she asked.

He shrugged. "I have a friend who knows a guy."

She arched an eyebrow. Clearly, Zeke had some interesting friends.

As the elevator moved upward, Zeke leaned over and picked something up from the floor.

"Here, you might want these."

She stared at his hand to see her white panties. Her cheeks

flushed at the thought she'd almost left them lying on the elevator floor. When she reached for them, he closed his fingers around them and tucked them into his pocket and winked.

"A little souvenir."

Souvenir? Did that mean he figured their relationship wouldn't last very long? Did he just consider her a short-term distraction?

As soon as Marie opened the door, Jade trotted up to her and meowed.

"Hey there, little fella." Zeke picked up Jade and stroked her, immediately triggering a loud rumbling purr. "How about I feed the fur-ball—"

"Jade." Why couldn't guys keep track of a cat's name or gender?

"Right." He stroked behind Jade's ears and she tipped her head up, her eyelids falling closed. The purring got louder. "I'll go feed Jade and order the pizza, while you change."

Marie went into her bedroom and changed from her work clothes, then returned to the living room and settled beside Zeke. Jade draped herself over Zeke's lap until the pizza arrived, then Marie and Zeke enjoyed dinner.

Marie popped the last of the pizza slice into her mouth and leaned back on the couch while she chewed thoughtfully, watching Zeke take a swig from his bottle of beer. That escapade in the elevator had been absolutely sensational. And not just the location. Remembering the way he'd commanded her still sent thrills through her.

A part of her was uncertain, though. Women had worked so hard for so long to ensure they were respected and treated as equals to men. Why did the thought of a man ordering her around . . . treating her like a plaything . . . turn her on?

"Zeke, this thing we're doing . . . with me calling you Master . . ."

He put his beer down and his intense gaze locked on her.

She tugged on her thumb, not sure exactly what to say. "I . . . uh . . . really like it."

"Good."

"But . . . I don't want you to think that—"

He tugged her into his arms and kissed her, his mouth mastering hers, his tongue pushing between her lips and swirling inside. It was cool, with the yeasty taste of beer. She caressed it with her own tongue, her lips moving in response to his.

Then he drew back.

"I would never assume the dominant role outside the bedroom, nor expect you to defer to me."

She stared at him, his gaze insistent and intense. She smiled and stroked back the hair that had fallen over his eye.

"Well, you are a strong man who likes to take the lead, so I expect you to be a little dominating, but that's what I like about you. As long as we both understand the limits."

The intensity of his stare did not change.

"Marie, if you feel things are going too far, or you simply don't want to continue, tell me."

His intense concern touched her. She nodded.

"And if we decide to take the role-playing further, then I'll give you a safe word to use. The split second you say that word, everything stops cold. Do you understand?"

She nodded again.

"This is all about your pleasure. Nothing else. It's not

meant to be an ego boost for me. All I need to know is that you're enjoying yourself. That's *all* that's important."

She nodded again, beginning to feel like a bobble-head doll. "I understand."

He kissed her, gently this time, and for some reason that tenderness, in contrast to his usual masterful use of her mouth, sent her senses spinning.

When he released her, she felt light-headed, and positively ebullient.

"Now, take off your clothes and get me a cold beer."

Four

Marie's jaw dropped open at Zeke's transformation back to dominant male.

"I said, take off your clothes." His olive green eyes stared deep into hers, as if challenging.

She hesitated for only a second, wondering if she should tell him no. But she realized she didn't need to test him. He'd told her this was about her pleasure and she totally believed him.

He raised an eyebrow. She stood up.

"Yes, Master."

She tugged her T-shirt over her head and tossed it onto the easy chair, then unfastened the button and zipper on her jeans. As she pushed them down, his gaze followed every movement. She stepped out of the denim and stood before him in only a racy red bra and thong.

His simmering gaze assured her she'd made the right choice when she'd gone to change out of her work clothes while he'd ordered the pizza.

She reached around behind her back to unfasten her bra.

"Wait. Come here and turn around."

She turned around and sat down beside him. His fingers worked at the hooks and the garment loosened. He slipped the straps off her shoulders and she allowed the bra to fall onto her lap. His hands glided around her waist, then cupped her naked breasts. He squeezed and stroked, sending her senses spinning. Her nipples thrust forward. He squeezed them and she sucked in a breath.

His hands slipped away and she stood up, then tucked her thumbs under the elastic of her thong and pushed it down. He stroked her naked butt as she pulled the tiny garment over her feet and discarded it. She stood up slowly, enjoying his hands circling over her round flesh.

Then he smacked her bottom.

"Now for that beer."

She scurried into the kitchen and retrieved a beer from the fridge. What had he meant when he'd suggested they might take the role-playing further . . . doing something that would require a safe word? She'd never tried domination and submission role-playing before she'd met Zeke, but she understood the concept of a safe word. Wasn't that usually used when the woman . . . or rather, whichever partner played the submissive role . . . would want to struggle? When she was being overpowered and might want to tell him to stop in the context of the roles?

Might Zeke want to overpower her? The very thought sent a vibrant yearning pulsing through her. What if he forced her down on the bed and held her hands over her head, then climbed on top of her and . . . ?

Oh, she could just imagine his big, hard cock sliding

into her as she struggled against him. Powerless to stop him. He could do anything he wanted to her.

What if he tied her up? Held her head still while he slid his cock into her mouth?

She began to tremble at the intensely erotic images flashing through her brain.

She opened the beer, then pressed the cold bottle against her chest, to cool herself down. As she walked back into the living room, she continued holding it against her body, but as she walked toward the couch, Zeke watching the bottle against her skin, she dragged it over her breast, then pressed it against her right nipple, which puckered into a tight bud. She stood in front of Zeke and poured a little beer over her left breast.

She grinned. "Oops."

She handed him the beer, but he shoved it onto the side table and grabbed her waist, then drew her toward him. She gasped at the feel of his mouth surrounding her cold wet nipple, then his tongue swirling over it. Round and round.

"Beer-flavored nipples. Wonderful."

He grinned at her and she smiled back, but she wanted more. Thoughts of him throwing her to the ground and ravaging her sent her temperature rising.

She stroked her hands over her breasts, then down her stomach and between her legs. Him sitting there fully clothed while she stood before him totally naked turned her on immensely.

She crouched in front of him and reached for his belt and released the buckle, then unzipped his jeans. In a second, she drew out his raging erection and tugged. She eased herself back, allowing his cock to slip from her fingers, and stretched out on the floor.

She opened her legs and dragged her finger along her slick opening.

"Zeke, I want you to fuck me."

He grinned and reached for the hem of his T-shirt.

"No, leave it on. Just fuck me. Right now."

He prowled over her and kissed her neck, then downward to her breast. He sucked hard as he pressed his cockhead to her opening.

"Oh, yes. Push that magnificent cock of yours into me right now."

He followed her command and drove into her, pinning her tight to the floor.

She gasped, then wrapped her legs around him. He drew back and drove into her again. She moaned, so close she could barely hold herself together.

"Fuck me. Faster."

He thrust into her. One stroke. Two. She wailed as an explosive orgasm catapulted her to ecstasy. She clung to him as he hammered into her. Deep. Hard. Her wail turned to a moan as ecstasy blossomed into blissful surrender. He groaned and she felt his liquid heat inside her, then her body turned to mush.

A soft giggle slipped from her lips as he lifted her in his arms and carried her to bed.

Ty grabbed his mail from the box then headed toward the elevator. He stepped inside and, as the doors closed, saw Marie racing toward him.

"Ty, wait."

He pressed the Open button and she rushed inside, panting.

"Thanks." She sucked in a deep breath as the door closed. "I've got a date tonight and I'm running late."

The elevator moved upward, the floor numbers increasing on the LED display above the panel of buttons.

"Again? You're seeing this new guy a lot." He succeeded in making his voice sound teasing, despite his clenched jaw.

She grinned. "I don't know. It's been a whole two dates so far . . . not counting the weekend."

He hated the wistful look in her eyes as she thought about her new lover. Damn, it should have been him!

As soon as the doors opened on their floor, she flew out of the elevator and down the hall.

"Sorry, gotta run. See you later." Her voice trailed down the hall, then she disappeared into her apartment.

As Ty walked down the hall, he heard the elevator bell and glanced back as the door of the second elevator opened.

A tall man in worn black denim jeans and vest, a black leather jacket thrown over his shoulder, stepped from the elevator. His sleeveless black T-shirt accentuated the tattoos on each bulging bicep. The long, colorful tattoo on the right Ty recognized immediately, though it had obviously been updated with newer pigment since he'd last seen it five years ago.

"What the hell are you doing here?" Ty's voice grated harshly through the hallway.

"Ty?" Zeke pulled the sunglasses from his face, revealing olive green eyes, a little warmer and more vivid than Ty remembered.

At Zeke's surprised expression, Ty immediately realized Zeke wasn't here to see him. That meant . . .

"You God damned son of a bitch, you'd better not be

here to—" Ty bit off his sentence as he heard a door open. He jerked around to see Marie peer down the hallway.

"Ty? Is something wrong?" she asked.

He gritted his teeth, shot a sharp glare at Zeke, then turned back to her.

"Of course not. This your friend?" He almost choked on the last word as he nudged his head toward the bastard standing just down the hall from him.

She spotted Zeke and the concern in her eyes melted to a soft, wistful gaze, her lips turning up in a smile. Ty's chest clenched at the sight.

"Zeke. You're here. Sorry, I haven't started dinner. I got in late."

"No problem. We can just order in."

Marie's gaze switched from Zeke to Ty then back again. "Do . . . you two know each other?"

Ty's eyes blazed as his teeth grated together.

"Yeah, we . . . went to the same high school," Zeke answered.

Ty strode toward his apartment and unlocked the door, then disappeared inside without another word.

Zeke watched Marie stare at Ty's closing door. Zeke walked toward her and resisted the urge to take her in his arms and kiss her, not wanting to further antagonize Ty if he happened to come out of his apartment again.

"Sorry, Ty doesn't usually behave that way. Did something happen?" she asked.

"He was just . . . surprised to see me here, that's all."

"I was sure I heard raised voices."

"I didn't say he was *happy* to see me."

Her eyebrows arched. "I take it it's a long story?"

He nodded as they entered her apartment and shut the door.

She sat down beside him on the couch. "I've got the time."

He shrugged. He did not intend to tell her about the rift between him and his old friend. He didn't know what kind of relationship existed between Ty and Marie. Even if he did, he wouldn't reveal any secrets from Ty's past. He wouldn't do anything that Ty might interpret as a further betrayal of their friendship.

Ex-friendship as far as Ty was concerned—Zeke's chest tightened at the thought—but Zeke would never give up on them. Ty had been the best friend Zeke had ever known, and if there was ever anything he could do to mend the rift between them, he'd do it. If it hadn't been for Ty, Zeke's life would be very different right now. In fact, he'd probably be in jail.

"How about you get me a beer instead?"

"Then you'll talk?"

He slid his arms around her and tugged her to his body, then devoured her lips until she was breathless. "I can think of way better things to do than talking."

He kissed her again, enjoying the sweet feel of her soft lips against his, the delicate fragrance of herbal shampoo from her hair, and the intoxicating sensation of her pebbling nibbles pushing into his chest.

He grinned at her. "Now, how about that beer?"

She blinked, then stroked his cheek with her soft hand, her delicate tender touch reaching a place deep inside him.

She smiled. "You're not insisting on naked this time?"

An instant replay of Tuesday night's request to bring him a beer naked flashed through his brain, making his cock swell.

"Not this time. I need to keep you on your toes. Anyway, we'd never get to dinner, and I'm hungry. How about you?"

"Oh yeah. I'm hungry all right." Her eyes filled with a simmering sexual hunger that mirrored his own.

But he didn't want to act on it yet. Not in his current frame of mind.

"Okay, that's it. Off with you, you vamp. Go get that beer." He lifted her by the waist and set her on her feet, then patted her firm round behind.

She laughed, then sauntered toward the kitchen with an exaggerated wiggle of her hips.

He watched as she disappeared into the kitchen. Sweet, loving, intensely sexy Marie. A woman he was sure he could fall for completely.

He remembered Ty's protest when he realized Zeke was here to see Marie. Clearly, he hadn't wanted Zeke anywhere near her. In fact, given Ty's possessive reaction, Zeke suspected Ty had a thing for her. How could he not? The woman was beautiful, sweet, sensual. The whole package.

Ty had been his best friend, and at a time when he'd needed a friend badly. Ty had saved Zeke's butt more than once.

Damn, Zeke knew he'd give up anything to mend the rift between him and Ty.

But would he be able to give up Marie?

Marie opened the fridge and pulled out a tall brown bottle of beer. She set it on the granite counter and opened the drawer, then rifled through for the bottle opener. Jade leapt onto the counter to see what Marie was doing. She picked up the cat, snuggled her close, then put her back on the floor.

What was the deal with Ty and Zeke?

She couldn't believe they knew each other. They were totally different types. Of course, knowing each other didn't mean they'd been friends. Might Zeke have been the school bully, leaving hard feelings between him and Ty? But despite his tough-guy nature, she didn't believe Zeke to be the bullying type.

She'd love to talk to Ty about this and find out what happened between them, but she suspected Ty would be just as tight-lipped as Zeke.

She found the opener and flicked the metal cap off the bottle. The frosty brown glass and the yeasty smell made her mouth water. She grabbed another bottle from the fridge and opened it for herself. In her short time with Zeke, she found she was acquiring a taste for beer. She smiled. Especially when running her tongue past his full sensual lips into his hot mouth.

She wrapped her hand around the cold bottle and took a sip, the bubbles dancing across her tongue with potent flavor. But despite the delicious eye candy sitting in the next room, she couldn't stop her mind from returning to the scene in the hall. She was sure she'd heard Ty swearing, which was totally unlike him. There were definitely hard feelings between these two men, though more on Ty's side than Zeke's, judging from Zeke's reaction. Now how to get it out of them . . .

Zeke glanced away from the sports report on the news as Marie walked into the room, a beer bottle in each hand. She held one out to him and he took it and sipped deeply as she sat down beside him. He stared at her thoughtfully.

"So, I've been wondering . . . why are you attracted to

41

a guy like me? I assume I'm not the usual type you go out with."

"True. I usually go out with . . . you know . . . the Mr.-Nice-Guy types. Like Ty."

His eyebrows jolted upward. "Mr. Nice Guy? Ty?"

Man, if she only knew. Ty had been one of the toughest guys in the old neighborhood. A real badass. Which is why they had been such great friends.

She tipped her head. "Yeah. You know. The dependable type. Someone you can talk to. A guy who listens to your problems."

He narrowed his eyes. "You don't think you could tell me about your problems?"

She pressed her lips together. "I didn't mean . . ." She curled her legs up and pushed herself onto her knees, then leaned in close and kissed him. "Of course I do. It's really more that . . . you have . . ." She shrugged, her lips turning up in an impish smile. "An edge. You're sort of . . . unpredictable."

"Admit it. You think I'm a badass, don't you?" He flipped her onto her back, her sky blue eyes wide. He leaned down and consumed her lips in a fervent kiss. "All you women want is a bad-boy type." He grinned. "Someone intent on dominating you, then walking away, leaving you broken-hearted. But deep inside, you believe you'll tame his spirit and win him forever."

She wrapped her arms around his neck and pulled him down for another kiss, then smiled up at him. "And if we don't, we know it'll be a wild ride. Well worth the risk."

His smile faded and he dragged her against him, his tongue driving between her lips, consuming her mouth with deep plunging strokes, leaving her breathless.

"Are you absolutely sure about that, Marie?"

She stared back at him, her blue eyes wide and filled with uncertainty. He silently cursed himself, then drew her onto his lap and kissed her again, this time with just as much passion, but with a gentle pressure of his mouth on hers, while he stroked her back in soothing circles.

When he finally released her, she stared at him, dazed. "Uh . . . you're certainly in a weird mood tonight."

He laughed. "Yeah. I told you, I need to keep you on your toes." He eased her off his lap onto the couch beside him, then took a sip of his beer. "I think you want to go out with me because you know I'll show you some thrills in the sack."

She grinned. "Well, that's not such a bad thing, is it?"

A broad smile claimed his face. "No. It's the best. Now, I think we should order Chinese for dinner."

"Sure. I'll go get the take-out menu for the place in the strip mall down the street."

She returned a moment later and they selected several dishes, then Zeke called in the order.

"You didn't ask them to deliver," Marie said once he'd hung up.

Zeke stood up. "No, I'm going to go pick it up."

"You're not going now, are you? It'll be a while before it's ready and the place is just a block away."

He smiled. "That's okay, I'll take the long way. I'm in the mood for a walk."

She wrapped her arms around his neck before he could pull away. "You really are in a weird mood today." She kissed him, spearing her delicious tongue between his lips, sending his cock pulsing with need.

Her sweet seductive manner almost made him forget

his intent, but he drew back and unwrapped her hands from his neck, kissing them briefly before releasing them.

"Down, sweet thing. I'll be back before you know it."

Zeke walked toward Ty's door and knocked. A moment later, the door opened and Ty glared at him with chocolate brown eyes.

In fact, both eyes were brown, which meant he was wearing colored contact lenses to hide the fact that one eye was actually soft green with gold specks. Zeke shouldn't be surprised. Although the women had always found Ty's odd eyes sexy as sin, Ty had always felt it made him . . . flawed. In the old days, he'd embraced his so-called flaws . . . odd eyes, anger, dominant nature . . . but Zeke had a feeling the new Ty had decided to clean up his act and eliminate the flaws he could . . . and hide the rest.

Too bad he was so totally misguided.

"What the hell do you want?" Ty said.

Five

Zeke stared hard at his friend. Ex-friend actually. But by Ty's choice, not his. "To talk to you."

"Forget it."

Ty pushed the door to close it, but Zeke flattened his hand against it.

"I need to talk to you about Marie," Zeke said.

The ice from Ty's gaze chilled Zeke to the bone, but Ty finally stepped back, allowing Zeke to enter.

He glanced around at Ty's apartment. Brown leather and dark oak furniture suited Ty. The colorful artwork was unexpected. A nice touch. And the place was exceptionally tidy. Same old Ty, in that respect, at least.

"Nice place."

"What do you want, Zeke?"

Zeke faced Ty, who stared at him with a glower, his arms crossed.

"After that incident in the hall, it's pretty clear you don't want me seeing Marie."

Ty just continued to glare.

Damn, after five years, clearly his anger was still fresh.

"Were you two involved?" Zeke asked.

"Not that it's any of your business, but . . . no."

Ty's words echoed through Zeke's mind.

You God damned son of a bitch, you'd better not be here to—

See Marie. Clearly, that was how Ty had intended to end that sentence.

Zeke gazed at him thoughtfully, then nodded to himself. "But you want to be."

Ty clenched his jaw. "As I said, it's none of your God damned business."

Zeke drew in a deep breath, undeterred. "Do you want me to step aside?"

Ty stared at him, his glare turning to an assessing scowl.

"You think that'll make up for what happened with Ashley?"

Zeke sighed. "I told you, I never tried to steal your girlfriend."

"So you've said."

Zeke's chest clenched. And that's what had hurt the most. That despite the close bond that had always existed between Ty and Zeke, and even though the woman had shamelessly thrown herself at Zeke, Ty hadn't even listened to Zeke's side. Ty had simply assumed the worst.

"So do you want me to step aside or not?" Zeke hated being in this fucking position. He didn't want to let Marie go, but he respected Ty's feelings and the close bond they'd once shared.

A bond he wished they *still* shared. Their close friendship had turned sour overnight after that threesome with Ashley . . . which *she* had suggested. And it seemed pretty clear to Zeke, she'd done it specifically to get an in with Zeke. She'd been ready to dump Ty, but she'd wanted a new boyfriend lined up first.

Zeke wondered if this was finally his chance to set things right between them. He and Ty shared too much to just let their friendship die. Too much history. Too much pain.

"What about Marie?" Ty asked. "Don't you care how she feels about it?"

"Of course I care. But we haven't been going out very long. She'll get over it."

Ty's fists clenched at his sides. "Don't do me any fucking favors."

He couldn't stand how callously the guy was willing to treat Marie. As much as he didn't want Zeke anywhere near Marie, he didn't want to see Marie hurt.

He also didn't want Zeke thinking he could even begin to make up for the pain he'd caused.

Zeke shrugged. "Whatever."

God damn it, had he created a monster when he'd pushed Zeke to try the role of sexual Dominant so many years ago? Ty had naturally leaned to that role and found it very liberating. He'd thought that it would help give Zeke, who'd had so little control over his life, a sense of power. Ty never would have suggested it if he hadn't believed Zeke respected his women, and that he'd understand the responsibilities of the role; specifically, to give his partner pleasure. In return, he got the sense of power that would help him get past his feelings of helplessness.

But now, it seemed Zeke might have gone astray.

He tugged a card out of his inside pocket and tossed it on Ty's coffee table. "If you change your mind, call me."

Ty's jaw clenched tightly and he picked up the card and crumpled it.

"Not going to happen."

Zeke's olive eyes turned cold and he strode out of the apartment.

Zeke opened the hard saddlebag on the back of his Harley, grabbed his helmet and snapped it on, then climbed on the big bike. The engine roared to life and he zoomed out of the parking lot, then dodged around the traffic and headed for the highway, needing to feel speed.

Damn it. The thought of letting Marie go burned through his gut. The woman had definitely insinuated herself into his deepest desires. But not quite as deep as his desire to mend things with Ty.

Ty had done so much for Zeke. He'd kept him motivated to stay in school, allowing Zeke to make something of himself. Now he owned his own business, doing something he loved. Restoring vintage cars. But more, Ty had kept Zeke on the straight and narrow. Stopped him from winding up in jail. Or worse, dead.

The bond he had with Ty was too important to let anything stand in the way. Even Marie.

He took the ramp onto the highway, then accelerated, roaring past the other traffic.

Twenty minutes later, he parked his bike in the parking lot outside Marie's building and carried the bag of Chinese food, and an extra little surprise he'd picked up for tonight, to the main door. Once in the lobby, he pressed the call button for Marie's apartment.

"Hello?" Marie asked over the speaker.

"Hi, babe. It's Zeke. Sorry to take so long."

A loud buzzing sounded, indicating she'd released the door lock. Three minutes later, he got off the elevator on her floor. When he got to her door and knocked, he was extremely conscious of the fact that Ty was only yards away, in his apartment down the hall from Marie's, but he tried to overwhelm that with thoughts of Marie. He might be letting her go, but he still had tonight to make some memories he'd never forget . . . for him and for her.

The door opened and Marie smiled at him.

"I thought you'd run out on me."

At the sight of her wide, sky blue eyes gazing up at him, the silky waves of dark brown hair brushing her shoulders, her full heart-shaped lips, he wanted to say *never*. But he couldn't do that. Because this would be the last time he saw her. The last time he would touch her. Suddenly, his heart ached with a desperate desire to pull her into his arms and keep her there forever.

It had been so long since he'd felt this kind of connection to a woman that he'd started to wonder if he was just a loner . . . meant to live out his days on his own, without a partner. And then Marie had come along and made him realize how wonderful life could be with the right person. How could he even consider letting her go?

As she stepped aside and let him in, then closed the door, he realized this was insane. He'd only known her for a week. It's not like he'd fallen in love with her.

Though as she took the paper bag with the food from his hands, her fingers brushing his, shooting a jolt of pure awareness through him, he wondered if he was wrong about that. If two people were right for each other, why wouldn't they know it right away? Maybe it was only caution that made people wait to decide they were actually in love.

His jaw clenched. Not that love was an option for him and Marie. Because he'd told Ty he'd give her up. And he didn't go back on his word.

"What's that?" Marie asked, gazing at the black plastic bag he still held.

He grinned at the reminder of the special treat he had picked up.

"I'll tell you after dinner."

"Oh, a surprise?" She smiled and the delight shining in her eyes sent cascades of warmth washing through him. She walked to the rectangular dining room table and put down the bag of food. "I'll go get some plates."

He tucked the black bag in her entrance closet, then followed her into the kitchen. As she closed the cabinet door, he stepped up behind her and wrapped his arms around her waist, drawing her close to his body. He nuzzled her neck as his hand cupped her soft breast and squeezed. She turned around in his arms and tilted her chin up. He captured her lovely, full lips and kissed her, loving the feel of her soft mouth under his. The tip of her tongue pressed shyly against his lips and he opened, suffered the delightful torture of her delicate strokes inside his mouth, then tightened his grip on her delectable curvy body and drove his tongue deep into her soft depths, devouring her sweetness.

Finally, he released her. She gasped for breath, her eyes wide.

He grinned. "I'm not sure we have time for this. I'm taking you to a movie at eight and it's . . ."—he glanced at his watch—"seven now."

"A movie?" She seemed disappointed. "I thought we'd stay in tonight and—"

He wrapped an arm around her waist and pulled her in for another kiss. "You are going to a movie. Understand?"

At his authoritative tone, she nodded. Oh God, his pulse quickened as she fell right into the submissive role.

"I asked if you understand."

"Yes . . . Master."

His cock throbbed at the word *Master* on her delicate lips. He kissed her. Hard and thoroughly.

After they finished eating, he helped her clear the table and carry the dishes and empty food containers into the kitchen.

"I guess we should get ready for the movie now," she said. "I think I'll change into my jeans."

"I have a better idea." He took her hand and led her into the living room, then smiled. "Take off your underpants."

Her eyes widened a little, then a grin curled up her lips. She reached under her skirt and fidgeted, then wiggled as she eased the small black garment down her thighs and dropped it to the floor. He held out his hand and she picked the panties up and handed them to him. He closed his fingers around them, feeling the heat of her and . . . oh God, the slight dampness. His cock twitched.

"Now I want you to sit in the chair."

She sat in the chair, which formed a ninety-degree angle with the couch.

"Great. Now, draw your skirt up a little and press your knees against the armrests of the chair."

She tugged her short skirt a little higher and pressed her knees against the armrests as he'd instructed, which essentially opened her legs and gave him a spectacular view of her delightful pussy. She had trimmed the hair to a neat little heart shape.

He nodded and smiled his approval as he sat on the couch and picked up the remote. He turned on the TV and flipped through the channels, occasionally casting his gaze from the screen to her exposed pussy. Each time he looked at her, he couldn't help but imagine his tongue gliding along her slick passage. As he stared at her, she began to squirm and he was sure he could see glistening moisture from her exposed slit.

"Master, it's almost eight. Are we leaving for the movie soon?"

"Right now, I'm enjoying the show in front of me." He smiled and clicked off the TV. "We can always go to a later show. Now, stand up and go to the closet. Bring me the black bag."

She stood up and retrieved it.

"No peeking," he said.

She returned and gave him the bag. He reached inside and pulled out a box, then handed it to her.

"What is it?" She took it and stared at the little device visible through the clear plastic window on the box.

"It's something I want you to wear tonight." *Wear* wasn't the most accurate word. It would actually be embedded inside her.

Marie glanced at him uncertainly. The thing he presented to her was . . . well, it was a dildo that was designed for . . . her back opening. She had never used something like that. Now he was going to command her to use it. Or he'd use it on her.

Of course, she could say no. He'd been very clear about that.

Did she want to say no?

He took the box from her and opened it, then pulled out the black, plastic, roughly conical shaped object with a stem and flat end. He touched the tip, then stroked the length of it. She had a sudden desire to see him take it in his mouth and suck on it. He held it toward her and she licked it, then took it in her mouth, thinking of his big cock. He watched her, clearly thinking the same thing as a bulge formed in his jeans.

He took the dildo from her and dragged it along her cheek, then down the front of her blouse.

"Marie, I want you to go into the bedroom and run your fingers over your pussy. I want you to ensure you are really . . . *really* wet." He dragged the dildo lower, then rested it against her stomach, below her navel. "Then slide this into your pussy and glide it around slowly."

Oh man, she wanted him to slide it into her right now.

"Get it really slick and wet. Then . . ."

He grasped her hips and turned her around, then lifted her skirt. He caressed her ass with delightful round strokes. She tingled inside. Then she felt the dildo glide between her cheeks and press lightly against her small, tight opening.

Oh God, was he going to push it in right now? The pressure of the small rounded tip against her puckered opening increased and she sucked in a deep breath, realizing she wanted him to.

". . . then I want you to push it in here."

A shiver rippled through her. She wanted to lean back against it. Take it right now.

But he drew it away and placed it in her hand.

"Then come back out here. Understand?"

"Yes, Master."

She walked toward the bedroom, the sexy device in her hand.

"And, Marie . . ."

She stopped and glanced back at him. "Yes, Master?"

"Do not come."

Oh, damn.

Six

Sitting behind Zeke on the bike . . . clinging to him as they sped along the highway, her breasts crushed against his broad muscular back . . . the big machine vibrating beneath her hot, wet pussy . . . was sheer torture. And the whole time she could feel the unaccustomed pressure of the dildo in her back opening.

When they arrived at the cinema, she held her skirt carefully so she didn't flash anyone as she climbed off the bike. She lifted her leg and had to hold back a gasp as her behind rotated on the seat and the butt plug shifted inside her.

Zeke led her into the movie and they sat at the back. Only a few people were in the theater and none in the back few rows. She didn't even notice the action on the screen as Zeke's hand glided along her inner thigh, then under her skirt. His fingers stroked along her slick, swollen lips. She opened her legs, giving him easier access. He stroked her slit, then glided inside. He delved deeper and stroked her inner passage, building an incredible heat inside her. Her G-spot . . .

oh God, he knew where it was and how to use it! Warmth suffused her entire body. Pleasure built within her, gaining momentum . . . then he stopped and pulled his hand free. She almost whimpered out loud.

She tried to pay attention to the movie . . . some cars chasing across the flickering backdrop of city streets . . . but she couldn't concentrate. She wanted his hands on her. After an agonizing wait, his hand returned to her thigh, then stroked her slit again. This time, he pressed against her clit. She almost cried out. He eased off, then stroked lightly. She sucked in air, then tilted her pelvis forward, trying to get more pressure, but he drew away entirely.

Damn. Punishment for her eagerness.

Finally, he stroked her again. Lightly. Teasing.

Oh God, not enough.

During the entire movie he tortured her like that. Giving her a little, then leaving her breathless and wanting. Occasionally, he would slide his fingers under her and grasp the flared end of the butt plug with his fingers and pivot it a little, sending quivers through her. When the movie ended and she sat behind him riding the motorcycle home, she almost came several times just from the vibration of the leather seat beneath her.

But she fought the urge to let go. Fought the intense desire to soar to heaven on the back of this big machine while flying through the night.

By the time they got to her apartment, she was practically panting. When the door closed behind them, she turned to him and thrust herself against him, wrapping her arms around him tightly and devouring his mouth. He lifted her, their mouths still locked together, tongues delving deep. She wrapped her legs around him as he carried her backward. His denim-covered erection pressed against her, driving her wild. She wanted him inside her. *Needed* him inside her.

Her tongue stroked inside his hot mouth hungrily as he pushed through the kitchen doorway. She felt something hard and cold beneath her and realized he'd set her on the counter. She stroked down his chest and fumbled for the zipper of his jeans and dragged it down, stroking the bulge of his cock with her other hand, anxious to feel it in the flesh. She reached inside, rewarded with the feel of his marble-hard cock. She wrapped her fingers around the hot, hard flesh and pulled it out, then stroked. He groaned. His hand cupped her breast and her nipple pushed into his palm in desperate need. She leaned back against the cupboard behind her and pushed her pelvis forward.

"I want you inside me." She placed his cockhead against her aching vagina.

"God, you are so wet." His guttural words grated through her.

She pivoted her hips forward, trying to take his hard shaft inside her, but his cockhead simply nudged her wet flesh. His tongue thrust into her mouth.

"Oh please. I need you now." She tugged on his erection.

He sucked on her tongue, pulling her deeper into his mouth. She moaned, overwhelmed with the intense need to join with him.

She pulled her mouth free. "Master, please fuck me!"

He groaned, then drove forward. One fast, hard thrust. Stretching her. Impaling her completely. She wailed at the intense ecstasy of his hard cock filling her. The tightness in her ass from the dildo still inside her heightened the potent pleasure.

She clung to his shoulders, her legs wrapping around him, and moaned as he thrust again. Hot waves of intense pleasure rippled through her. Another thrust singed her nerve endings. His hard cock glided into her again and again. His body claiming hers. Consuming her. Filling her with mind-numbing pleasure until she plummeted to a heavenly place of total bliss.

She moaned, the sound reverberating through her, carrying her further into that joyful place of pure sensation.

His cock jerked deep, then throbbed within her, pulsing with heat. He groaned, holding her tight against him, her head tucked tightly against his chest. Both of them panted for air.

As she nuzzled the soft leather against her face, she realized he still wore his jacket. In fact, he was still fully clothed. Both of them were . . . except for her lack of panties.

He stroked her hair, then pressed his lips to her neck. After nuzzling for a moment, he eased back and smiled at her.

"I think you enjoyed our evening out after all."

She wrapped her arms around his neck and kissed him.

"It was sensational. Especially the last part."

"You know we're not finished yet." He stroked her thigh, then tucked his hands under her knees and lifted, tipping her hips up. He stroked her ass, then she felt something move inside her.

The dildo. She'd almost forgotten.

He carried her into the bedroom and laid her on the bed. The feel of his fingers brushing against her feet as he removed her shoes sent tingles dancing through her. He stripped off her skirt and blouse, leaving her lying on the bed in only her navy lace bra. He grinned as he tugged off his leather jacket and tossed it onto the chair. He sat down beside her and stroked his hands over her body. Broad strokes from ankle to hip, up her ribs and over her shoulders, then down again, never touching her breasts or the aching—and quite naked—mound between her legs. She arched and pivoted as his hands stroked over her hips, but he chuckled and deftly avoided contact with her needy opening.

Finally, he arched his leg over her, pinning her thighs between his knees, and stroked along the bottom of her bra, then tucked his hands behind her and unhooked it. As it released, her breathing accelerated, knowing his hands would be on her soon. He peeled away the bra and his sexy olive green eyes darkened as he gazed at her nipples, which tightened at his intense scrutiny.

Now she was totally naked—pinned between his denim-clad legs—while he was fully clothed. As if she were his own private sex slave. He stroked his hands up her ribs, then glided over her breasts, stopping short of her aching nipples. Oh God, she wanted him to touch her hard buds. He grinned, then stroked one with his fingertip. She moaned at the delightful sensation.

Then he leaned down and licked the other nipple and she grasped his head tight to her chest as she moaned again, running her fingers through his shoulder-length black hair. She arched her hips upward, hoping to grind against him, but his knees kept her in place. He released her nipple and straightened, smiling as he pulled off his black denim vest, then grabbed the hem of his black T-shirt and pulled it up his torso, revealing tight, well-defined muscles along his abs and chest, then tugged it over his head and tossed it aside.

She ran her fingers along the golden serpentine dragon tattooed across his chest, down the hard ridges of his stomach, then released his silver-studded leather belt from the stainless steel buckle. He shifted to his feet and dropped his jeans to the floor, then divested himself of his slate gray boxers. She rolled onto her side and reached for his swelling cock. She wrapped her hands around his thick shaft and stroked. Hot flesh gliding over granite.

He stepped closer and she shimmied around until her head hung over the end of the bed, then she licked the mushroom-shaped tip. She swirled her tongue over and around, then wrapped her lips around him and swallowed his broad cockhead. It filled her mouth beautifully. She dragged her teeth lightly along the ridge, then sucked. His moan delighted her. She took him deeper, sucking and squeezing. He groaned again as she stroked her hands over his hard butt and opened her throat, then pulled him closer so he glided deep into her. In this position, she could take almost all of his impressive length down her throat. He glided in and out several times as she cupped his balls in one hand.

"Oh, sweet thing, you are something else." He cupped her cheeks, gently stroking under her chin as he slowly thrust into her. "That feels so damned good." He stiffened. "Oh damn, I'm too fucking close— I—"

He groaned, stiffening as hot liquid erupted down her throat. A thrill shot through her that he couldn't control himself around her. She squeezed and sucked as he continued to climax.

"Damn, woman, you are so fucking hot."

He pulled his cock from her mouth, then leaned down and captured her lips, gliding his tongue deep into her mouth and thoroughly exploring. When he released her, she gasped for air.

"Got a vibrator?" he asked, his dark green eyes darting to the bedside table. "In there?"

She nodded, then pivoted around to rest her head on the pillow again. He opened the drawer and she blushed as she realized he'd see that she had three different ones in there. He grinned and pulled out the biggest one. It was thick and long, with a very realistic shape, including veins and ridges.

"I see you like big."

He dropped it back in the drawer and tugged out the one with a clit stimulator next to the shaft. That one got the job done every time.

He slid the lever and it hummed to life. The familiar sound sent heat thrumming through her. He pressed his finger to the tip of the clit stimulator and grinned.

"Interesting." He stared at her, his olive eyes heating. "I would love to watch you use this sometime." His cock swelled as he spoke.

He turned off the device and discarded it, too, then pulled out the last one. Like the first, it was also realistic looking, despite the shocking pink color, but this one was a more modest size.

"This one will do nicely." He shoved the drawer closed, then sat beside her again. He turned on the device and glided it along her chest, then over one mound. He dragged it lightly over her nipple, sending rippling pulses through her. He slid it upward, then along her collarbone, up the side of her neck, then along her jaw.

"Open your mouth."

She opened, automatically obeying his commanding tone. He dipped the pulsing member into her mouth, briefly, then held the tip against her lower lip. Her tongue dodged out and licked the vibrating tip.

"Wrap your lips around it and suck."

She arched her neck forward and obeyed. The silicone

shaft vibrated against her lips and she sucked. Her mouth quivered with the gentle vibration of the device.

He drew it free, then pressed it to her thighs, then nudged it between them, pushing across her aching vagina. He glided it along her slick opening, back and forth.

She wanted it inside. Actually, she wanted *him* inside, but it would do for now. She opened her thighs and arched upward.

"Anxious, are you?"

He glided over her again, then leaned forward and kissed her thigh. She sighed. Then he covered her slit with his mouth and licked. She moaned in agonized pleasure. When he sucked on her clit, she gasped and clutched his hair.

He lifted his head, then the vibrating cock touched her clit and spasms of pleasure rocketed through her in an instant orgasm. He quivered the vibrating device against her and she wailed her release.

He glided the shocking pink cock inside her. Deeply at first, then in and out a few times.

"Okay, now we're ready."

Ready for what?

With the cock still inside her, he grasped her hips and dragged her to the edge of the bed. She dropped her feet to the floor and he helped her up.

"Turn around," he instructed.

She obeyed and he grabbed a couple of pillows and dropped them in front of her.

"Lean on the bed."

She leaned forward, resting her head on the pillows, leaving her back end high and accessible. He stroked over her ass, then she felt the dildo inside her back opening swirl around. Then he drew it out. Before she could get used to the resulting feeling of emptiness, he turned off the vibrator and drew it from her wet slit, then pressed it against her ass.

"Oh."

The cockhead nudged her back opening, then he pushed forward and the cock slowly glided into her. Excitement quivered through her as his real-flesh cock nudged her vagina. He drove forward, filling her with hot, hard cock. With his arm wrapped around her waist, he held her tight to his body.

As he drew his own cock back, he also drew back the cock in her ass. When he drove forward again, he did so with both cocks. He increased the rhythm, pulsing in and out of both her openings. Like two men. Both fucking her.

Images of Ty also thrusting into her sent her pulse skyrocketing.

Her hands clutched at the pillows as intense pleasure built within her.

"Oh God, yes." She sucked in air and moaned as he kept thrusting.

In and out. Deeper and faster.

Zeke. And Ty. Both inside her.

He nuzzled her neck. "Do you like the idea of being fucked by two men? Both of us driving into your sweet little body."

She nodded, unable to utter a word as pleasure blossomed into full-blown bliss. Every nerve ending electrified.

"Are you coming, sweet thing?" he asked as he drove deeper.

She nodded again, then wailed in ecstasy. She lost all sense of time and space as she simply rode the wave of sheer unadulterated joy.

Zeke tensed behind her, his groin shuddering in spasms. Then he collapsed against her back, sucking in air. Both cocks slipped away.

"My God, woman, fucking you is intense."

A jubilant energy bubbled through her and she began to giggle. She rolled onto her side, then slipped off the edge of the bed, her giggles turning to full-out laughter. As he tumbled on top of her, he rolled onto his side, tugging her against his body, chuckling the whole time.

As she lay on the carpet, tucked against his strong, warm body, she smiled, still high on the overwhelming erotic experience they'd just shared. That had certainly blown the doors off any doubts she might have had about getting involved with a man like Zeke. Good God, she'd never felt as alive as she had in his arms. And she'd certainly never felt as incredibly sexy.

Zeke held Marie close, watching her lovely face in the moonlight as she slept. Shit, he would never have believed a woman could get under his skin like this one had. Her love of adventure and willingness to try new things made her exceptionally fun to be around. And her endearing sweetness paired with her exuberance to explore a whole new world of sexual experience proved to be a powerful aphrodisiac.

But more than that, he felt special when he was with her. Her delicate femininity made him feel strong and powerful, yet her obvious strength of will assured him she wasn't fragile. He could dominate her knowing she would keep her sense of self. And her sense of humor.

He smiled as he remembered rolling on the floor with her after their intense lovemaking. Laughter paired with sex.

He loved it. Since he'd met her, he'd found himself looking forward to each new day just so he could be with her.

He tightened his arms around her. A huge thing was that she accepted him for who he was. Most people saw no further than the tattoos on his arms, the way he dressed, and the pierced spikes in his eyebrows. Many became anxious or intimidated, or reacted with disdain. Of course, some women found his rough edges sexy. But typically, they either wanted a short fling to satisfy their sense of danger then they'd move on, or they had a tough edge of their own.

But not Marie.

He stroked her cheek. So feminine and so sweet.

All the things he found so alluring in Marie were probably what Ty found attractive, too. He and Ty were both men looking for acceptance.

His heart ached at the thought of taking the woman Ty wanted. And it had been clear Ty wanted her. Zeke had seen that look in Ty's eyes before. He'd probably had a plan. Marie had mentioned she'd ended a long-term relationship recently. Knowing Ty, he'd been waiting for the right time. Unfortunately, Zeke had shown up before Ty had made his move.

Damn, Zeke couldn't steal the woman from Ty. He wouldn't do something to hurt Ty again.

Even if it meant giving up the best thing that had ever happened to him?

What if Marie wasn't interested in Ty? Or what if they started dating and it fizzled out? Zeke would have lost Marie for no reason.

Except that if he didn't give her up, Ty wouldn't get his chance to pursue Marie, and his resentment would build.

If only there were some way he could find out if Marie were interested in Ty before giving her up.

Marie awoke to the feel of a hard male chest against her cheek. She opened her eyes and found herself staring at a pair of blue eyes. She blinked. Dragon eyes. On the large tattoo covering Zeke's chest, the colors delightfully bright in the dazzling sunlight streaming in the window.

She nuzzled her cheek against the dragon, then kissed its nose. Her lips grazed along the neck of the beast, until she reached Zeke's beadlike nipple. She nipped, then licked. He murmured approvingly. Her hand stroked down the hard contours of his stomach, then trailed lower, anticipation thrumming through her. Just as her fingers stroked over his already rising cock, with a quick movement he grabbed her wrist, then rolled her onto her back. Catching her other wrist, he prowled over her, and pinned both her hands above her head. He smiled down at her, then nuzzled her neck, sending her hormones swirling.

She gazed up at his handsome, rugged face. Light glinted off the metal spikes in his eyebrow.

"Good morning." She smiled.

"Yes, it is." Still holding her hands pinned, he eased back onto his knees and gazed down at her naked breasts. The nipples tightened into hard nubs. "An amazing morning. Ripe full of possibilities."

He pressed one knee between her thighs, then the other, and she widened her legs to accommodate him, her vagina aching with need. Would he drive into her now, with no foreplay, just a rough, raw coupling? Her insides throbbed with need.

But he simply watched her.

"I think we should have a little talk," he said finally.

"Talk?" That's not exactly what she felt like doing right now.

"I just want to know what your intentions are," he said.

"My *intentions?*" She smiled. "Well, right now . . . to get laid."

He chuckled. "That sort of takes me to my point."

"I'd really like to take your *point.*" She wriggled against his knees and arched, trying to get closer to his steadily rising cock, but with no luck.

"I'm starting to think you just want me for my body," he said.

"Well, it's a damned fine body." She grinned impishly. "And you use it so well."

He pressed her legs wider apart and stroked his leg against her slit. She moaned at the feel of his muscular flesh stroking her.

"Now, be good and pay attention."

She nodded. "Yes, Master."

"Now right there. That's part of what I want to talk about. You and I have been playing at Dominance and submission, but it's been pretty light. What I want to know is . . ."

His pause lingered until she finally prompted him. "Yes?"

"What if I ramp it up several notches?"

Seven

Adrenaline rushed through her, shooting her level of *excitement* up several notches.

"I . . . uh . . . yeah . . ." Her stomach quivered. "That would be . . ." *Exciting. Intoxicating.* ". . . great."

He brought his face close to hers. "So if I asked you to be my slave, and do anything I want . . . would you agree?"

Anything?

She gazed into his warm, olive green eyes. Despite his tough looks, the tattoos, piercings, and rough demeanor, she knew he was a good man. She could feel it.

"I trust you. What do you have in mind?"

"I want you to push past your comfort zone. I like to push the limits and I need a woman who's willing to take a chance. Go for some adventure. But I've yet to meet a woman who can handle me, and I want to give you a chance to end this thing before we go any further."

She almost got the impression he was trying to scare her away.

"I'm willing to give it a try." She widened her thighs and pressed her breasts higher. "Master."

He gazed at her peaked nipples and smiled, his olive green eyes darkening. He dipped his head and nipped one hard nipple, then sucked. She moaned at the exquisite pleasure. He kissed down her ribs, to her navel and swirled his tongue inside it, then proceeded lower. Her heart thumped loudly as she anticipated his touch down below.

But as soon as he reached her pubic curls, he changed directions, kissed her navel, and sat up.

He released her wrists, rolled her onto her side, and smacked her bottom.

"Now, slave. Go make breakfast."

"What?" This was not at all what she'd expected.

"The correct response is 'Yes, Master.'"

She stood up and narrowed her eyes as she gazed at him. Was she supposed to defy him to trigger some kind of punishment? Or would her refusal signal an unwillingness to follow his commands?

She decided to play it safe. "Yes, Master." She reached for her clothes.

"No clothes. I want you naked."

Okay, this was a bit more like it.

"Yes, Master."

She strolled into the kitchen and began preparing bacon and eggs. Jade, who lay on her carpeted cat tree, bathed in a sunbeam of light, opened her eyes to watch Marie for a few moments. When no cat treats were forthcoming, she closed her eyes and went back to sleep.

Breakfast was well under way when Zeke showed up in the kitchen, fully showered and dressed, but still sporting an incredibly sexy shadow of bristles across his face and chin. He poured himself a cup of coffee while he watched her cook. She could feel his gaze glide over her body . . . and linger on select places.

She grabbed a spatula and scooped the eggs on two plates, then added bacon. She'd set a place for Zeke at the round kitchen table, and one for herself beside him. She'd already placed a plate of toast on the table, along with a jar of jam and of honey.

She stood by the chair, waiting for him to sit down. He grabbed her hand and tugged her into his arms. Her heart thundered as his tongue spiked into her mouth and thoroughly explored her inner heat. He pulled her pelvis toward his and she could feel his bulge press against her belly.

She wanted to drop to her knees right that second and tug out his cock and feast on it. He stroked his hands over her bare buttocks, then he gave her a light smack.

"Sit and eat," he said.

"Yes, Master."

She sat down, as did he, and she began to eat her eggs. Zeke sipped his coffee, then picked up his fork and took a bite. At the same time, his hand glided up her thigh. He found her mound and stroked it.

"Delicious," he said as his fingers dipped inside her.

She widened her legs and he pressed in deeper. Two fingers, then three.

"Keep eating," he said, and she realized she'd paused, enjoying his touch.

His fingers withdrew and slid to her aching clit. He dabbed at it, then stroked lightly. She arched forward a little, wanting more, but he withdrew.

Damn!

He ate some more, and before long, his hand found her

again. He stroked her clit and she remained still. He rewarded her by stroking until she could feel the pleasure build . . . washing through her as an orgasm drew near . . . then he stopped.

He sipped his coffee and ate a little more, ignoring her fidgeting. A few minutes later, he stroked her again, until she was oh, so close . . . then he stopped. Again.

By the time she finished breakfast, she wanted to beg him to give her the pleasure she so desired.

But she didn't. She'd learned that Zeke knew how to prolong her pleasure, and the prize was worth the wait.

He pushed his plate aside and turned his gaze to her. She stood up, her knees rubbery, and carried the two empty plates to the dishwasher, then retrieved the empty coffee mugs. Zeke followed her, and watched her place the dishes in the dishwasher. Once she closed the appliance door, he wrapped his hands around her waist and turned her around, then captured her lips again. Her bare breasts, the nipples aching, pressed against the soft cotton of his T-shirt, stretched across his hard male muscles. She leaned toward him, wanting to feel him against every inch of her body.

"Slave, kneel down and take out my cock."

Oh, yeah, baby!

She dropped to her knees and unzipped his pants, then reached inside for the prize. Her fingers wrapped around his thick, hard cock and she drew it out.

Hot. Hard. And enormous.

She wrapped her lips around him. His cockhead filled her mouth. She swirled her tongue around and around, loving the moan of approval he made. She glided down his shaft, taking him as deep as she could. She relaxed her throat and took him deeper still. He moaned again.

His fingers stroked over her hair. "Make me come, sweet thing."

She dove up and down on his hard cock, sucking and squeezing, as she stroked his gloriously hard butt. He tensed and his cock twitched, then he groaned as hot liquid filled her mouth. She swallowed, then smiled and stood up. He tugged her into his arms and kissed her passionately, his hands stroking her ass in a very encouraging manner.

"You deserve a reward for that."

He turned her around and bent her over the kitchen counter. The cold granite countertop startled her, sending her nipples pulsing with sensation, but she ignored it, concentrating on his hands gliding between her legs, stroking her wet slit.

Would he press his mouth to her opening? Or glide his cock inside and fuck her silly?

She felt his deflated cock press against her, instantly swelling as it slid against her wet flesh. He pressed it tight against her slit and it glided forward and back over her throbbing flesh. When it was long and hard again, he nudged it against her opening. His finger lightly tweaked her clit as the hard shaft slid into her.

Deep inside.

He didn't draw back, just stayed buried inside her. He fingered her clit again and she thought she'd burst with pleasure, but he released the sensitive bud. His pelvis still pressed tightly against her, his hands glided under her body and cupped her breasts. She pushed back against him, wanting his cock deeper still, but it made little difference. She squeezed him inside her, clutching him tightly, then releasing, then tightening again.

Oh God, she wanted to come.

He tweaked her nipples, then drew back. His cock slipped away, leaving her empty. She continued leaning on the counter, hoping he would thrust into her again. Hoping he would fuck her until she exploded in ecstasy.

"Stand up," he said.

She stood up and turned to face him, knowing her need must show clearly in her glazed eyes and burning cheeks.

"Follow me." He led her into the bedroom and her hopes soared. "Lie down on the bed and spread your legs."

"Yes, Master." She hopped onto the bed and lay down, then opened her legs, a big grin on her face.

He picked up a blue cloth cuff and wrapped it around one of her ankles. It attached with Velcro. Then he attached another cuff around her other ankle. She hadn't noticed the cuffs when she'd walked into the room, but now she saw that there were also two lying beside the pillows. All four cuffs were attached to straps that disappeared around the edges of the mattress. He attached the unused cuffs around her wrists and adjusted the straps until her arms and legs were pulled wide apart.

"Wait here," he said, then turned to leave the bedroom.

Like she had a choice.

As she lay there alone, spread-eagled on the bed, her whole body thrummed with anticipation. She remembered the feel of his enormous cock inside her just minutes ago, stretching her. Now she thought about it moving inside her, of his hard masculine body pumping into her.

Zeke returned ten minutes later carrying a piece of paper. He set it on the dresser then grabbed a black strap from the bedside table.

"Open your mouth."

She did and realized the strap was actually a gag as he

pushed a ball into her mouth. As her mouth closed around it, she realized the ball was actually the shape of a cockhead. Her tongue explored it as he attached the strap behind her head.

He stroked his thumb over her clit and she arched against him.

"You are totally ready and want me to fuck you, right?"

She nodded.

"You really, really need a man inside you, right?"

She nodded again, squeezing the cockhead in her mouth.

"I don't intend to fuck you . . ."

Her eyes widened and the throbbing between her legs intensified.

"Not now, anyway." He smiled. "Are you ready to push your limits?"

Oh God, she wanted him to fuck her.

She nodded.

"Okay, here's what's going to happen."

Eight

Ty put down his newspaper and stood up to answer the door. As he walked toward it, he saw an envelope sitting on the floor in front of the door. Someone must have slid it underneath. He peered out the peephole but didn't see anyone on the other side, so he picked up the envelope and opened it. He pulled out a piece of paper with a note in a neat computer script.

> *Ty,*
> *I need your help. Please come over and let yourself in.*
> *Marie*

Odd that Marie would leave him a note when she could have simply waited for him to answer the door. And why type the note on the computer rather than write it by hand? He walked into the kitchen. What kind of help did she need that she couldn't have asked Zeke for? After all, the guy had been over just last night.

Probably *all* night.

His gut tightened at the thought of Zeke over there in bed with Marie. Making love to Marie. Zeke had stolen Ashley from Ty years ago and now he'd stolen Marie. God damn it. Why the hell did he have to show up now and ruin everything?

He grabbed Marie's key from the drawer then headed down the hall. He knocked, but she didn't answer, so he let himself in, as she'd instructed.

"Marie?" he called. When she didn't answer, he walked into the kitchen, but she wasn't there. "Marie?" he called again.

The fur-ball trotted into the kitchen, meowing loudly. Ty noticed a note on the counter and before he could pick it up, the cat bounded onto the countertop and sat on it, then thrust its head against Ty's hand. Ty picked up the animal and petted it absently as he glanced at the piece of paper.

I'm in the bedroom.

Ty's heart rate doubled at the thought of Marie inviting him into her bedroom. His cock twitched, but he pushed aside lusty thoughts, knowing this might not be what he was hoping it was. He strode down the hall and peered into her spare bedroom. The computer was turned off and the room was empty. He continued down the hall, and noticed a note on her bedroom door.

Come in.

A quiver raced through him. All kinds of exciting ideas scurried through his head, but he thrust them aside, unwilling to get his hopes up.

He pushed the door open.

Marie heard the key in the lock of her apartment door. Oh God, was that Ty, or had Zeke come back? Then she heard Ty call her name.

What would Ty think when he saw her? She felt her cheeks burn. Plagued with second thoughts, she wished she could scurry from the bed and hide.

When Zeke first told her that he was going to send Ty in here, she'd balked, but the reality was that she had wanted Ty for a long time. Zeke knew Ty well and assured her Ty would be up for it.

She remembered that first morning-after in her apartment when Zeke had playfully talked her through a threesome with Ty as Zeke had made love to her. As he'd fucked her, he'd told her to imagine her neighbor's cock gliding into her as he watched from the chair. He'd had her repeat Ty's name, making it more real. Later in the fantasy, Zeke had told her to imagine both men pumping into her at the same time.

Her insides quivered in need.

Did Zeke hope to watch in real life like he had in the fantasy? To convince Ty to fuck her while he watched, then join them?

Ty called her name again, closer this time. She heard his footsteps in the hallway outside her bedroom. Oh God, what would Ty think when he saw her?

This whole thing was crazy—hands-down the craziest thing she'd ever done. But at the same time, it was also the most thrilling. She'd never felt so decadent . . . and so aroused in her entire life.

She remembered the heat in Ty's eyes when he looked at her sometimes. She was sure the attraction between them was mutual. When he saw her like this, would he find it as much of a turn-on as she did? And would he act on his attraction?

She drew in a deep breath as the door pushed open. God, she hoped so.

"Marie," Ty called as he pushed open the door.

He froze at the sight of Marie, totally naked and spread-eagled on the bed. His cock lurched to attention as he took in her bare breasts, her long slender legs, and a large round purple bow, about six inches in diameter, strategically placed on her pelvis, attached to a piece of notepaper jutting below.

Then he realized she was gagged and bound.

"Oh my God, Marie, are you all right?"

There were no sheets or blankets in sight to cover her, so he tugged off his T-shirt as he raced toward the bed ready to free her. Then he slowed down. What if he had just walked in on the middle of a kinky sex session with her and Zeke? He might walk in any second.

"Am I . . . intruding? Is Zeke here?"

He did *not* want to run into Zeke.

A memory of Ashley, bound and gagged, both he and Zeke pumping into her, flashed through his mind, followed by a surge of anger. At Zeke. At Ashley. At himself. God damn it, if Zeke walked in here right now, Ty would probably pound him one.

Marie shook her head, her gaze locked on his naked chest with hunger in her eyes. He continued to the bed and laid his T-shirt across her breasts. Her beautiful round, ripe breasts, the nipples puckered into hard tips. He sat down beside her and reached around behind her hair to remove the gag, but she shook her head and nodded downward. Toward the note.

He reached for the note, then realized he'd better leave it where it was. He shifted down the bed and gazed at the computer script.

> *Ty,*
> *I am hot and wet and ready for you.*
> *I want you to touch me. Everywhere.*
> *I am your love slave.*
> *Take me!*

His insides quivered as his cock twitched. His gaze flicked to Marie's. Her cheeks had stained crimson, but as he gazed at her, her sky blue eyes darkened. He reached behind her head and unfastened the gag, despite her protesting sounds. He drew it from her mouth and noticed it was a cock-head gag, which sent his tortured cock into another bout of twitching.

He wanted to ask her if Zeke had talked her into this, but if she answered yes, he wouldn't be able to go through with it and, right now, he could think of nothing else but running his hands all over her delightful naked body.

"Marie, did you write this note?"

"Every word is true."

So Zeke wrote it, but she was going along with it. Was this a lark for her? Sexual experimentation? Or had Zeke played the role of her Master and ordered her to do this? Could it be that Marie was a natural sub who couldn't say no to her Master?

The thought that Zeke had orchestrated this made Ty

angry, but his cock still throbbed with need. Damn it, he had to walk away. He couldn't let himself be pulled into this, no matter how much he wanted to touch her. To make sweet passionate love to her. He could *not* let Zeke use Marie to make up for the past. It wasn't fair to Marie, and . . . he sucked in a breath as he tried to ignore the almost overwhelming urge to push aside all reason and simply give in to his intense desire for her . . . Damn it, he just couldn't let Zeke control her this way. If Ty was going to be with Marie, it would be her choice, not Zeke's.

"Ty, I'm very attracted to you."

"Marie, are you saying this because you're following Zeke's orders in a Domination role-playing scenario?"

"No," she murmured.

His gaze locked on the tip of her tongue as it glided over her full lips, leaving them glistening.

"I want you," she said, "and I think the feeling is mutual."

Her words set his head spinning. His gaze locked with hers. Knowing she was attracted to him, too, sent hunger raging through him. This put a whole new light on things. *She wanted him.*

He stroked her long brown hair behind her ears, loving the feel of her silky skin under his fingertips.

"You have no idea how much."

She smiled. "Then how about you put the gag back in."

Ty picked up the gag, then paused to gaze at her lovely full lips. He leaned down and captured those lips, then glided his tongue into her silken depths. Heaven. He explored her warmth, his hands cupping her soft cheeks.

It was pure heaven. To touch her. To kiss her.

And his cock throbbed at the thought of what else he'd soon do.

He drew away and smiled at her, then he pushed the cockhead back into her mouth and fastened the gag into place.

"You want me to touch you everywhere?"

She nodded, her eyes twinkling. He grasped his T-shirt, loosely draped over her breasts, and slowly dragged it aside, watching as more and more of her delicate flesh became visible. The swell of her breast, then a hard dusky rose nipple. Another rising mound. Another hard nub.

The T-shirt dropped to the floor, leaving both of her breasts visible. Her chest rose and fell as she drew in deep breaths.

He smiled and reached for the note, with the bow attached, and picked them up. His gaze locked on her naked pussy. Shaved. Except for a tiny heart-shaped patch of curls at the top. Oh man, he wanted to run his fingertip through those curls, then glide lower and feel her wetness . . . but he wanted to do this right. He didn't want to spook her.

As his lips touched Marie's neck, tingles of excitement singed through her. He nuzzled, then kissed downward. He stroked over her breast, then cupped it in his warm hand. Her nipple thrust into his palm. When his mouth covered her other nipple, she thought she'd faint.

She had no idea Ty's touch would excite her so much. He was so much like the men she usually dated, yet his effect on her rivaled—if not surpassed—what she felt with Zeke. He sucked on her nub and she arched upward, murmuring around the cockhead in her mouth. She sucked on it, wishing she could see Ty's cock. Suck on Ty's cock.

When he'd taken off his shirt to cover her, her heart had melted at the lovely, protective gesture. That romantic notion had quickly turned to lustful thoughts as she gazed at his tight, hard abs and muscular arms and shoulders.

Ty released her nipple and stroked over her breasts, smiling at her.

"You are incredibly beautiful, Marie. I've wanted to do this for so long."

He leaned forward and kissed under her breast, then upward. Around the aureola, but never touching it. Then to her other breast. Kissing her. Lovingly. Tenderly. She felt warm and tingly all over. Cherished.

Then his mouth latched onto her nipple again and his tongue swirled over the hard nub. He sucked deeply.

She moaned.

His hands glided over her hips, then down her thighs. He caressed her calves, then stroked over her ankles and around her feet. He held one foot between his hands and caressed with light pressure. He massaged her foot until she turned to a boneless mass, then he gave her other foot the same treatment.

He smiled and pressed his mouth to the bottom of her foot, then dragged his tongue along her sensitive flesh. Oh God, it felt incredible. His gaze shifted from her face to her open thighs, and the slick opening between. Heat burned through her.

He released her foot and kissed along her calf, and up her inner thigh, his brown eyes simmering with heat. His hands glided over her hips, then he grinned and ran a fingertip through the small patch of curls.

"So just how wet are you?" He stroked along her slit and whistled. "Damn, you are wet!"

His finger pushed inside her and her eyelids fell closed at the intense excitement quivering through her.

"And pretty damned hot, too."

He stood up and her eyelids flicked open at the clunking sound of his belt hitting the floor. His jeans sat in a puddle at his feet. He stepped out of them, then tugged his boxers down.

When he stood up, she could see his large, hard cock standing at full attention.

Large? Good God, it was massive. Even bigger than Zeke's. The head, purple and straining, would fill her mouth. Her tongue glided over the cockhead of the gag.

He moved to the end of the bed and knelt between her legs. He stroked her thighs, then glided his fingers along her wet slit. The feel of him touching her there sent her heart fluttering into a wild erratic beat. Two of his fingers dipped inside her and she squeezed them. He chuckled.

His thumb brushed over her clit and, at the intense sensation, she moaned, though it came out as a dull mumble. He toyed with her, his fingers stroking inside her and his thumb brushing her sensitive button. Waves of pleasure rose in her and she could feel that sweet release swelling toward her.

Then he stopped.

God damn it, did these two guys work from the same playbook? Then his mouth covered her and pleasure spiked through her again. She mumbled her appreciation, arching against him, wanting more . . . more . . . *more!*

But as the wave rose again, promising to carry her to heaven, he stopped again.

He pushed up on his knees and grinned at her. "I think I'm frustrating you. Believe me, I want to give you an orgasm, I just want our first time to be . . . together."

Her gaze locked on his full, hard cock. Together. His huge cock driving into her. Oh yeah!

"Do you want me to make love to you now?"

She shook her head. Well, she did, but first, she wanted to taste that big cock of his.

He looked confused. "You don't want me to?"

She nodded her head, then mumbled against the gag, hoping he'd get the idea to take it off. He reached behind her head and unfastened it, then removed it.

As soon as the cockhead popped from her mouth, she said, "I do, I just . . . want something else first."

"What?"

She gazed at his cock and he smiled.

"What do you want, Marie?"

Nine

Marie rolled her eyes, knowing Ty was going to insist she say it.

"I want to suck your cock."

He grinned, then prowled over her. She licked her lips as the giant straining purple cockhead drew close to her mouth. With a knee on each side of her chest, he pressed his pelvis forward, his cock in his hand. She opened, welcoming his hot, hard cock. The bulbous head slid into her mouth, filling it. She licked him, swirling her tongue around and around the little hole on the tip.

She squeezed him inside her mouth, then tipped her head forward to take him deeper. He pressed in a little, then drew back . . . gliding in and out in short strokes. She squeezed and licked. His short thrusts sped up and she sensed him getting close. She sucked, loving the feel of his hard flesh in her mouth, anticipating his release. Wanting to make him climax.

But suddenly he pulled free.

"Damn it, woman, I told you I want us to come to-gether."

She smiled at his tremulous voice . . . and his sweet romantic notion. He wanted their first time to be special.

"Sorry . . . Master."

The hot look in his eyes as she said *Master* enthralled her. Could Mr. Nice Guy Ty be a closet dominant?

"Damn, you're sexy." He shifted downward and kissed her neck, then he captured her mouth and kissed her passionately, taking her breath away.

She felt his cock nudge her opening. "Oh yes."

His cockhead pressed inside her, stretching her.

"Oh God, Master, fuck me."

He groaned, then thrust deep inside her.

She moaned, startled—and totally enthralled—at the feel of his huge cock totally filling her. He held her tight to his body. His cock twitched inside her, almost sending her over the edge.

"Ty, if you . . ." She gasped as he started to ease back, his cockhead dragging against the sensitive walls of her vagina, sending electric pleasure sparking through her. "Oh . . . if you want us to come . . ." She sucked in another breath at the exquisite sensations flickering inside her. "Together . . ."

He glided into her again and she felt light-headed.

"You'll have to . . ." She moaned as waves of pleasure wafted through her. "Hurry."

He drew back and, as he thrust into her again, she arched forward to meet him. She wailed at the intense joy shooting through her. His cock drove deep and she plummeted into ecstasy, barely aware of his loud groan as he pulsed within her, filling her with liquid heat.

Collapsing on top of her, he nuzzled her neck. Then his lips found hers and caressed them in a tender kiss.

He sat up and unfastened her ankles, then her wrists, then drew her into his arms. His lips caressed the top of her head as he enveloped her in his embrace, holding her tight to his broad, strong chest.

Never had she felt so cherished or protected.

Zeke lay in bed, staring at the ceiling, wondering what Marie and Ty were doing right now. He could imagine Ty finding Marie sprawled naked on the bed, her arms and legs bound. Ty's immediate thoughts had probably been to set her free—and likely to beat Zeke to a pulp. Until he found the note.

Then things would have changed. Ty would have realized that Marie was all laid out, gift-wrapped in her birthday suit, complete with a bow, just for him. Zeke could imagine Ty reading the note, then—after he got over the shock—drawing aside the bow and touching her. Sliding his fingers into her and feeling how hot and wet she was.

Zeke's cock pulsed with need. He grasped it and stroked as he thought of Ty stroking Marie's body, then succumbing to his need and thrusting inside her. Zeke's cock hardened even more at the thought of what Ty felt as he glided inside Marie.

Ty had probably wanted her for a while now. It would be an intense experience for him. Thrusting into her hot, wet body, hearing her soft murmurs around the gag.

Zeke continued to stroke his rigid member, faster and faster, until he stiffened and released in a gripping climax. Within moments, he fell asleep.

Zeke stepped into Marie's apartment and heard moaning in the other room. He walked down the hall, then pushed open the door to her bedroom. He saw two naked bodies as Ty thrust into Marie, her hands clinging to his shoulders. Ty thrust, and thrust again. Marie wailed her release.

Zeke's cock swelled to life.

Ty rolled back and flopped beside her.

"Hey, buddy." Ty's eyes lit up as he saw Zeke standing in the doorway. "Come on in."

Marie glowed with happiness as she gazed at him. "Zeke, I'm glad you're here. Ty was fabulous . . ." She stroked a hand over Ty's chest. "Thank you so much." She stroked her hands over her breasts, then widened her legs. "Now I'd really like you to fuck me, too."

"I'd love to watch that," Ty said, his eyes lighting up as he pushed himself to a sitting position. His sagging cock began to harden again.

Zeke's cock strained against his jeans.

Marie sat up. "Come over here." Her voice, low and sultry, drew him like a siren's song.

He stepped beside her and she unzipped him and tugged out his throbbing cock. She licked the tip of him, then her mouth—hot and moist—surrounded him. He groaned. Her hand stroked his balls while she dove up and down on him, then she sucked on his shaft until he thought he'd burst. She released him, then lay back and opened her arms.

He prowled over her and nudged his cock to her opening. Ty watched with interest as Zeke's shaft slowly glided into Marie. She squeezed him inside her and he groaned again. He drew back and thrust forward. She moaned, clinging to him.

It was heaven feeling her hot body grip his cock as it stroked inside her. He thrust faster and deeper and she moaned again. He could tell she was close.

"Oh Zeke. Oh . . . you're making me come." She arched against him as he kept thrusting. "Oh God, I'm . . . I'm coming." She wailed long and hard as he thrust and thrust.

Finally, she flopped back, exhausted from a long, intense orgasm. He drew his cock from inside her, still hard. Still needy. He stood up, a little disoriented. Ty got up and circled around the bed toward him.

"Zeke, I want to thank you for your gift," Ty said.

While Ty spoke, Marie's hand wrapped around his cock and stroked. Ty grasped Zeke's head, then pressed his lips to Zeke's.

Startled, Zeke stood frozen. Ty's tongue—warm and firm— delved inside his mouth. Marie's hand stroked Zeke's straining cock and hormones raged through him. Suddenly, Zeke found himself kissing Ty back. Ty's hands stroked down Zeke's back and he pulled him closer. Another hand encircled his cock. A bigger, firmer hand.

Zeke jerked back and gazed down to see Marie and Ty holding his cock. Marie released him and Ty knelt down in front of him. When Ty's lips encircled Zeke's cockhead, then drew him inside, Zeke could feel an intense need building in his gut.

He wanted this. Oh God, he wanted Ty to suck his cock. To give him an orgasm.

Ty dove down, taking Zeke deep, then slowly glided back. Forward again, then back. Pleasure washed through Zeke in intense waves. Two more strokes and Zeke felt it happening. His balls tightened. His nerve endings quivered. Heat shot through him as he ejaculated inside Ty's mouth.

Zeke's eyelids jerked open and he stared at the darkness around him. A *dream*. It had been a fucking *dream*.

As he felt the damp, sticky fluid on his belly, he realized it had been a very hot . . . and very *wet* . . . dream.

What the fuck was going on?

Marie felt Ty's firm masculine back against her cheek. She wrapped her arms around his waist, snuggled closer, and sighed. Slowly, she opened her eyelids to the bright morning sunlight streaming into the room.

A blue eye stared back at her.

She started, then realized it was a tattoo.

Tattoo? But Ty didn't have a tattoo. A fog surrounded her brain as she grasped at memories of last night. It had been Ty she'd gone to bed with, not Zeke. Hadn't it? But . . .

She stared at the tattoo, then lurched back.

"Zeke?"

Something was very wrong. The dragon on Zeke's *chest* had blue eyes, but wasn't the tattoo on Zeke's back a large green-eyed dragon? But this was a bird of some sort. Long and stylized with blue eyes, and crimson and blue feathers.

Abruptly, he rolled over and glared at her. Strands of straight sandy brown hair—not black waves—fell across his forehead.

"Ty!" Oh God, what the heck was going on?

"That's right. And don't forget it."

The brimstone in his brown eyes and the commanding note in his voice startled her. It was so unlike him. So . . . intimidating. So . . . *sexy*.

He grabbed her and dragged her into his arms, then captured her lips in an aggressive, passionate kiss. Overpowering her with intense masculinity.

"*I'm* the one who made love to you last night. Not Zeke."

She nodded, wide-eyed. Saturday morning Ty had found

her sprawled on her bed, naked and bound. He had made love to her then . . . and again later. And again in the evening. They hadn't been able to get enough of each other. They had finally collapsed in each other's arms and fallen asleep.

"I know . . ." she said. "I . . . It's just that . . . I didn't know you had a tattoo. I thought I must have . . . gotten confused."

The thunderous expression seeped from his face.

"Tattoo? Right. I was going to explain about that. I—"

He seemed about to apologize, so she silenced him with a finger over his lips.

"No, I like it. I find it . . . sexy."

He smiled. "Really?" Then his smile faded. "Because it reminds you of Zeke?"

"No, because it shows me another side of you. A sort of . . . *dangerous* side."

His eyebrows lowered. "And you like that?"

She smiled. "Oh yeah."

She cupped his whisker-roughened cheeks. The sheer masculinity of it sent chills through her. Oh God, he was so intensely sexy! She brushed her lips against his. His arms tightened around her and he pulled her closer, crushing her breasts against his solid chest. Her nipples puckered immediately. His hand glided down her back and he pulled her hips tight to his pelvis. His hard cock pressed against her belly.

When he released her lips she gazed up at him, catching her breath.

"I . . . want you to turn around," she said.

"Why?"

"I . . ." She licked her lips. "I want to see it."

"Okay, but that's the wrong direction."

She smacked him lightly. "I mean your tattoo."

He grinned, then rolled over. She traced her finger along the bird's head, which curved up across his left shoulder blade, then down the feathers along its back, which roughly paralleled Ty's spine.

"It's a phoenix," he said.

"Rebirth."

"That's right. I had it reworked from a dragon—in fact an exact duplicate of Zeke's—but then I decided to . . . change some things in my life, so I thought it was appropriate."

She wanted to ask if it had anything to do with what had happened between him and Zeke, but decided now wasn't the time.

"Sit up. I want to have a better look," she said.

He pushed himself up and sat on the edge of the bed, his feet on the floor. She sat behind him and traced the large tattoo with her finger. It stretched about twelve inches long, covering most of the left side of his back. She sat with her pelvis tight to his back, her legs dangling over the edge of the bed, and snuggled her cheek against his sexy tattoo. She reached around his waist and stroked his belly . . . then lower, until she found the tip of his erection. Her hand glided over his shaft, then she wrapped her hand around his hard cock.

"Mmm. I like that," he murmured.

"Me, too."

She hooked her legs around his thighs and pulled her pelvis tighter against him. As she stroked his cock up and down, she pulsed her hot opening against his hard butt. His muscular cheeks stroked her sex, her soft flesh pressing between them, not quite giving her the stimulation she needed. His hand slid around behind him and his finger glided along her slick slit. He found her clit with his fingertip and stroked it.

"Oh yes. That's good," she murmured against his back. She rocked her pelvis as she stroked his long cock. Up and down. His breathing accelerated right along with hers as he toyed with her clit, sending pleasure catapulting along her nerve endings. She nuzzled the phoenix as she stroked, then moaned at the blissful waves flooding her senses. Her eyelids fluttered closed.

He squeezed her button and she gasped. The feel of his rigid cock gliding past her palms heightened the delightful sensations streaming through her . . . then sparks flared behind her eyelids as she shot off to heaven.

"Oh God, sweetheart." He turned and rolled her backward as he spoke, then climbed over her. "I want to—"

But his cock exploded in a stream of white, pooling on her chest, as he groaned. She grabbed his cock and stroked while he continued to climax, his face taut with pleasure.

Then he stared down at her and the white fluid covering her breasts.

"Oh sweetheart, I'm sorry."

"Don't be." She dragged her finger through the pool, then licked her fingertip.

His eyes darkened as he watched her intently. She cupped her breasts and pushed them upward, the nipples standing tall and proud.

"Oh God, you are so sexy." He leaned forward and wrapped his lips around one taut nipple, then sucked.

Tremors of need shot through her. She grabbed his cock and squeezed. It immediately grew hard in her hands. Thick and long.

"Fuck me, Ty."

His eyes widened, but he pressed his finger to her wet slit and glided along it.

"I want that hard cock of yours inside me," she insisted. "Now."

"Whatever the lady wants."

He pressed his tip to her opening and propelled forward, skewering her with one deep thrust. She gasped at the exquisite pleasure.

He drew back and pulsed deep again. She wrapped her legs around him, drawing him deeper still.

He leaned forward and kissed her. Deep and passionate. Then he began to thrust with a vengeance. Hard. And fast.

Her internal muscles tightened around him as she rode the wave of intense sensations. Magnificent pleasure seared every nerve ending. She clung to him as an incredible orgasm tore through her, flinging her to a place of pure ecstasy.

He groaned as he filled her with liquid heat.

As she lay in his arms, his cock still buried deep inside her, he kissed her cheek. She snuggled against him, not wanting this closeness to end. But knowing it would. It had to.

Ty gazed at her and felt his heart compress. This was uncharted territory for them, and he knew he had to tread lightly.

He didn't want to turn her off by overanalyzing things, but he had to know what this meant to her. Did this mean they were together now, or had Zeke merely pulled him in as a one-time thing?

He watched as she hopped from the bed and grabbed her robe.

"Marie, I have to know. Are you with me or are you with Zeke?"

Ten

Marie had to be careful here. She didn't want him to feel used, but she didn't want him to think they were more than friends either.

She had been clutching her robe around her waist, not having wasted time tying it. Now she allowed it to slip from her shoulders, intent on keeping his full attention.

"Zeke suggested what we did last night. But the truth is, I've been attracted to you for some time."

The robe dropped lower, and his gaze remained fixed on the sliding fabric. She allowed it to fall to the floor. His brown eyes darkened as he stared at her hardening nipples.

"How attracted?"

She noticed his cock rising.

She stepped toward him. "*Very* attracted." She pressed her hand to his chest and pressed him back until he sat down, then she settled on the bed next to him. "But I think that's a perfectly natural response. I mean, we're very compatible as friends—there's definitely a strong connection between us. And you're a great-looking guy—"

"And you're a beautiful woman." He put his hand on top of hers.

She closed her eyes, enjoying his warmth.

"But relationships come and go . . . For me anyway," she said. "I'm still figuring out what I need in a guy. But I feel like our friendship is something that can last forever and I want to hold on to that."

He cupped her cheeks and stared into her eyes. "If you think our friendship can last forever, then maybe a relationship could, too."

Uh-oh. This was going in the wrong direction.

"I'm not willing to take that chance."

She saw a stricken look in his eyes, and knew she'd just hurt his feelings.

"I'm just trying to be clear about things so neither of us ends up hurt. You're my best friend, Ty, and knowing I hurt you would break my heart. The only thing worse would be losing you."

"I understand where you're coming from. But there's something I want to know. If Zeke weren't in the picture, would you and I have a chance?"

"Ty, don't ask me that."

"I am asking." He squeezed her hand and gazed deep into her eyes. "Tell me."

"Zeke is a little wild. A little . . . dangerous."

"Whereas I'm like every other guy you've ever dated."

"Ty, you mean the world to me."

"But I'm safe? Predictable?"

"Of course you are, and that's not a bad thing. You're also kind, thoughtful, sensitive—"

"What if I was dominating and . . . dangerous."

"Ty, that's not it."

"What is it then? Tell me."

"I've already told you . . . There isn't much more to it. Romantic relationships end. If I go out with you . . . and it doesn't work out, then . . . I might lose you." She stroked his sandy brown hair, her gut tensing at the thought. "I couldn't bear that."

"You'll never lose me," he murmured, then kissed her temple.

Ty strolled into the kitchen and started the coffee, then grabbed the eggs from the fridge. The fur-ball rubbed around his legs, meowing. He picked her up and stroked her back, enjoying the soothing purring sound emanating from the small creature.

He still couldn't believe what had happened last night, and this morning. Making love to Marie . . . holding her in his arms . . . had been a dream come true. A dream he couldn't bear to have come to an end.

He grabbed a cat treat from the little tin on the counter and held it in front of the cat. She sniffed it, then Ty placed the animal on the floor with the treat in front of her. She picked up the morsel gingerly, then carried it to the window to devour.

But Marie was dating Zeke, and if Ty stole her away, wouldn't he be repeating exactly what Zeke had done when he'd stolen Ashley? Except that Ty had had his sights on Marie long before Zeke stepped into the picture.

Not that Zeke had known that. Damn, what an annoying situation. Marie was Zeke's girl, but she should be Ty's. But Ty couldn't steal her away from Zeke because . . . that wouldn't be right.

On the other hand, Zeke had offered to step aside. Could Ty really ask him to do that? Damn it, this was too important to let stupid male pride get in the way. If Zeke was willing to—

But then, Marie was a part of the equation. Ty wasn't stupid enough to believe that he and Zeke could decide who Marie would want to be with. Only she could make that decision. All Ty could do was let her know how much he wanted her and see if he could get her over her fear of falling in love with him.

And hope she would choose him over Zeke.

To do that, he'd have to stay in the picture. Essentially, he'd have to be the third in their threesome. *Just like Ashley had asked Zeke to be with her and me.* The difference being that Zeke knew the possible outcome and was okay with it.

Damn, if this was going to work, he'd have to drop the animosity between him and Zeke. Ty had been angry for five years. Maybe it was time to let it go. He had to give Zeke credit for the fact he wanted to do the right thing by Ty and help him win Marie, especially since he clearly wanted her for himself.

If Zeke could take that step, then maybe Ty could have the woman he loved after all.

Marie stepped into the living room, her hair still slightly damp from her shower. The sun shone brightly in her large living room window and soft rock music played on the radio. At the delicious aroma of bacon, she headed straight to the kitchen.

Ty stood at the stove stirring half-cooked scrambled eggs with a wooden spoon.

"Smells great," she said, admiring his tight butt, shown off to perfection in his snug jeans.

He turned around and pulled her into his arms. "You smell great, too."

He kissed her, his lips lingering a moment longer than they would have for a friendly kiss, but she didn't seem to notice.

"Well, good morning to you, too."

He grinned. "It has been so far."

"Want me to set the table?" she asked.

"Already done. I thought we'd eat in the dining room today."

Ty grabbed a plate and spooned a helping of eggs onto it, set it aside, then poured the rest of the eggs onto a second plate. He opened the oven and pulled out the bacon on a warming tray, then placed several strips on each plate.

He carried them through the door into the dining room and they both sat down. He already had the cutlery laid out, along with a jug of orange juice, jam, honey, and a basket with two croissants and some toast. She plucked a piece of toast from the basket and buttered it, then spread it with jam.

"So, was yesterday's fun and games a one-time event, or do you think I'll be included in future adventures?"

"Oh, well . . . I don't know." She shifted in her chair. "I doubt Zeke will want to repeat the same thing, especially since he wasn't . . . you know . . . involved."

"So what about doing something where he is involved?"

"You mean . . . both of you?"

He nodded, gazing at her over his mug as he sipped.

"Since you and Zeke don't seem to get along, I sort of figured that you wouldn't want to," she said.

"But if I was agreeable, and so was Zeke, would you want to?"

A shiver danced down her spine. Would she ever!

"Well . . . I . . . uh . . . would consider it."

She put down her fork.

"If you don't mind me asking . . . Zeke said you both went to the same high school. Were you friends?"

"Yeah. We were."

"How did you meet?"

He sighed. "When I was in my early teens, my dad lost his job, so we moved to a low-income neighborhood in Jersey where my dad got a job in a factory. It was a tough neighborhood, people just scraping by. Zeke lived in the house next door and we became friends. He showed me the ropes, helped me avoid trouble." Ty sipped his coffee. "That was when he lived with the Johnsons. They were good people, but they were just his foster parents."

"Zeke's an orphan?" she asked.

Ty shook his head. "His parents abandoned him when he was twelve. He lived on the streets for about three months before anyone realized he had no home."

Her heart clenched at the thought of young Zeke, only twelve years old, wandering around without a home, without anyone to look out for him or take care of him.

"So these people he was living with when you moved there, they adopted him?" she asked.

"No, they were his foster parents. Then things changed and for some reason, they couldn't keep taking care of him, so he moved in with another family. Things weren't so great for him there. The old man beat him up a lot and every time he did, Zeke took off. He bounced from home to home for quite a while, with no consistency, no . . . love."

Zeke's story broke Marie's heart.

"Finally," Ty continued, "when Zeke was seventeen, childhood services put him in a group home. Zeke started hanging out with members of a local gang." Ty stared into his coffee mug, swirling it around. "I could see he was heading for big trouble. We were still friends and I told him I wouldn't have any part of a gang, but that we could be our own gang of two."

"You basically made him choose between the gang and you?"

Ty shrugged. "It was the only way. What he really needed was a sense of belonging. A family, of sorts, that would look out for him. I convinced him we were tough enough to make it without them. That's when we got the matching tattoos." He smiled wistfully. "My parents nearly killed me over that."

By the look of affection in his eyes, she knew he meant they'd shown typical parental concern. He set down his mug on the table.

"Did they try to stop you from being friends with Zeke?" she asked.

Ty shrugged. "They were worried, but they could tell Zeke was basically a good kid in a bad situation. They believed, like I did, that he just needed a little friendship and support."

"And you gave him that." Her heart swelled at Ty's compassion and loyalty to his friend. "How long did you remain friends?"

"Until about five years ago."

Her eyebrows arched upward. She knew Ty had gone

to college and studied computer science—he now worked as a software architect at a major high-tech company—so she had assumed that their friendship had waned when Ty left for school. Of course, that didn't explain the animosity Ty held for Zeke.

"So what happened?"

Ty's jaw clenched and his eyes turned hard.

She rested her hand on his. "I'd really like to know."

His lips compressed into a tight line, but he nodded.

"I was dating this girl a while back . . . her name was Ashley. Very sexy. Zeke found her attractive." He took a sip of his coffee, then pushed his mug aside. "Ashley and I had been dating for a couple of months and . . . she was pretty adventurous. She knew Zeke and I were good friends, and . . . she told me she'd had this fantasy for a long time. To have a threesome with two men. She wondered if . . . Zeke might join us sometime and help fulfill that fantasy."

Marie felt her cheeks flush a little. Zeke had returned the favor, having invited Ty to join them. She felt sure Zeke hadn't intended this to be a reversal of that earlier incident, but she couldn't help feeling a bit strange about the whole thing. Of course, in this case, Zeke had merely shared his girlfriend—her—with Ty, while not actually participating in the sharing. Was that his way of making sure it didn't get weird?

"So the three of you . . . did it?" She sipped her coffee, trying to appear nonchalant.

"Yeah. And Ashley loved it. So much so, that a few days later I caught her draped all over Zeke, practically sucking his face off."

"Are you saying Zeke stole your girlfriend?"

"He said he didn't, but the evidence was right in front of me. Ashley broke up with me right after that."

Marie decided not to ask if this Ashley woman had started dating Zeke afterward. Better not to fan the flames.

"You didn't believe Zeke? Even though you were such good friends?"

His hands rolled into fists, his eyes flashing. "A woman can come between the best of friends."

He tossed back the rest of his orange juice and thumped the glass on the table. He then picked up his fork.

They continued eating in silence, except for the music playing on the stereo.

What if she had met these two men when they'd still been buddies? Would she have been the woman to come between them? Because with the chemistry she shared with both men . . .

Damn, she would never want to be responsible for breaking up a close friendship. She drew in a deep breath and gazed at Ty as he finished his eggs. Would it be possible to use this situation to do the opposite? Could carrying on a relationship with both men . . . forcing them to be together . . . actually help patch things up between them? It would be a fine balance, but if they went into this with both men knowing firmly where they stood . . . that she was Zeke's girlfriend, not Ty's . . .

Ty finished eating and he set his plate aside and sipped his coffee.

"Marie, I'm sorry I snapped at you. And . . . I know you're going out with Zeke. I shouldn't have brought it up."

"Not at all. I asked you." She gazed at him. "Earlier you asked if . . . well, if I might consider being with . . . you know, both of you. If you and Zeke are at odds, why would you even consider it?"

His gaze locked with hers. "To be with you."

Eleven

"Oh." She would love to be with both men at the same time. It would be a fantasy come true. Especially with *these* two men.

But would she be sending the wrong message? Remembering the look in Ty's eyes this morning, she worried that Ty might hope that their sexual relationship would turn into something more.

But he knew she was dating Zeke. And she'd made it abundantly clear to Ty that she did not want to pursue a romantic relationship with him.

So the fact that he had asked her about starting a threesome proved to her that he would be happy with a no-strings-attached sexual relationship.

Well, why not? Most guys would love it. She really needed to stop overthinking things. It's not like she was torturing the guy. If anything, she was giving him a male fantasy come true.

"Um . . . well, if you're okay with it, I think Zeke would go for it."

His gaze locked with hers. "Did he say something?"

"Not as such, but that first night he was here . . . and you came to feed Jade in the morning . . . I told him my neighbor was here to feed the cat and he . . . sort of suggested inviting you to join us."

He raised an eyebrow. "Really?"

"He thought my neighbor was a woman, but when I told him you were a guy, he told me to close my eyes and he talked me through a fantasy with you joining us. He didn't know it was you, of course."

"What did he say?"

"He . . . uh, first he said to imagine that you were making love to me and he was watching from the chair. Then we . . . pretended that both of you were . . . well, you get the idea."

"No, tell me." He grinned. "What did you pretend?"

She smiled, her cheeks heating. "You're bad."

"At least tell me . . . was I front or back?"

She remembered the feel of Zeke's finger slipping into her back opening as he filled her vagina with his cock, telling her he would slide into her ass while Ty fucked her.

"Uh . . . the first time you were in front."

"The first time? Sounds like I've starred in a few of your fantasies."

The hot look he sent her heated her insides.

She smiled. "The next time, he got one of my vibrators and used it to actually play out the scenario. You were the back that time."

His eyebrow arched again. "How many vibrators do you have?"

Her cheeks grew hotter. "Just the right number," she quipped.

"So I've been back and front." His gaze intensified. "Are you as totally turned on as I am?"

Oh God, her insides were melting. "Oh yeah."

She shoved back her chair and lurched to her feet. Ty met her, wrapping his arms around her and capturing her lips, his tongue gliding into her mouth. She opened, her tongue meeting his. Her nipples pressed hard against his solid chest as his hands stroked up and down her back, stoking the fire within her.

She dropped to her knees, then grabbed his zipper tag and pulled it down. She tugged down his jeans, and stroked over the bulge in his boxers.

"Sit," she said.

He sat down and she reached inside and drew out his cock, already rock hard. She wrapped her fingers around the shaft—so thick she couldn't close her fingers around it. She stroked. From bottom to top, then down again. She leaned forward and brushed her lips against the bulbous head.

She trembled at the feel of his hard flesh pressed to her mouth . . . at the power she felt as she licked the tip of his enormous erection and it twitched in her hold. She lightly brushed her teeth over the big straining head, then opened wide and drew it inside. It filled her mouth. She swirled her tongue over the tip, then spiraled downward until she caressed the underside of the corona.

His fingers stroked through her hair. "Oh sweetheart, that feels incredible."

She licked around and around, encouraged by his increasingly rapid breathing and his fingers tightening around her scalp.

She glided downward, taking him as deep as she could. She squeezed him in her mouth, then sucked. She dipped a hand into his boxers and stroked his balls lightly with her fingertips. She glided up, then down again, squeezing his cock within her mouth in a pulsing motion.

"Damn, sweetheart, I won't last with you doing that."

She sucked harder, then bobbed up and down on him faster. His breathing accelerated and she cradled his balls and stroked delicately as she sucked and squeezed, continuing to move up and down. He stiffened, then groaned. Liquid heat pulsed into her mouth.

When he was done and slumped back in the chair, she released him and smiled.

He drew her to her feet and tugged her onto his lap, then kissed her, his lips caressing hers with passion. His hands stroked over her back. She reached for the hem of her T-shirt and started drawing it up, wanting to feel his hands on her breasts.

"Wait."

She stopped, and gazed at him. He took her hands and kissed them, then slid his arm around her waist and stood up, taking her with him. He wrapped his hand around hers and led her to the couch.

"Bring me a silk scarf." His authoritative tone sent a chill through her. Goose bumps quivered across her flesh.

Zeke had commanded her many times, but Ty's tone had an incredibly sexy effect on her. Maybe because of the contrast to his usual sweet, considerate demeanor.

"Yes, Master."

She scurried to her bedroom, pulled open the top drawer of her dresser and scooped up a handful of scarves, then grabbed the black glittery one. It wasn't silk, but it was a soft delicate texture and that's probably all he cared about.

When she returned to the living room, he was just saying good-bye to someone on his cell phone. She handed him the scarf.

"Good choice. Now turn around."

He placed the scarf over her eyes, then tied it behind her head.

"Can you see anything?" he asked.

"No, Master."

"Very good."

She felt his hands grasp her hips and he guided her forward, then he let go.

"Now, take off your clothes." From the direction of his voice, he was in front of her now. Maybe he was sitting in the armchair.

Her nipples hardened and heat melted inside her as she grasped the hem of her T-shirt and drew it over her head, then let go of it. She unfastened her silver-edged denim belt, then unzipped her jeans and pushed them over her hips. They fell to the floor and she kicked them aside.

She stood there in only her bra and thong, totally aware of Ty's gaze on her. She reached behind her and unhooked her bra. She suddenly felt a little shy. He could see her but she couldn't see him. It felt . . . wicked . . . sexy. She stroked her hands over her breasts, still covered by the lacy cups of her bra . . . then slowly eased the fabric forward. Cool air caressed her skin as she dropped the garment to the floor. Her nipples grew harder still.

"Lovely." He seemed to be across the room now.

"Where are you?" she asked.

"I'm just getting my coffee mug. Keep going."

As she tucked her thumbs under the waistband of her thong, a knock sounded at the door. Damn, what rotten timing.

"I'll get that," Ty said.

She reached for the blindfold to pull it off. "Uh . . . I'd better—"

"Leave the blindfold," he commanded.

Her fingers jerked from the fabric at his tone.

"I just looked through the peephole. It's Zeke."

A quiver raced along her spine. What would Zeke think if he saw her like this with Ty? Sure, he set things up so Ty would find her bound to her bed and make love to her, but maybe he'd only meant for them to have that one encounter. Maybe the fact Ty had even slept over was more than Zeke had intended, let alone the sexy encounters they'd already had this morning. Guilt crept through her. Had she been cheating on Zeke?

A knock sounded again.

"You stay exactly as you are. I'm going to get it."

"But—"

"Don't worry. I'll just step outside and talk to him."

She heard the door open, then close again. She stood in the room, practically naked, goose bumps quivering along her flesh. A couple of minutes later, the door opened again, then closed.

"I told Zeke a little of our conversation. That I think you would like the idea of him watching us make love. He's willing if you are."

A quiver raced through her.

"You mean . . . now? He'd come in and . . . watch us?"

"That's right."

Oh God, Zeke was standing outside the door right

now, awaiting her answer. Did he know she was practically naked?

"He's really excited by the idea, Marie."

Her head started to nod before she'd even consciously decided, but she knew it's what she wanted.

"Good."

She heard the door open, then close a few seconds later. She trembled and felt a little weak in the knees.

"Zeke wants you to pretend he's not here. He wants us to carry on as if we're alone."

She nodded. She might be able to *pretend* he wasn't here, but she sure wouldn't be able to ignore the effect of knowing he sat in the same room as she stood here naked . . . as Ty touched her, then made love to her.

"Zeke is sitting in the easy chair, watching you. I can tell by his face that he is totally turned on by the sight of you."

"I thought I was supposed to pretend he wasn't here."

"Let's say it's more that he wants you to *behave* as if he's not here. Now, take off your panties."

"Yes, Master."

What would Zeke think of her calling Ty "master" instead of him? Would he be angry? Would he punish her? And why did the idea of being punished make her so hot?

She sucked in a breath and hooked her thumbs under the waistband of her thong, then pushed it down her legs. She flicked it over her feet, then tossed it aside . . . then slowly stood up, quite aware that as soon as she straightened up both men would see her entirely naked body.

"Gorgeous. Zeke has pulled out his cock and is stroking it as he watches you."

The thought sent a thrill through her.

She heard a zipper, then the clunk of pants and a belt

hitting the floor. A moment later, Ty's hands stroked over her back, then settled on her shoulders and he drew her back against his hot—and very naked—body.

He stroked around her body and cupped her breasts. The nipples pressed into his palms. One hand continued downward, over her belly, then over her pubic curls. He cupped her mound, then he stroked her, gliding over her damp slit.

"You're very wet." One finger dipped into her. Then a second. "Do you like that, Marie?"

Tingles raced through her insides.

"Yes."

Zeke could see her . . . could hear her . . . responding to Ty.

He kissed her cheek. "Don't worry about Zeke," he murmured in her ear. "He's very excited watching you."

"Ty, is—"

Ty's finger swirled inside her and she sucked in air.

He kissed her neck. "What is it?"

"Is . . . uh . . . Zeke really here?"

He slid his hands to her waist and drew her tighter to his body.

"Do you want me to take off the blindfold so you can see?" His fingers settled lightly on the back of the scarf.

She wondered if he'd only told her Zeke was here to increase the excitement . . . which certainly was working.

Did she want to know?

She shook her head, almost sure Zeke wasn't there, but unwilling to give up the fantasy.

"I'm sitting down on the couch." Ty's hands glided down to her hips. "I want you to sit on my lap."

He eased her down and she followed. She felt his legs

beneath her and settled onto his lap. His hard cock pressed against her back.

"Bring your legs up and kneel on me."

She lifted one foot and tucked it beside him, then the other, settling on her knees facing away from him.

"Now I'm going to shove my cock inside you and fuck you in front of Zeke."

His words sent a thrill through her. Zeke watching them while Ty thrust into her, bringing her to orgasm.

His cockhead nudged her slick slit, then glided inside, filling her with his thick length. He went deep, stretching her all the way. She squeezed him as his hands stroked over her breasts. She arched forward, filling his hands.

"You are so God damned sexy," he murmured in her ear.

He wrapped his hands around her waist and guided her body upward. The ridge of his cock stroked her inner walls, sending intensely erotic sensations dancing through her. He guided her downward again, and she gasped as his huge cock filled her again.

She moved up and down as waves of pleasure rose within her. Zeke watching her. Ty fucking her. She moaned as his cock thrust deep . . . then drew back. Then thrust deep again. Her body tightened, then exploded in blissful waves of intense pleasure. Ty groaned, filling her with liquid heat and she gasped, then wailed in ecstasy. Still Ty thrust into her, extending her pleasure on . . . and on.

Finally she collapsed against him. His arms curled around her waist and they sat together, catching their breath.

A few moments later, Ty nuzzled her neck.

"Zeke's gone now," he said as he drew the blindfold from her eyes.

As soon as the fabric pulled free, her gaze dodged to the

armchair where Zeke had supposedly been sitting. No sign of him.

She had no idea if he'd really been there or not.

Zeke walked toward the phone and reached for the handset, wanting to call Marie and tell her he wanted to come over. He wanted to hear all about what had happened with her and Ty . . . to have her tell him every last, intimate detail.

He clenched his fist, resisting the urge to just pick up the phone and call her. The whole idea had been to give Ty a chance with her. If things had gone well, Ty would still be with her. Zeke didn't want to mess things up by getting in the way.

No matter how much he wanted to see Marie.

He turned away from the phone and walked toward his computer. He'd distract himself by reading e-mails, then maybe hop on his Harley and go for a ride. Clear his head.

He turned on his monitor and opened the browser. His inbox popped into view. Of the ten unread messages, the one on the top caught his attention. It was from someone called yes.master.0. He would have thought it was a spam message trying to attract him to some porn site, but the subject was "Don't tell Zeke."

What the hell?

Twelve

Zeke opened the message and noticed Marie's name at the bottom. Had she mistakenly e-mailed it to him instead of Ty? He began to read.

Master Ty,
Thank you for fucking me while I was tied up and gagged last night. Your huge cock driving into me made me come . . . and come . . . and come.

Zeke's cock shot to attention. This did not sound at all like Marie. In fact, he was pretty sure Ty had written it— Marie glancing over his shoulder—with the express intention of sending it to Zeke. A way to include him in the experience.

He leaned back in his chair, settling in to enjoy the e-mail.

The four times you fucked me this morning were sensational, too. I'm still aching from your big cock driving into me. Even as I stand here, bent over the counter, my arms tied to the other side, ready for whenever you want to drive into me, I long for your cock inside me.

He grinned. They were really getting into it all right. Knowing Marie, she'd probably pointed out that she couldn't very well be writing this e-mail if she was tied up, but Ty would have assured her that accuracy wasn't the main point of this e-mail.

As instructed, I will meet you at the indoor swimming pool tomorrow morning at 6:00 A.M. It's great that your friend in maintenance can arrange for us to have access to the pool two hours before it opens. Knowing no one can see us (unless they know that your friend will set a temporary combination on the door of 5, 6, 2, 9) means I'll be delighted to skinny-dip with you. I'm looking forward to you stripping off my clothes and fucking me on the diving board . . . in the water . . . or anywhere else you please.

Looking forward to tomorrow.

Your servant,
Marie

Well, Zeke certainly knew where he was going to be at six o'clock tomorrow morning!

Marie woke up to the sound of her alarm. She glanced at the time with bleary eyes.

5:30. Oh man, why was it going off so early?

Then she remembered Ty's suggestion. To go skinny-dipping in the pool this morning before it opened. No one would see them and . . . thanks to that e-mail they sent to Zeke . . . most likely he would be watching them from some invisible vantage point.

Heat quivered through her. She leapt from her bed and opened her drawer, then tugged out her sexiest, most revealing bathing suit . . . a blue and purple bikini. She raced to the bathroom and shed her pajamas, then showered and brushed her teeth. She combed her dark brown hair, then twisted it behind her head and captured it with a clip.

She pulled on the tiny bathing suit, then glanced critically in the mirror, adjusting the underwire cups to hold up her bosom in an enticing manner. She adjusted the high-cut bottoms, which made her legs look longer, and turned around to check out her butt in the mirror.

A thong would have been super sexy, but it didn't really matter, since she doubted the bathing suit would stay on for long. She waltzed back into her bedroom and found the matching sarong, then wrapped it around her hips and tied it. As she passed by the linen closet, she grabbed a big fuchsia beach towel and glanced at the clock. 5:45. Ty would be over in five minutes. She tossed the towel on the couch, then sat and gazed out the window at the blue, cloudless sky as she waited for him to arrive.

A knock sounded at 5:50 on the button. She grabbed the towel and raced across the living room, then opened the door.

"Hey, sweetheart. All ready?"

She smiled. "You bet."

As she stepped out of the apartment, he tugged her into his arms and treated her to a sound kiss, stroking her lips with his tongue. She melted into his arms, kissing him back with bold strokes of her tongue inside his hot, coffee-flavored mouth.

He took her hand in his. "Let's go." He led her down the hall toward the elevator at a quick pace, clearly as full of anticipation as she was.

A few moments later, they approached the dark brown door labeled CHANGING ROOM. Ty punched in the combination, then pulled open the door. Inside was a tiled area with change rooms on the right and a glassed-in area on the left. Beyond the glass, they could see the pool surrounded by lounge chairs. They walked toward the glass doors and pushed them open. The humidity and the distinct smell of chlorine hit them as soon as they stepped inside.

Marie tossed her towel onto one of the chairs by the edge of the pool, then untied her sarong and tossed it on top. She glanced around, wondering where Zeke was. Or if he was here at all.

"Don't worry. I'm sure he's watching," Ty murmured.

Despite the warmth of the room, her nipples peaked at the thought. Zeke would be watching every move they made.

Ty pulled off his white T-shirt, revealing his rippling abs and broad shoulders. He tossed it on a chair, then turned and walked toward the concrete steps leading into the pool. Her gaze lingered on the colorful phoenix tattoo across his back as he walked down the concrete steps into the crystal water. Very sexy.

Continuing to watch him, Marie settled on the side of the pool, dangling her legs into the water. It was cooler than the air, sending goose bumps racing along her skin.

Ty smiled as he walked toward her. He stopped in front of her and stroked his hands up her thighs, sending heat along her nerve endings.

"Are you ready to get . . . wet?"

His fingers stroked along the edge of her bikini bottom, near the crotch.

Oh God, she was already getting wet.

He dropped back in the water and swam backward.

"Go stand on the diving board," he said, with that note of authority.

She stood up and walked along the side of the pool toward the deep end, extremely conscious of Ty watching her behind shift from side to side as she walked.

And what angle was Zeke watching her from?

She stepped up to the diving board and stood on it, facing Ty in the pool. He treaded water, watching her.

"Remove your top," he said.

She shivered and glanced around, suddenly wondering if anyone might actually walk in on them. But Ty had assured her his friend could be trusted.

"Yes, Master." She reached behind her and unclasped her top. The elastic around her chest loosened.

Slowly, she peeled the fabric from her breasts and tossed it aside. Her nipples hardened and thrust forward. He stared at her bare breasts with frank male appreciation.

"Now, touch those beautiful breasts of yours."

She cupped her hands under her breasts and lifted them, then stroked over her hard buds, dragging her fingertips back and forth. Quivering pleasure rippled through her.

"Lovely. Now slide one hand inside your bottoms."

She slid her right hand down her body to the edge of the fabric, then slipped underneath the small V of her bottoms. The small patch of pubic curls tickled her fingers as she continued downward. She stroked over the folds of flesh, then over her slit.

"Push your fingers inside and tell me what you feel."

118

She slid two fingers inside and found slick, wet flesh.

"It's hot. And very wet." And touching herself like this felt very good.

"Take off your bottoms."

"Yes, Master."

She slid them off, then tossed them aside. Ty's hot gaze seared her flesh. And she could imagine she felt Zeke watching her. Maybe his cock was hard and ready just from seeing her standing here stroking herself. Maybe he wanted to race over here and drive his hard cock into her.

"Sit down, straddling the diving board."

She lowered her body and draped her legs on either side of the board.

"Now show me your pretty pussy."

She stroked her fingers along the soft folds on either side of her vulva and drew the flesh apart, revealing her slick opening. Watching Ty's gaze on her . . . knowing Zeke was hidden somewhere nearby, she stroked her wet slit.

Ty swam beneath the diving board and nibbled the bottom of her foot, then took her big toe in his mouth. He sucked as he stroked her calf. When he released her, he nipped her toes, then swam to the side and pushed himself out of the water with his powerful arms. He stripped off his swimming trunks and, as he stood up, she could see his huge cock standing straight up. And his balls and groin were clean-shaven.

He sat on the side of the diving board and she stared at his impressive erection.

"Come and suck my cock."

She smiled. "Yes, Master."

She climbed down from the board and crouched in front of him. She grasped his thick cock in her hand and stroked a few times, loving the feel of his hard shaft in her hand. She leaned down and lapped at the end with her tongue, then took his cockhead into her mouth. He stroked her shoulders and along her upper back as she licked and squeezed him.

She opened her throat and dove down, taking him as deep as she could. He was so big she couldn't go very far.

She released his cock from her mouth, then encircled it with both hands, stroking up and down.

"You are so big, Master. I don't think I can take you inside of me again. You're too much for me."

"You can and you will . . . But first, I want you to do more of this." He guided her head to his groin and gently fed her his cock.

He stroked his fingers through her hair as she licked, then took him to her limit again. She began to bob up and down, sucking, but he stilled her head.

"I think it's time to cool off a little." He slipped from her mouth and offered his hand. "Come swim with me."

She took his hand and followed him to the shallow end of the pool, then down the concrete steps. As they walked deeper into the water, the cool liquid climbed her body. She shivered as it lapped across the undersides of her breasts, then over her nipples. They tightened into hard buds.

He turned and pulled her into his arms. Trembling pleasure jolted through her as his lips nuzzled the side of her neck at the shoulder. He stroked a hand over her breast, and the already hard nipple burned with need for him. Her senses reeled.

He released her and swam backward. She followed him, swimming into deeper water. She couldn't believe how sexy it felt having the water sluice over her bare breasts, especially with Ty's hot gaze following her the whole time.

She watched as his penis bobbed around in the water. Miraculously, even in the cool water, it remained erect. He swam to the side of the pool and stood on the narrow ledge under the water, then beckoned for her to join him. He drew her into his arms and kissed her. The feel of his hard flesh against hers sent tingles through her. He pressed her back against the side of the pool.

"You are so sexy with your breasts floating in the water."

She glanced down at the tops of her white mounds visible above the surface of the water.

"You're pretty sexy yourself." She wrapped her hand around his wet member.

His hand slid between her legs and stroked her slippery slit. He wrapped an arm around her waist and lifted her a little, then sucked her nipple into his mouth. She sighed. His fingers slipped inside her, his thumb stroking over her clit. He moved his fingers in and out of her. Spiraling need coiled through her.

He leaned his face toward her ear. "What do you think of the idea of flushing Zeke out of his hiding place?" he whispered.

Zeke. She'd almost forgotten about him. But yes, she'd be thrilled to have him come out and join them. She nodded.

"Okay, pretend you hear someone come in and say so loud enough so he can hear you. Then scoot into the ladies' changing room."

She nodded against his neck, then drew her head back suddenly. "What was that?"

"What?" Ty asked innocently.

"I think I heard someone."

He helped her out of the pool and she raced to her

towel, then wrapped it around herself. Ty followed on her heels and they both dodged through the change room door.

"So this is what a ladies' changing room looks like inside." Ty glanced around.

It was so odd to see Ty, a tall, broad, incredibly masculine hunk—totally naked—standing in the middle of no-man's land.

"Now what?" she asked.

He nodded his head toward the curtained shower stalls. "Let's go in there."

She followed him behind the curtain and he drew her close, tugging at her towel at the same time. It pulled free and her bare breasts fell against his hard, muscular chest. Her cold nipples seemed to cling to his warmth. He smiled broadly. Swirling tendrils of need spiraled through her, originating from her tingling breasts.

He turned on the water and she yipped then giggled as a cold stream flooded over them. She flattened herself against the back wall, flinching at the cold tiles against her back, waiting for the water to heat up.

Ty took her hands and held them against the wall on either side of her head, their fingers interlaced, as his lips found hers in a hungry kiss. The water warmed as he shifted his body closer to hers. She was so aroused, she could barely catch her breath. His erection pushed against her and she desperately wanted him inside her.

He continued to hold her hands firm and she pushed against his grasp, trapping her.

"You're a dirty girl, fucking Zeke and then fucking me. I need to wash you off before I fuck you again."

He pushed her wrists together above her head and held them with one hand, then smacked her ass with the other, which made her flesh tingle in the most erotic way imaginable.

He shifted his knees between hers and eased them apart, opening her to him. Using the thumb of his free hand, he pumped shower gel onto his palm from the dispenser on the wall, then he stroked over her folds with his slippery hand, rubbing until the gel foamed up. Then he pressed forward, his hard swollen cock gliding over her intimate flesh. His hips undulated forward, pressing the length of his cock against her soapy folds, stimulating her. She pivoted her hips upward to gain more contact with that lovely, hard cock.

Her head drooped back against the wall as he positioned his cock against her opening. He pushed the head in slightly, then drew back. Her insides quivered. He glided forward again, barely entering her.

A soft moan escaped her lips. "Please, Master, I need you in me."

He slapped her ass again. "Haven't you had enough cock today, you dirty girl?"

He pulled her sideways, still against the tiled wall, but farther into the spray of water, then pinned her wrists against the tiled wall with both his hands again. The warm water rushed over their bodies as he continued to pulse forward and back, his cockhead nudging into her opening, but never fully penetrating her. Her body trembled with need.

Then he pressed forward with purpose and his cock began to slide into her slowly.

"Oh, yes." She groaned.

Deeper.

Her breath quickened as pleasure built in her like steam in a pressure cooker.

His cock filled her more and more, until he pressed her

tight against the wall, his cock fully immersed in her. She pushed against the pressure of his hands and moaned.

"Marie? Are you in there?"

Zeke's voice cut through her sensual daze.

"Answer him," Ty whispered against her ear.

"Yes, Master Zeke."

Ty nodded with a big smile.

The curtains flew open and Zeke peered into the stall. Ty drew back and thrust into her. She moaned again at his hard cock driving deep.

"What's going on in here?" Zeke asked, his hand stroking his own cock.

"Ty is fucking me," she answered, then moaned again as he drew back, then drove forward.

Zeke's olive green eyes had darkened to a forest green as he watched Ty thrust into her. Her eyelids fell closed at the exquisite pleasure.

"Are you enjoying it?" Zeke asked.

Ty drove into her again.

"Oh, yes, Master."

Ty glanced around at Zeke. "Thanks for your gift. Why don't we share?"

Zeke stripped off his trunks and stepped into the stall with them. Ty pulled out and Zeke's cock pushed into her. He thrust a couple of times, then drew out. Ty glided into her again, then pulled her against him. He leaned his back against the wall and suddenly she realized what was going to happen next. Zeke pressed his tip to her back opening and eased forward.

She relaxed, letting his cock slowly stretch her as the head slipped inside. Sandwiched between the two men, both standing still, allowing her to get used to Zeke's cockhead inside her ass, she took a deep breath. Oh God, she felt so full. Yet in a few moments, Zeke would be fully immersed in her. Both men's cocks filling her.

Zeke kissed the back of her neck. "Okay, sweet thing?"

She nodded, ready for more. He pushed forward . . . slowly, but insistently . . . filling her with his hot, hard cock.

It slid deeper, and deeper, until he was fully inside her. She sighed. "God, it's so . . . intense."

Thirteen

Zeke's cock twitched inside Marie. It was incredible being tightly gripped by her back opening. Zeke found it just as incredible knowing Ty's cock filled her other opening.

Ty's cock was only a hairbreadth from his. Zeke kissed Marie's shoulder, then gazed at Ty. For a split second, their gazes locked and an insane urge to lean forward and kiss Ty almost overwhelmed him, but Ty immediately jerked his gaze to Marie.

Oh God, what was wrong with him?

Ty began to move and Zeke followed suit. Marie moaned between them. Zeke tucked his hands around her, cupping her breasts, feeling Ty's hard muscular chest pressing against the backs of his hands.

Man, he'd missed Ty's friendship, but these intense feelings Zeke was having . . . these odd desires . . . were throwing him off.

Ty thrust again, and Zeke followed. Marie moaned. Her nipples thrust into his palms, sending his hormones spiking. God, she was incredibly sexy. Soft. Feminine. And so God damned tight.

She gasped at Ty's deep thrust. She tightened around Zeke's cock as she wailed in orgasm. Ty groaned, clearly shooting his load inside her. Zeke's balls tightened, too, then he erupted inside her, holding her tight against him. Intense pleasure blasted through him and his whole body seemed to explode in a blaze of searing ecstasy.

I just had a threesome! Marie tightened her arms around Zeke's waist, clinging to him, as he dodged through traffic on the way downtown. *With two gorgeous, sexy . . . ripped men!*

The big motorcycle rumbled between her legs as they raced along the highway. The memory of the two men's cocks inside her—both at the same time—sent thrills through her as the wind whipped past her face. She felt a little tender inside, but in a good way. She leaned her head against Zeke's leather-clad back and sighed.

Zeke took the off-ramp and the traffic around them became more dense, forcing Zeke to slow down, which suited Marie just fine. The first time she'd gotten on the big motorcycle, he'd had her so turned on, she'd welcomed the big leather seat between her legs. This morning, however, without the distraction of her hormones, it had intimidated her, but Zeke had insisted she'd be fine and, if she hadn't accepted his ride, she would have been late for work. Their fun-time at the pool had gone on longer than she'd expected and she'd missed the last express bus.

It came down to the fact that she trusted Zeke totally, so she knew she'd be all right riding with him. He would handle the motorcycle as he did all things . . . with confidence and skill.

Traffic slowed and he stopped at a red light.

"How you doing?" he asked over the rumble of the engine.

She squeezed him. "Just great."

He chuckled. "How do you like riding on the bike?"

"It takes a little getting used to, but I like it."

He laughed. "Not very convincing, sweet thing, but you get points for trying."

The light turned green and the cars ahead of them began to move. Zeke pushed forward and they moved slowly behind the cars. She clung tighter to his waist, almost preferring the fast pace of the highway to the closed-in feeling of the traffic. A feeling that only got worse as they reached the downtown core where they were surrounded by tall office buildings that cast long morning shadows along the busy streets.

Finally, Zeke pulled up in front of her building. She lifted her leg over the seat—no way to look ladylike doing that—and glanced around to see if anyone had seen her. She felt a little unsteady on her legs as she unfastened the helmet and pulled it off her head. A quick glance in Zeke's side mirror and she realized she looked a fright. She thrust the helmet to Zeke and quickly smoothed down her hair, hoping none of her coworkers had seen her hair sticking out in all directions. It's not that she was Miss Priss at work, but she liked to at least appear to have it all together.

Zeke climbed off the machine and retrieved her soft leather briefcase from the hard-shell saddlebag where he'd stowed it. He handed it to her and she smiled as she took the strap and pushed it over her shoulder.

"Thanks again. For the ride and for . . ." She felt her cheeks heat. ". . . everything."

He wrapped his arms around her and pulled her close to his body, then captured her lips. His mouth moved on hers with passion and his tongue glided into her mouth. She stroked in return, clinging to his broad shoulders. God, this man was sexy and she couldn't believe how lucky she was to be with him.

Zeke finally released Marie, knowing she had to get to work. But he didn't want to. He wanted to scoop her up and drive away with her, then make sweet passionate love to her. Somewhere warm and sunny, maybe by a lake. Something quite different from this concrete jungle.

She smiled timidly. "Talk to you later."

Then she turned and walked away.

He'd noticed her uncomfortable glance around after she'd dismounted the Harley. Like she was embarrassed to be seen with him. Well, what did he expect? There she was looking gorgeous and very professional in black pants and a blazer with a red silk blouse. And him . . . torn jeans and leather chaps, black leather jacket, pierced eyebrow. She probably thanked her lucky stars the jacket covered the tattoos.

As Marie walked toward the double glass doors, another woman approached her and they chatted. They both glanced back to him and Marie nodded, then the other woman giggled. Marie's cheeks reddened, then she turned to the door.

Shit! Why did he ever think a woman like Marie would want to hang with a guy like him? He'd only embarrass her. Maybe Ty had the right idea after all with his change of image. Marie seemed to want a change of pace with a guy like Zeke, but she'd probably tire of it pretty fast when she had to introduce him to her friends.

He jumped on the Harley and gunned the engine, then roared away into the traffic.

As Marie got on the elevator, she saw Zeke zoom away. Judy stood beside her as they rode up to their floor.

"So where did you meet him?"

"At my friend's cottage when I went up for the Labor Day weekend."

"He is so *hot*." Judy nudged her arm. "You're so *lucky!*"

Marie smiled. She was indeed.

"So, you got any more like him?"

Marie thought about Ty and realized he was more like Zeke than she'd ever thought. He might seem like a Mr. Nice Guy, but then, deep down inside, so was Zeke. And that wasn't a bad thing. Caring, sensitive, being a good listener were all great qualities. Wrapping it up in a bad-boy exterior made a dynamite package. And it wasn't just the exterior. It was the confidence. The authority. The *dominating* manner.

And Ty had proven he had that all right.

Judy nudged her arm again. "Hey, you're a million miles away."

Marie glanced at her and smiled. "Yeah, I guess I was."

"So, how about it? Any more like him?"

"Yeah." At Judy's hopeful gaze, Marie grinned. "But I'm not sharing."

What the hey. She could be a badass, too.

Fuck! What the hell have I gotten myself into?

Ty stared at the computer screen, not seeing the window of text in front of him. Damn it. It had been incredible fucking Marie right along with Zeke this morning. Too damned incredible! He had almost imagined he'd felt Zeke's

130

cock gliding against his as they'd both driven into her at the same time.

Then Zeke had gazed at him and . . . God, the look on his face. As if . . . as if he'd been having the same feelings about Ty that Ty had been having about Zeke. Feelings he shouldn't be having for another *guy*.

Feelings Ty had experienced for the first time five years ago when they'd had the threesome with Ashley. Which was the only other threesome Ty had ever had. Those feelings were the reason he'd never had a threesome again. And maybe, he had to admit, part of the reason he'd stayed angry at Zeke all these years. Because it made more sense and was easier to deal with than the alternative. But he'd put it out of his mind since his falling-out with Zeke. Buried it away, hidden it deep in his subconscious . . . until today when sharing a woman with Zeke again had brought it all back. The uncomfortable, yet intense attraction . . . for another man. For Zeke.

Had Zeke seen the desire in Ty's face?

Damn, what the hell was he going to do now? He wanted Marie. And even though she was dating Zeke, she had given him the chance to be with her . . . at the same time as Zeke. It was a chance he had to take because he needed to convince her he was the man for her. Zeke was okay with it and he knew Ty wanted her, so why the hell not?

But, damn, how could he fuck Marie while Zeke was part of the picture? He shouldn't be feeling these things for Zeke. Shouldn't be getting turned on by the sight of Zeke's broad sculpted chest . . . his bulging, muscular arms . . . his stiff cock . . . But he was and that scared the shit out of him.

As much as he wanted Marie . . .

Damn it, maybe he should just wait until this thing between her and Zeke burned out.

Zeke stepped back and stared at the beautiful 1968 Mustang 428 Cobra Jet he'd just finished priming. He pulled the mask from his face and set it on the workbench, then headed toward the office. He poured himself a cup of coffee and sat back on the desk chair, then glanced out the glass door and watched Henry, his cousin and partner, talking to a fellow standing in front of a red 1971 Corvette Stingray with a wicked scratch along the side.

Damn, it bugged him that someone would key a beautiful car like that. He had no patience for blatant vandalism.

Zeke and Henry's paint shop, Classic Lines, specialized in classic cars. Zeke loved doing custom paint jobs on the beautiful vintage automobiles their clients brought in.

He sipped his coffee and remembered his cell phone had vibrated when he'd been spraying the driver's door of the Mustang. He pulled his cell from his pocket and flipped it open. A text message from Marie.

Hi. Forgot my shoes in your saddlebag. Want to grab lunch? Tired of wearing running shoes at work. :-) Marie

He glanced at the clock on the wall. It was eleven. He could make it, no problem, but . . . did he want to? He would drop off her shoes, of course, but . . . did he want to extend this thing with Marie? Sure, she was sexy and fun to be with, but they were entirely different types of people. It would never last.

And . . . things were getting a bit weird. First that dream

about Ty and then, this morning, Zeke's crazy urge to kiss him. Ty would totally freak out if he knew Zeke was thinking about him like that. They'd finally begun to mend the rift between them. He didn't need something like this to throw a monkey wrench in the works.

Why not just step aside? Marie would be better off with Ty anyway.

Of course, stepping aside didn't guarantee she'd continue with Ty. Zeke hadn't even had a chance to find out her impression of her escapades with Ty. Sticking with it a bit longer would allow him to assess the situation. See if he could do anything to ensure Marie would want to continue a relationship with Ty when Zeke moved on.

And, damn but he wanted to see her again. And he loved watching her with Ty.

Ah, who the hell was he kidding. He wanted to see this thing through.

He pressed the reply button on his cell.

Marie walked the two blocks from her building to the park where she'd agreed to meet Zeke for lunch. The sun shone brightly—a warm day for September—as she walked along the paved path toward the river's edge. She spotted Zeke sitting on a bench, gazing across the water.

She sat down beside him. "Hi, stranger. Mind if I sit down?"

He glanced around and smiled. "A beautiful woman like you? I'd be a fool to say no."

He lifted a chunky rectangular bag onto his lap and unzipped it. When he opened the flap, she saw it was insulated. He pulled out a couple of individual-size bottles of fruit juice and two sandwiches.

They ate their lunch and enjoyed the sunny day, people-watching. A woman walked by pushing a baby stroller, with a young boy following on her heels. Two people on bicycles rode along the path that ran along the other side of the river.

"So I haven't had a chance to ask you how it went with Ty on Saturday," Zeke said.

She took a sip of her juice.

"I . . . uh . . . was surprised you didn't call Sunday." She'd figured he'd want to talk about it.

"I wanted to give you space. Allow you to enjoy whatever happened after waking up together."

She glanced at him. "What makes you think we spent the night together?"

He shrugged. "Ty's a smart guy. Finding himself in bed with a gorgeous woman . . . I figure he'd want to make the most of the situation." He stroked her cheek with his finger. "I certainly would have."

She'd felt guilty making love with Ty after the initial scenario—and several times—but Zeke seemed to be okay with it.

"So . . . ?"

"It was . . . really sexy."

"You're not going to tell me what he did when he found you? How he stroked your breasts? Maybe kissed along your thighs? Interesting details like that?"

She didn't intend to talk about it, but this gave her just the lead-in she needed to talk about Ty joining in the relationship.

"Maybe tonight we could invite Ty over to . . . act it out," she suggested.

"With me watching?"

She smiled. "You watching . . . you joining in . . . it's all good."

He tucked his arm around her waist and pulled her close to his body. "You little vamp. You're turning into a wild woman."

"And you love it, right?"

Fourteen

Damn, Marie had meant it as a flip remark, but it had come out sounding like she was seeking his approval.

But he just chuckled and planted a light kiss on her lips. "Damn right I do." He took a sip of his juice. "I guess the question now is will Ty go along with it? With the rift between us, I'm surprised he went along with this morning's adventure."

"He actually suggested it. Sending you the e-mail and all."

He grinned. "I figured that."

"Before that, he asked me if having him involved in our . . . sexual play . . . would be a regular thing. I asked him about it since it's obvious there's some resentment between the two of you."

She didn't intend to tell him about the rest of their conversation, where Ty had told her about Zeke's tragic past. The story still made her heart ache . . . made her want to take him in her arms and hold him tight . . . but she didn't take Zeke for the kind of guy who'd want to talk about it.

"On his side, not mine," Zeke said. "I'd like nothing better than to mend our friendship."

She nodded. "I figured. And I think this arrangement could help do that."

"You could be right."

"So you're okay with it becoming a regular thing?"

"Better than okay." He sent her a heated gaze that sent her insides fluttering. "I can hardly wait to get started."

Thinking about this morning's lovemaking, how erotic having both men make love to her in the changing room had been, sent thrills through her. If only she could grab Zeke's hand and drag him to a secluded spot right now and tear off his clothes. Memories of their first encounter at the lake . . . in the water . . . sent her body tingling for his touch.

"I . . . uh . . ." She drew in a deep breath. "There was something I wanted to ask you about. When Ty and I talked, he said he wanted to do this because . . . it gives him a chance to be with me." She gazed at Zeke. "I'm a bit concerned. I don't know if it's just a physical attraction he has for me or . . . something more. Do you think it's something I should worry about?"

He took a sip of his juice. "How do you feel about him?"

"Well, he's a great guy but . . ."

"Are you attracted to him?"

"Yeah, sure," she said.

"So would you consider being in a relationship with him?"

Marie shifted on the bench. Zeke seemed very casual asking all these questions, but Marie found the situation uncomfortable.

She took Zeke's hand. "I'm in a relationship with you."

"Sure, right now. I meant if I wasn't in the picture."

Right now? Was he tiring of her already?

She drew in a deep breath, pushing aside her feelings of insecurity. "No."

He raised an eyebrow. "If he's attractive and you think he's a great guy, why not?"

"Because I like him so much."

He shook his head. "You're not making much sense."

"If I went out with him, we'd eventually break up. When that happened, our friendship would end, too."

"Why are you so sure you'd break up?"

She sighed. "Because every time I go out with a nice guy like him, it ends. I'm tired of failed relationships and I've heard that people tend to fall for the same type of person over and over again, repeating a failing pattern."

"Do I fit in that 'nice guy' category?"

She smiled. "You're better than nice. You're hot and sexy."

"Does that mean you think our relationship might last?"

She'd expected him to laugh and maybe tease her, but his tone was serious, and when she gazed into his olive green eyes, she saw a curious vulnerability.

She wrapped her hand around his raspy jaw and kissed him. "I think we've got a fighting chance," she said, thinking maybe there was a happily-ever-after in her future after all.

Marie knocked on Ty's door. A few moments later, he opened it and peered out at her . . . without his usual welcoming smile.

"Hi." She felt a bit nervous. But maybe that look on his face was just because he'd had a bad day. "May I come in?"

"Sure." He opened the door and stepped aside to let her in.

She followed him to the kitchen and they sat at the table, which had always been their favorite place to sit and talk.

"I talked to Zeke today . . . about the three of us. He thinks it's a good idea, too."

Ty shoved his hands in his jeans pockets. "Yeah, about that . . . I'm thinking that might not be such a good idea after all."

Her pulse started to race. "But, you liked the idea yesterday."

She hoped what they'd done this morning hadn't damaged their friendship.

"Yeah, I know. I did think it was a good idea, but . . . I've had time to think about it. You and Zeke need time to yourselves. You're just starting to build a relationship."

"Sure, but . . . the three of us don't always have to be together."

Ty's face turned grim, as if he didn't like that idea. "Yeah, I get that. I just think . . . I'd be in the way."

"Ty, is it because . . ." Oh damn, how did she finish that sentence? She couldn't ask him if he had deeper feelings for her.

"Because what? Because I want to go out with you, too?" He shrugged. "I admit it. If you and Zeke break up, I'd like a chance to date you. I like being with you." His gaze heated. "I like *touching* you."

At the thought of him touching her, heat pulsed through her.

"Well, then . . . wouldn't this be a good thing?" Her voice came out husky. "I mean . . . I like *being* touched by you."

Oh God, she felt like a siren trying to lure him to the rocks, but she couldn't help herself. She wanted to be with him so much right now.

She stepped toward him and stroked his cheek. As he gazed into her eyes, she could feel his jaw clench. She knew she should walk away . . . respect his decision . . . but she couldn't. She wanted him. She tipped her face up, showing him just how much.

He hesitated, then his hand came around the back of her head and he pulled her into a kiss. His lips moved on hers. Sure and firm. His tongue swept into her mouth and seared her desire. She wrapped her arms around him and kissed him back.

The phone rang, but he ignored it, pulling her tight against his body. Her breasts swelled and she stroked along his raspy jaw to his strong neck, then down his chest until her fingers tangled around his shirt button.

The phone continued to ring as she released the next couple of buttons, then ran her hand along his sculpted chest.

The answering machine picked up, giving Ty's brief message . . . then Zeke's voice came on the line.

"Hey, buddy. We should talk about Marie and—"

Ty released her and snatched up the phone.

"Yeah, I'm here." He glanced at Marie. "No, I don't think that'll work." His hand refastened his shirt buttons as he listened. "Marie's right here. You can talk to her yourself."

He handed her the phone.

"Hi, Zeke."

"Hi. Is something wrong?" Zeke asked. "I thought you said Ty wanted to do this."

She gripped the edge of the kitchen counter. "He seems to have changed his mind."

"Okay, we'll talk about this when I get there. I'll be over in about an hour."

Marie stared at the thin straps of leather connected with various black rings that Zeke held out to her.

"Don't you think we should respect Ty's decision?" she asked.

"No."

She raised an eyebrow. "Why not?"

"Because we all enjoyed being together and whatever is bugging Ty is probably a result of his mixed-up notion that he shouldn't be himself and I think we should help him past it."

She took the leather from him and eyed it warily, wondering exactly how she would even go about putting on this . . . garment.

"So you're saying we're actually helping him?"

"That's right. Now go put that on." Zeke winked. "Or do I need to order you to do it?"

She shrugged. "Either way, I think I'll need your help."

Zeke grinned wickedly. "Well, that sounds like fun." He followed her into the bedroom, carrying a shoe box under his arm.

Ty picked up the phone on the second ring. "Hello?"

"Hi, Ty. This is Marie. Could you come over for a minute?"

"Why?" He knew Zeke was over there. He'd heard them make the date.

"Um . . . Zeke and I just want to talk to you."

"I don't think that's a good idea."

"Please?"

Ah, damn. "All right. I'll be over in a minute."

He finished putting his dishes in the dishwasher, wondering why the hell they were pushing this. His anger with Zeke had fizzled in the face of discovering these strange feelings for him and Ty had started to wonder if the real reason he'd rejected Zeke was because of this disturbing attraction rather than because he really believed Zeke had stolen Ashley from him.

He poured the detergent in and started the machine, then walked down the hall to Marie's apartment. He knocked on the door.

Zeke opened the door almost immediately.

"Hey, man. Come on in."

He stepped inside, noticing Marie standing in the middle of the room, wearing a black coat. Were they on the way out?

"Look, I already talked to Marie," Ty said to Zeke, "and—"

Marie flung open her coat and dropped it to the floor. Ty's jaw nearly dropped to the ground after it.

Ty stared at Marie as she stood there in a black leather harness held together with black O-rings, straps crisscrossing her body, but covering nothing. His cock swelled at the sight of her perfect round breasts surrounded by the black leather straps, the dusky nipples tightened to hard nubs. A patch of leather covered her pussy, but it looked like it could peel away easily.

She wore six-inch black spike heels that made her legs look sensational. She turned around in a slow circle, and he saw that the patch of leather covering her pussy narrowed to a strap gliding between her cheeks to attach to another strap at her waist.

"Marie told me you were reluctant to join us again, but we thought this might convince you otherwise," Zeke said.

Ty could barely stop from drooling.

"We have a little game we thought you might like. Basically, we'll take turns ordering our reluctant slave to perform whatever actions we like. Are you up for it?" Zeke asked.

Up for it? Damn, his cock was nearly splitting his pants open.

"Uh . . . yeah."

"Okay. First things first. Ty, why don't you sit on the couch. Marie, the drinks."

"Yes, Master."

Oh God, he loved hearing her say that.

She turned and disappeared through the kitchen door. Ty sat down, folding his hands together on his knees. Why the hell wasn't he racing for the door?

Marie returned, her breasts softly bouncing as she carried a tray to the coffee table in front of him. He couldn't prise his gaze from her breasts. *Yeah, that would be why.*

They swayed nicely as she bent in front of him to set down the tray. She picked up one of the tall, frosty glasses of beer and handed it to him, then picked up the other one and carried it to Zeke. Her nearly naked ass also swayed nicely as she walked.

"Thank you," Zeke said.

She stood beside him and waited.

Zeke took a sip of his beer, then stood up. Ty followed suit.

"I'll go first," Zeke said. "Marie, come here."

She leaned close and he whispered something in her ear.

"But, Master—"

"No buts. Just do as you're told."

She hung her head. "Yes, Master." She walked toward Ty, then crouched in front of him. Despite her mock resistance, her dusky rose nipples were tight beads.

She placed her hand on his cheek, her fingers curling around his ear, and she pressed her lips to his. Her tongue pressed between his lips and curled inside his mouth. He wrapped his free arm around her waist and drew her closer and sucked her tongue deep inside, then stroked it with his own.

He kissed her hungrily. Her hard nipples spiked against his chest as they elongated even more. He tugged her against him, gliding his tongue inside her, kissing her more deeply.

Finally, he released her. She nearly panted for breath as she pushed herself to her feet, then stood beside him, awaiting his command.

"Your turn," Zeke said.

Fifteen

Okay, this could get very interesting.

"Go to Zeke and take off his shirt."

Ty watched her walk toward Zeke, her gorgeous behind swaying. She stroked her hands over Zeke's shoulders, then down his chest to his shirt button and released it, then the next. With each new button released, his shirt parted more, revealing hard muscle and ink beneath. She eased the fabric from his shoulders and the shirt fell to the floor, revealing Zeke's broad chest.

An impressive tattoo of a heavily scaled dragon, its long serpentine body coiled around his upper left arm, extended across his chest. Rather than fierce, its expression seemed almost benevolent. The three claws and the slender body indicated a Japanese dragon, which often represented strength, power, and protection. The golden color of the striking creature indicated attributes such as wisdom, kindness, and perseverance.

Zeke had grown since their younger days, stepping

away from the fierce western dragons that represented dark emotions, such as anger and aggression. Like the matching ones they'd had inked on their backs. That's why Ty had had his reworked to be a phoenix, wanting to leave that fierceness behind him.

"Stroke the dragon," Ty said and watched in fascination as Marie's delicate hand stroked over Zeke's chest, following the line of his elegant tattoo. "Now kiss it."

She leaned forward and kissed the dragon's nose, then along its head. Her hand flattened below his right shoulder as she glided down to the dragon's mouth, then dragged her tongue along its tongue.

He wanted to stroke his cock as he watched her tongue caress Zeke's chest, but he held himself back. His gaze glided over Zeke's hard nipples and he wanted Marie to do more.

"Toy with his nipples."

Her fingers found Zeke's nipple and Ty licked his lips as he watched her tweak it, then take the other in her mouth and nibble, then suck. Ty's own nipples hardened to beads and his mouth went dry.

He couldn't decide what he wanted more. To be Zeke feeling Marie's hand and mouth cajoling his nipples to hard arousal. Or to be Marie, toying with Zeke's hard little bead in his mouth, and feeling the firmness of his other nipple between his fingertips.

"Now stroke his cock," Ty said, barely aware he'd spoken, mesmerized by Marie's hand stroking over Zeke's chest.

He imagined he was one with Marie, her hand now stroking down Zeke's abs, feeling those sculpted muscles beneath his fingertips, then over his low-hanging jeans. She stopped, just a hairbreadth from the bulge pushing along his fly.

"Our slave is resisting," Zeke said.

"Do as I commanded, slave," Ty said, his excitement lending a sharpness to his voice.

She ran her fingers along the tip of the bulge, then stroked up and down several times, slowly. Ty could imagine the feel of Zeke's big cock under the denim, pushing against it to be freed.

Ty licked his lips again, his own cock squeezing hard against his jeans.

Zeke took her hand and guided it to the tab of his zipper. "I'm sure Ty meant my naked cock. Right, Ty?"

He should say no.

But he couldn't. He wanted to see Zeke's cock.

Damn, he wanted to *feel* Zeke's cock.

"Do it, slave," Ty commanded.

She tugged down the zipper and reached inside, then drew out Zeke's impressive erection. Her lovely hand wrapped around it and she stroked. Zeke murmured approval.

Ty's gaze shifted to Zeke's face and the expression of pleasure lighting his features. A deep yearning burned through Ty.

Ty drew in a breath, collecting his composure.

"Your turn, Zeke," he said.

Marie released Zeke's cock, but he grasped her wrist and held it in place, then urged her to stroke a couple more times. Ty gazed longingly at the huge cock. Finally, Zeke let go of Marie's wrist and she stood up.

Zeke sucked in a deep breath, then released it slowly. "Okay." He grinned at Ty.

The smile sent tremors through Ty. He'd missed Zeke more than he'd realized and he savored this opportunity to get to know him again. And, he couldn't believe how much he wanted to share a woman with him again, despite all the pain he'd suffered after the last time.

"Take Ty's shirt off," Zeke said.

Ty's gaze switched from Zeke's cock to Marie's breasts as she walked toward him. She stroked her hands along his shoulders and down his chest, then she grasped the hem of his T-shirt and lifted it up his body, slowly revealing his stomach, then his chest. Just before she pulled it over his head, Ty glanced toward Zeke and noticed a hungry look in his eyes. He raised his arms and as the black fabric blocked his vision, he realized that Zeke had not been staring hungrily at Marie's delightful naked backside, but at Ty's chest.

Did Zeke feel it, too? This strange attraction between them? Or had it been only his imagination?

The shirt disappeared and she discarded it.

"Now turn around and press against Ty. Take his hands and place them on your breasts."

"Oh, Master, I can't do that."

Ty grasped her shoulders and turned her around, then drew her tight against his body. Despite her resistance, she pressed her beautiful ass against his groin. His cock twitched at her softness against him.

"Keep going, Marie," Zeke urged in a steely voice.

She took Ty's hands and placed them over her round breasts. He cupped her, her nipples pressing into his palms. Watching Zeke, he lightly squeezed, then cupped underneath and opened his curled fingers, allowing her nipples to peek out, her lovely mounds of flesh resting in his hands.

"Very nice," Zeke said. "Now press your lovely ass back against Ty's cock."

Marie obeyed, her round naked flesh pressing harder against his rock-hard cock.

"Good. Now turn around and take it out."

She moved away from Ty and turned, then unfastened the metal button on his jeans and dragged the zipper down.

She hesitated, but her eyes gleamed with hunger as she gazed at his crotch.

"Do you want me to come over there and punish you?" Zeke threatened.

"No, Master."

But Ty could see the flash of excitement in her eyes at Zeke's suggestion. Her fingers slipped inside his jeans, and when her soft hand grasped his cock, he sucked in a breath. She drew his erection out of his jeans and continued holding it in her hand.

"Now kneel down in front of him."

She obeyed and Ty's cock twitched at the thought of her lips surrounding his cockhead . . . of her sucking him deep into her mouth.

But instead, Zeke said, "Now describe it to me."

She gazed at his cock, her soft blue eyes almost adoring. "It's big and hard. Almost too big to get my hand around."

"Tell me more."

She leaned in close. Ty could feel her breath on his cockhead.

"The head is really big. It would fill my mouth."

"Show me," Zeke said.

When she hesitated, Ty wrapped his hand around her head and drew her forward until her lips brushed him. She wrapped her lips around his corona and took him in her mouth. The feel of her surrounding him sent heat rocketing through him.

"Very good," Zeke said. "Now tell me more."

She released Ty's cock from her mouth and stroked her

fingertip down the shaft. Her delicate touch sent tremors through him.

"It's very long," she said. "Probably about twelve inches."

Ty figured about ten, but clearly Marie knew being generous was better for a man's ego. She cupped his balls and stroked lightly with one hand while the other stroked the length of his shaft again, then circled under the corona.

"The head is purple and very firm. There's a clear drop of liquid on the tip."

Ty couldn't help feeling somewhat . . . exposed . . . with both their attention so focused on his cock. Marie's soft touch. Zeke's intense gaze.

"Okay, good. Take off his jeans and boxers."

Marie stood up, reluctantly releasing Ty's cock. She tugged his jeans down his legs, then pulled his boxers down. Ty stepped out of them.

Zeke grinned at Ty. "Your turn."

"Okay," Ty said. "Marie, kneel down in front of Zeke and stroke his cock."

She moved to Zeke, then knelt in front of him. She wrapped her hand around his long, hard cock and stroked. Ty watched her hand move along Zeke's shaft in fascination.

"Now, kiss the tip," Ty instructed.

She leaned closer and puckered her lips, then kissed the tip.

"Lick it."

Her pink tongue lapped over the tip of his cockhead.

"Take it in your mouth," Ty said.

At her hesitation, Zeke grasped her head and pressed his cock to her mouth. As she wrapped her lips around Zeke's cock and took it into her mouth, Ty's cock twitched, the memory of her hot mouth surrounding his own cockhead still fresh in his mind.

"Now make him come." Ty's commanding tone made it clear he would brook no disobedience. When she didn't immediately start to move, he added, "Do not fail, or you will be punished. Understand?"

"Yes, Master."

Shivers danced along his spine at her response.

Her hand slipped underneath and she cradled Zeke's balls in her hand while she dove down on his cock, taking him deep. Zeke groaned as she drew back then dove deep again. She sucked, her cheeks hollowing. She drew back and stroked up and down his shaft with her hand, as she sucked his cockhead, probably swirling her tongue around the tip.

Ty's insides thrummed as he watched her, wanting her mouth on him, too. He wanted to stand beside Zeke and have her switch from one cock to the other so they could both enjoy her together. But that wasn't what they were doing tonight. Maybe next time.

Damn it. There shouldn't be a next time, but . . . this was just so fucking *hot*.

He could see Zeke's balls tighten and pull close to his body, then Zeke groaned and Ty knew he was coming. Pulsing into Marie's hot mouth.

Finally, Marie released Zeke's cock, then stood up.

Zeke took a few deep breaths, then smiled. "Yeah, okay. Now, Marie, go stand in front of Ty."

As Marie walked toward Ty, he noticed her distended nipples, her flushed face. Clearly, she was as turned on as he was.

"Take Ty's hand and kiss it."

She lifted his hand and pressed her delicate lips against his palm, setting his heartbeat racing.

"Are you wet, Marie?" Zeke asked.

"Yes, Master."

"Good. Place Ty's hand on your pussy. Let him feel how wet you are."

"But, Master, I can't—"

Ty grasped her hand and tugged her to him, turning her around to face Zeke, then he wrapped a hand around her waist, pulling her tight to his body. He glided his fingertips down the soft skin of her stomach, then underneath the leather, past her silky curls. Then he cupped her mound. She grabbed his wrist and drew it back, as if resisting his caresses, causing him to stroke her pussy. It was so soft. With his other hand, he grabbed her wrist and drew it upward, until her fingers *accidentally* rested on her breast, then he extended his middle finger to run along her slit. He slid a finger into her silky wetness. So hot and juicy.

"Marie, lie down on the floor and open your legs," Zeke said.

Ty released her and watched her lie down, his cock twitching at the sight of her breasts staring straight upward . . . her long legs opening to him.

Zeke knelt beside her and tugged on the leather covering her. It unsnapped from the straps, revealing her cute little pussy. Ty loved how she'd trimmed it into a neat little heart. Zeke tossed aside the scrap of leather.

"Do you want Ty to lick your pussy?"

"Um . . . no." But the low timbre of her voice and her heated gaze betrayed just how much she really did want it.

"I think you do. Tell him."

She gazed at Ty with wanton need in her eyes.

"Ty, please lick my pussy."

Ty dropped to his knees between her open thighs and leaned forward. He kissed her navel, then stroked her inner thighs. She moaned and he couldn't wait. He leaned forward and licked her hot, wet slit. When she moaned again, he drove his tongue into her. She arched against him and he found her clit with his finger and stroked it lightly. She cried out. He left it, not wanting her to come just yet, then drove two fingers inside her.

Oh God, she felt so good. He sat up, watching her face as pleasure washed across her features. He glanced toward Zeke, now standing a foot from her head, his cock standing straight up while he stroked it. Ty had to willfully stop himself from reaching forward and grasping that cock in his hand to take over the stroking, then . . . God help him . . . from taking it in his mouth and sucking it until it blew.

He gazed back to Marie. Her glorious breasts, nipples puckered to tight nubs . . . her pelvis arching up against his hand . . .

Damn, but he needed to release this insane tension.

"Marie, do you want Ty to fuck you?" Zeke asked.

"Oh yes. Ty, please fuck me. Please fuck me now." All pretence of resistance had faded.

Ty almost burst on the spot. He grabbed his swollen shaft and pressed his tip to her wet slit, then eased forward. Slowly entering her. Enjoying the feel of her wet passage swallowing him.

She arched her pelvis forward. "Oh God, please fuck me. I'm going to come."

He thrust forward, fully impaling her. She gazed up at him, blue eyes bright. He twitched inside her and . . .

"Oh God, I'm . . ." She threw her head back and moaned. "I'm . . . coming."

She tightened around him and he realized she was in full orgasm. He began to thrust, the sight of her flushed cheeks and pleasure-washed face driving his need higher. He drove into her, again and again, as she clung to his shoulders, wailing in ecstasy.

He thrust deep again and . . . yeah . . . heat washed through him . . . his balls tightened and . . . the tension released as wild pleasure pounded through him like a herd of wild stallions.

"God, you two are so fucking hot." Zeke's hand stroked up and down his hard cock.

Ty caught his breath as he watched, his own cock still buried within Marie's tight passage.

"My turn," Ty said, brushing aside his desire to stroke Zeke's cock. "Marie, do you want Zeke inside you, too?"

"Yes," she replied eagerly.

Ty held her close to him and drew her forward. "Wrap your legs around me, sweetheart."

He felt her long legs twine around him and her ankles cross behind his back. He moved to the desk and turned around, then leaned back against it for support.

"Tell Zeke what you want," he murmured in her ear.

"Zeke, I want you to fuck me from behind . . . while Ty is still inside me."

Ty watched Zeke as he stepped toward them. Zeke's olive green eyes had darkened. He grabbed a tube of lubricant from the desktop—trust Zeke to be prepared—and he slathered his cock with the gel, then pressed the tip to Marie's ass.

"Are you ready, sweet thing?" Zeke asked.

"Yes."

Zeke pushed forward. Ty watched Zeke's long cock disappear into her ass. Marie sighed against Ty's shoulder.

Ty gazed into Zeke's eyes, now inches from his own . . . and saw a mirror of his own desire. Not just for Marie, but for Ty. Ty was sure of it. Zeke wanted Ty, too.

Before he could freak out about it, Zeke began to move, his cock gliding in and out of Marie. She gazed up at Ty as she clung to his shoulders, desire filling her features.

"I am so close," she murmured.

Ty lost it. He began to thrust along with Zeke. Marie's face pressed to Ty's cheek. Zeke's face only inches away. His cock throbbed with the need to come again. Marie moaned and her head fell back on Zeke's shoulder. Zeke kissed her cheek, then smiled at Ty, still with that heated expression in his eyes. Ty could almost believe Zeke was going to lean forward and . . .

Marie moaned. "Oh God . . . This feels . . . so good."

Zeke groaned. His hand stroked over Marie's hip, then between them. Ty felt Zeke's hand stroke down Marie's stomach to her clit, but at the same time, his fingertips brushed Ty's cock as it thrust in and out of Marie. Ty gazed into Zeke's intense olive green eyes. Zeke's eyes darkened and he turned his hand, then his fingers glided under Ty to cup his balls. As Zeke kneaded him, Ty sucked in a breath, intense heat washing through him.

Marie gasped. Ty's balls tightened painfully, then he erupted inside her in a huge explosion of pleasure, catapulting him to a state of ecstasy beyond mind-expanding. He groaned, and Zeke immediately followed suit. As he continued to pump into Marie, pleasure continued to flood through him. She wailed in her own ecstatic orgasm.

Finally, Ty slowed and she collapsed against him. He held her tight, intensely aware of Zeke's closeness, too.

Ty had never experienced such intense pleasure before.

God, how the hell could he say no to continuing this sexual relationship?

Ty awoke to the feel of Marie's soft, warm body snuggled against his chest, her arm around his waist, her cheek pressed against his shoulder. He could feel the wisp of her breathing against his skin. He pressed his lips to the top of her head, then wrapped his arms a little tighter around her.

Moonlight washed across her features, so relaxed in sleep. His heart ached for her. He wanted her in his life. Just the two of them. His gaze shifted to the pillow behind her . . . and Zeke's sleeping face.

Zeke lay facing Marie, moonlight glinting off the metal studs in his eyebrow and his dark hair hanging over one eye. Ty had to stop himself from stroking the hair back, then dragging his hand along Zeke's whisker-roughened cheek. He looked incredibly sexy, his arm slung carelessly across the pillow, his full lips slightly parted.

God damn it, I shouldn't be feeling these things.

Ty slowly rolled to his back, then carefully drew Marie's arm from his waist and slipped off the side of the bed. He glanced around the floor, the moonlight barely illuminating his surroundings, and found his boxers. He pulled them on then sought the rest of his clothes, gathering them up in a heap. He couldn't find his socks in the darkness, so he gave up and simply pulled on his jeans, then turned toward the door, his shirt in his hand.

"Where are you going?"

Zeke stood in front of him, a softly illuminated shadow between Ty and the bedroom door.

Ty glanced at Marie, still sleeping on the bed. Zeke jerked his head toward the door and Ty nodded, then followed Zeke out of the room. Ty closed the door behind him, quietly so as not to awaken Marie, then followed Zeke to the living room.

Zeke leaned against the back of the couch. "Where are you going, Ty?"

"I thought I'd give the two of you space."

"Why? You want Marie. We both know that. You should be taking all the time you can to get close to her and convince her you're the right guy for her."

"But you're the one she's dating. I'm just a sexual accessory."

Zeke stared at Ty, knowing the bitterness in his voice and his need to flee had nothing to do with the fact they were both vying for the same woman. It had more to do with the look on Ty's face as he'd stared back at Zeke with hunger in his eyes.

It wasn't just shared lust for Marie. Ty wanted Zeke. And, Zeke realized, he wanted Ty, too. Zeke had gotten caught up in the moment, and that had scared the shit out of Ty.

"Ty, there's something more going on here besides the two of us wanting the same woman. When the three of us were together earlier . . . you and I . . . felt something."

Ty stared at him warily.

"Yeah, we both wanted to fuck Marie."

"That's not what I mean." He reached out and placed his hand on Ty's shoulder but Ty pulled back. "Hey, man, I don't get this any more than you do, but I want to understand what's going on."

"Two guys in bed with the same woman . . . both turned on. What's to get? It's pretty fucking straightforward. I'm hot for Marie. I look your way and you think my lust is directed at you." Ty shrugged. "That's it. Nothing to get bent out of shape over."

Clearly, Ty wasn't ready to handle this. In fact, Zeke had a hunch Ty had been struggling with it for a long time. Maybe he'd never be ready, which was too bad because Zeke was finally starting to understand why he'd missed Ty so much over the years. Why he wanted to do anything he could to fix their friendship, even risk the woman he knew he was falling in love with because . . . the truth was . . . Zeke realized he just might be in love with Ty, too.

That's why they'd always been so close. That's why it had hurt so much when Ty had walked away. That's why Zeke needed so desperately to make things right again between them.

And he suspected that's why Ty had walked away in the first place. He couldn't cope with the thought of being attracted to another man . . . especially his best friend. So he'd convinced himself that Zeke had tried to steal Ashley, even though they'd both known she'd flitted from man to man in the blink of an eye.

Ty had convinced himself Zeke had betrayed him because that was easier to accept than that he'd fallen for his best friend.

Now Ty had met a woman he truly loved . . . Zeke could see it in his eyes. The funny thing was, if he would just embrace his dominant personality again, he could win Marie's whole heart in the blink of an eye.

Damn it, maybe Zeke didn't have a chance in hell of winning Ty's heart, but he could be instrumental in Ty finding his true happiness. Right now, Zeke had the girl Ty loved. As much as Zeke would love to keep Marie for himself, two wrongs didn't make a right.

If Ty accepting his real self again—his dominant sexual self—would win Marie away from Zeke, then she was never really meant to be with Zeke. Zeke didn't want to win by default. He wanted to win because he was the right man.

And he really didn't want to hurt Ty.

"Okay, let's put this aside for now. Let's talk about Marie," Zeke said.

Ty's eyebrows quirked. "What about her?"

"In case you haven't noticed, Marie likes being dominated. And you, my friend, are the master of Domination. At least, you used to be. So if you want to win the girl, all you have to do is bring your full game."

Ty's eyes narrowed. "Why are you telling me this? Don't you want her anymore?"

"Of course I do. She's incredible. But what you and I want isn't really relevant. The question is, who does she want?"

"Would it make it easier or harder if I said I wanted both of you?" Marie stood in the doorway, a silk robe loosely wrapped around her body.

"How long have you been there, Marie?" Ty asked.

Sixteen

Zeke couldn't tear his gaze from Marie's softly swaying, incredibly sexy body, the silk of her robe caressing her curves as she moved toward them. She rested her hand on Ty's cheek.

"Long enough to know that you both want me." She opened her robe and dropped it to the floor, revealing her totally naked body. She ran her hands along the sides of her waist and up her ribs, then cupped under her breasts and lifted. Her thumbs stroked over her nipples, which instantly grew hard. "I want you both to show me how much you want me. I'd love to feel both of you sucking on my nipples."

Ty reached for one soft, round breast and stroked it. Her hand fell away as he cupped her, then glided his fingers over her hard nub.

Marie sucked in a breath as Ty's lips captured her nipple. Zeke stepped toward her and nuzzled her neck, then kissed down her chest and covered her other nipple with his mouth.

They both sucked and she gasped at the wildly erotic pleasure spiking through her. Her knees went weak, but Ty's hands coiled around her waist and held her steady. Zeke's hand brushed over her behind and he stroked. She pressed her hands against each man's stomach, swirling over hard, sculpted abs. She slipped one inside Zeke's boxers and grasped his hard cock. Ty released his zipper and kicked away his pants and boxers, then guided her hand to his cock. Her hand wrapped around him, too.

Two cocks. One in each hand. So big and hard.

As she stroked the length of their shafts, spurred on by the pleasure pulsing through her at their repeated sucking on her nipples and the stroking of their hands along her ass, hips, and thighs, she could feel melting heat between her legs. Zeke's hand stroked over her slit and she felt his fingers explore her wet folds. Ty's finger glided right inside her. Zeke slid a finger into her, too, and the two of them swirled inside her in unison.

Ty sucked hard on her nipple and she groaned.

She drew back and lay down on the big comfy ottoman in front of the couch, opening her legs in invitation. Zeke knelt between her legs and licked her navel, then nibbled downward until the tip of his tongue dragged over her clit. Ty captured her mouth in a passionate kiss, then cupped her breasts as he watched Zeke lick her slit. Zeke's mouth settled over her clit. Pleasure spiked higher and higher as he cajoled it with his tongue, alternating between sucking and licking. She covered Ty's hands, pressing them tight to her breasts as she rode a wave of intense pleasure, then wailed her release.

Zeke gazed up at her with a twinkle in his green eyes, then she felt his cock press against her wet opening . . . and slide inside. He stroked a couple of times, his cockhead dragging along the walls of her vagina, then he pulled free. Ty drew his hands from her breasts and positioned himself at her opening and pushed inside. His bigger cock stuffed her to the point of pleasure-pain. He plunged in and out, igniting her arousal to a new level.

Long slow strokes. Her body trembled with the intensity of the sensations rocketing through her. Then Zeke wrapped his hands around her waist and lifted her, then shifted her around until she lay bent over the ottoman. He pressed against her slippery opening, then slowly pushed forward until his cock impaled her. Ty stepped toward her, his huge erection pointing straight forward. She wrapped her fingers around it, then took it in her mouth. She squeezed her lips around his corona while licking his tip. As he moaned, she glided forward, relaxing and opening her throat to take him as deep as she could.

Zeke pushed forward again, gliding his cock deeper into her, inch by inch. Finally, both men were fully impaled in her. Zeke kissed the back of her neck, then began to move. Both cocks glided within her—Ty with short strokes, Zeke with long, deep strokes—filling her . . . easing back . . . then filling her again.

Pleasure rose within her, then fluttered along every nerve ending. Ty reached forward and stroked his finger into her folds, finding her clit. She caught her breath as ecstasy spiraled through her, then moaned—barely keeping Ty's cock in her mouth—as it burst in an explosion of intense joy. She squeezed her mouth around Ty's big cock and clenched around Zeke. Both men tensed and groaned as they released inside her.

Oh God, these men knew how to make love to her.

Finally, Marie shifted between them. Zeke pushed himself up and slipped away from her, then helped her stand up. He took her in his arms and kissed her. Ty stood beside her and when Zeke's lips released hers, Ty kissed her. She slid her arms around each of them, pulling them close in a loose hug, an arm around each male waist.

She nuzzled Ty's neck as Zeke kissed her temple.

"Come back to bed." She took Ty's hand and Zeke's and led them both to the bedroom.

Marie gazed at Zeke as the morning sun caressed his strong features. She mentally traced a finger along his square jawline. Felt the sandpaper texture of his whisker-roughened face. She glanced at the pillow on the other side of her, the indentation of Ty's head still visible. But no Ty.

Like a bandit, he'd stolen away in the middle of the night. It had been incredibly sexy being commanded by them. First by one, then the other. Zeke telling her to do erotic things to Ty. Ty telling her to do erotic things to Zeke in return.

Almost as if they'd wanted to do those things to each other.

Zeke rolled onto his side and his hand glided along her hip.

"Hey, sweet thing. You look deep in thought."

She gazed at his face. His olive eyes glowed warmly in the crystal clear morning light. She smiled and stroked her fingertip over the metal studs in his eyebrow.

"Just thinking about last night."

He chuckled. "It was pretty incredible." He glanced over her shoulder. "So where's our partner in crime?"

"I assume he decided to head back to his place. It's not like it's far to go."

He wrapped his arm around her waist and drew her close to his hot and hard body. "How he could prefer being alone in his bed when he could be so close to you, I can't figure."

His words sent a flush of pleasure through her, but she shrugged.

"Zeke, I know what caused the problem between you and Ty. He told me about the threesome with you and his girlfriend."

"And he told you I tried to steal her?"

"Yes. He also told me you denied it. I didn't understand why he hadn't believed you, but clearly the whole thing hit him pretty hard." She gazed at him. "Was he in love with her?"

"Maybe he thought he was, but he should have known better. She wasn't the type to settle into a committed relationship." He pushed himself up on his elbow. "Why are you asking about this?"

"Well, I'm just wondering . . . are you trying to make up to Ty for what happened? Maybe by . . . helping him win me?"

"Marie, how much of our conversation did you hear last night?"

"I came in when you were telling him that I like to be dominated and that if he put his mind to it, he could win me over."

Zeke nodded. "He could."

"Why would you help him? Do you want to get rid of me?"

"Marie, if you were listening, you heard me tell him that it's what you want that's important." He tugged her to his body and kissed her, his lips brushing hers in a tender, persuasive caress. "As much as I want you, if it turns out you're truly meant to be with him, then it doesn't do any of us any good if you stay with me."

She rested her hand on his cheek, a soft smile on her lips. "That is so sweet. I never realized what a true romantic you are." She stroked his raspy jawline. "And it only makes me love you more."

His eyes crinkled as he smiled. "You're saying you love me?"

She nodded, and gazed deeply into his eyes. "I do love you, Zeke."

His grin faded as her words sank in.

"Marie . . . I—"

She captured his lips, gliding her tongue deep into his mouth, staving off his words. She didn't want to know his response. Maybe he loved her. Maybe he didn't. Maybe he didn't know. But it wasn't a great sign that he was willing to push her into another man's arms. Still, she had to tell him what was in her heart.

Now she wanted to show him—physically—that she was his. She wrapped her hand around his swelling cock and stroked, while nuzzling the base of his neck. Within seconds, his erection was rock-hard. She climbed over him, then pushed herself down on his stiff rod, taking him deep. She moaned into his mouth, then kissed him with more passion as she lifted herself, then lowered again, impaling herself on his shaft.

She would make him want her more than ever. He was sexy and strong and . . . exactly the right man for her. She squeezed him inside her and he groaned.

She released his lips. "Do you want me, Zeke?"

He rolled her beneath him and drove deep. "Are you kidding? I've never wanted a woman more."

He drew back and thrust deep again.

Her eyelids fluttered at the wild sensations pulsing through her as his cock stroked inside her.

"Show me how much."

He kissed her again as he drove his cock deep . . . pulled back, then drove deep again.

As the first waves of ecstasy blossomed over her, she heard his guttural words.

"I love you, Marie."

Then he drove deep and fast until he sent her screaming over the edge in a mind-shattering orgasm.

Warm water streamed over Zeke's head as Marie stroked a soapy hand along his spine then in a meandering path across his shoulder blade.

"Why dragons?" she asked.

He smiled. He loved her fascination with his tattoos.

"Dragons represent strength and, in the case of western dragons like that one, aggression, both traits I needed when growing up."

"And the other dragon?" Her hand stroked along the dragon that coiled along his upper arm.

He turned and scooped her into his arms, her wet naked body pressing against his in a most enticing fashion. His cock hardened.

"That dragon is an eastern dragon. A protector. Strong, but wise."

She stroked around the dragon's ears. "Very nice." She leaned forward and kissed the dragon's nose. "I think I'll call her Julie."

His eyes narrowed. "You think my dragon's a girl?"

She gazed up at him, her blue eyes glittering. "Well . . . strong and wise." She shrugged.

He chuckled and pulled her tight against him, then captured her mouth. Her soft lips caressed his and his cock swelled against her stomach.

"Let's get this straight right now," he said as he gazed into her vivid blue eyes. "Every part of my body is totally male."

Her fingers stroked down his stomach, then wrapped around his growing cock.

"Well, this part certainly is." Holding his shaft firmly, she kissed along his chest, then licked his nipple, sending exciting tingles along his spine. "You don't want to think about me kissing your girl dragon?" She smiled, then licked along the dragon's mouth. "I could stroke Julie and lick the length of her body." Her tongue stroked along his chest, following the lines of his tattoo, then she sucked his nipple into her mouth. "Oh, I found Julie's nipple." She gazed up at him. "Do you like me sucking on Julie's nipple?"

His cock certainly did. He backed her against the tile wall and pinned her hands above her head.

"Of course, the thought of you licking and sucking on another woman's nipple gets me hot." He licked her breast, then wrapped his lips around her nipple and sucked hard until she moaned. He raised his head, then captured her lips and thrust his tongue into her mouth, plunging in and out until she was totally breathless. He pressed his forehead to hers. "But my body parts are male. Including the dragons. Got it?"

She gazed into his eyes, her blue eyes dark with desire. "Yes, Master."

"That's what I want to hear."

He released her hands and offered her the bar of soap from the wire holder on the wall. "Here, wash my back."

She took the bar and he turned around. Her soft, slippery hands stroked across his back and over his shoulders. Up and around in long strokes. Before long, her strokes focused on a winding path along his left back.

"You aren't coming up with names for that one, are you?"

"Would you like me to?"

"No." He could just imagine what she might suggest. He scrubbed his chest firmly. "You know Ty had one done exactly the same."

"But his is a phoenix."

"It is now, but when we had them done, they were both dragons. He's had his reworked. A talented tattoo artist can do phenomenal things. I had mine reworked, too, but just to enhance the detail and color."

"You didn't want to change it to an eastern dragon like the one on the front?"

"No, he's a part of my history."

"Just like Ty."

"That's true."

"Do you think you and I . . . being together . . . do you think that will jeopardize you and Ty being friends again?"

He turned to face her. "I hope not."

"But . . . you both think there's a chance he'll win me away from you?"

Zeke kept his expression fixed. In fact, Zeke was *sure* Ty could win her away from him. But he wouldn't tell her that.

She'd told him she loved him. And he *wanted* her to love him. Forever. But if he didn't give her the opportunity to see the real Ty . . . he would simply be hiding from reality. If she was meant to be with Ty, she and Zeke would never find true happiness.

On the other hand, if she didn't fall for Ty after experiencing his true dominant personality, then Zeke could truly accept her love.

"What should we do, Zeke? I don't want to lose Ty as a friend either."

"What about our current arrangement? Do you want the threesome to continue?"

"Oh, yeah. The sex is great. But . . . I'm just wondering if that's fair to Ty. Wouldn't that be leading him on?"

He drew her into his arms and kissed her, then held her with his arms loosely around her waist. "Here's an idea. I know this quaint little getaway where the three of us could go for an exciting weekend together. We could enjoy each other's company, go a little crazy, and figure out what we want to do as far as continuing our threesome goes. And don't worry, before we go I'll have a talk with him. Hint that you and I are getting pretty serious. Get him thinking about where he wants to fit in this relationship."

She pushed herself on her toes and kissed him, her eyes twinkling. "That sounds like a very interesting idea."

Ty peered through the peephole to see Marie's smiling face.

She knocked again. "Let me in, Ty."

He pulled open the door and Marie swept into his apartment carrying a large covered casserole dish, followed by Zeke carrying a plate of toast in one hand and a basket of pastries in the other.

"We brought breakfast." She set the casserole dish on the table and took off the lid, revealing a pile of fluffy scrambled eggs surrounded by bacon and sausage, the wonderful aroma filling the room.

"You have coffee on?" Marie asked. "If not, we've got a pot brewed at my place. We can bring it over."

Ty followed her into the kitchen. She grabbed plates and cutlery while Zeke headed straight for the coffeepot. Ty grabbed some mugs and followed them back into the dining room.

"You skipped out on us. What gives?" Marie asked.

Seventeen

"I thought you two would be more comfortable without a third wheel crowding you."

"Very noble of you," she said, "but I hate it when a man leaves in the middle of the night. Makes me feel like he wants to get away from me."

Ty's gaze caught hers. "That's not it at all. I love being with you."

Damn, he shouldn't be admitting that. Right now, she was dating Zeke.

"Sweet thing, I think we're going to need more coffee. Why don't you go grab that pot from your kitchen after all?"

She glanced at Ty, then back to Zeke. "Okay." She turned and headed for the door.

"What's up?" Ty asked. He knew Zeke had gotten rid of Marie so they could talk.

"Marie and I are going to a getaway next weekend and we're inviting you along. This is your opportunity to pull out all the stops and win her over."

"A romantic weekend for three?"

"That's right. And I've got to warn you. This thing between me and Marie is getting serious, so this'll be your last shot. So make it count."

Damn it. Ty's gut clenched at the thought of having to keep a leash on his wild reactions to Zeke for an entire weekend of close quarters. But he didn't want to lose the opportunity to win Marie. Especially since time was running out.

Marie returned with a thermos jug of coffee and set it on the dining table. "So, ready for breakfast?"

"Looks great," Ty said as he approached the table.

"Marie, I asked Ty if he'd join us next weekend." Zeke glanced at Ty. "So, will you come?"

"Where is this place?" Ty asked.

"It's the Forbidden Sanctuary."

Ty raised his eyebrows. He'd heard about the place. A BDSM bed-and-breakfast. Being there would certainly fire up their imaginations. If Zeke was right and Marie wanted the full experience of being dominated, that was the place to go. He gazed at Marie, imagining her naked and bound, her ankles strapped to a spreader bar, forcing her legs wide apart, leaving her open and accessible for all kinds of fun. His cock swelled.

Would she be ready and willing to do all he commanded? How far would he be able to push her?

Suddenly, he desperately wanted to know the answer. He pulled out a chair and sat across from her.

"Yes. I believe I will."

At five o'clock on the dot Friday, Marie plucked her bag from her desk drawer and headed to the elevator. Once on the street in front of her office building, she glanced around, watching for Ty's car.

She had packed her bags last night and left them in Ty's apartment before she left for work this morning. He'd planned to drive to work today, then pick her up from the office.

Excitement skittered through her. As the week had progressed, Marie had found herself getting more and more excited about the weekend. Well, who wouldn't. A whole weekend with two sexy men at a sexual playground, from the way Zeke had described the place.

Ty's car pulled up to the curb and she smiled and climbed in the passenger door. He pulled into the busy traffic again.

"You all ready for the weekend?" he asked.

She smiled. "I can hardly wait."

"Zeke called. He went ahead of us so he could pick up the key for the cottage, buy some groceries, and get everything organized before we get there."

Once they were outside the city, Ty stopped and picked up a case of beer, then they continued on their way. Forty-five minutes later, they pulled up to a small cottage right off a lake, surrounded by tall trees. Zeke's Harley stood outside.

"It's really pretty here," Marie said.

"Hey, there." Zeke walked toward the car and opened Marie's door.

As soon as she stepped out, Zeke pulled her into a tight embrace and kissed her.

Ty retrieved their bags from the trunk and took them inside. Zeke grabbed the case of beer from the trunk and Marie followed him into the cottage.

She glanced around, not quite sure what to expect. It

looked like a quite cozy, but average cottage. There was a living room right off the entryway, a doorway to a full kitchen, and a casual dining area off to the side. A large window overlooked the lake.

She followed Zeke into the kitchen where he placed the case on the counter and put the bottles in the fridge. She could see that the fridge was fully stocked.

As Marie stared out the window at the sun reflecting off the lake, she couldn't help thinking about what would happen later that night. Here she was with her two handsome men in this wonderful lovers' hideaway. The weekend was all about sex and . . . she quivered . . . she could hardly wait.

Even now, she could imagine the men undressing. Revealing their hard, muscled bodies . . . their long, hard cocks. Then undressing her. Stroking her body. Touching her breasts.

Their mouths covering her nipples.

She sucked in a deep breath, then distracted herself by walking into the living room. The furniture was a little old-fashioned, but clean and cozy. The front window offered another beautiful view of the lake, and the staff had placed a pretty vase full of daisies on the table to welcome them.

The place seemed so quaint and homey. Marie wondered why it was considered a BDSM bed-and-breakfast.

Once they were all in the living room, Ty wrapped his arm around her waist and tugged her to his body, then captured her mouth in a hungry, devouring kiss.

As his tongue thrust into her mouth, she melted against him, totally breathless at his ultra-masculine manner. He hadn't shaved, so his face was coarse and raspy . . . which was so sexy. When he finally released her mouth, she blinked at him, gazing into his warm brown eyes . . . but . . . something was different. She touched his cheek and stared at one eye, then the other. One was a cinnamon brown, as usual, but the other was a soft green with golden specks.

"Your eyes are different."

"Does it matter?" A hard edge tightened his voice.

"Only in that they're gorgeous. And incredibly sexy. Have you been hiding them with contact lenses?"

"Yes, but I've decided to let you see the real me this weekend." He smiled. "And that includes letting you see my more dominating nature."

"Really?" She smiled broadly. "That should be fun."

He grinned. "Zeke and I are ready to give you some rigorous training. Are you ready to submit to me totally?"

The words took her breath away. To submit to him *totally*.

"Yes, Master."

He smiled broadly. "Very good."

He pulled her against him and took her mouth again. Her breasts crushed against his hard chest, the aureolas pebbling and the nipples blossoming into hard nubs. When he released her, she noticed Zeke had returned to the living room and sat down in the chair by the window across from the couch.

"I'm going to say this once, Marie," Ty said. "Your safe word is 'fox.' If you can't say the word, tap three times, with a foot, a hand, or even a finger. *If* you use the safe word, the scenario will stop, no questions asked, but that's it. We stop and I leave. So use it wisely."

Shivers ran down her spine at the total authority in his voice. She never would have thought it from Ty, but he was being every inch the commanding dominant she'd dreamed of.

He released her and stepped away, then unfastened the buttons on his shirt. She watched hungrily as he removed it, revealing the rippling muscles across his chest. When he turned around to toss the shirt onto the easy chair beside the couch, her gaze locked on the colorful phoenix tattoo across his back. God, he looked so sexy and . . . *bad* . . . with that tattoo. He turned back to face her and his chest seemed almost too naked without a tattoo gracing the sculpted expanse of flesh. And she could almost imagine him with spikes through his eyebrows like Zeke.

Gone was Mr. Nice Guy. Enter Mr. Bad Boy!

"The only thing you are to say is 'yes, Master,' unless I ask you a direct question," Ty continued. "Do you understand?"

Excitement flooded through her. "Yes, Master."

"Good. If you do not follow my instructions, you will be punished. Do you understand?"

Her insides quivered. "Yes, Master."

"Good. Now strip."

She drew in a breath, but quickly unbuttoned her blouse, dropped it off her shoulders, and tossed it over the arm of the chair beside the couch. Ty's sensational odd-colored eyes fixed on her lacy red bra, right where her nipples were stretching the fabric. She unzipped her straight black skirt and slid it over her hips and down her legs, then stepped out of it and laid it on top of her blouse. Now she stood in front of him in only her bra and matching red lace thong, the heat of his intense gaze sending sparks along her nerve endings.

Suddenly, she remembered that Zeke still sat in the chair by the window, watching.

"Why have you stopped, slave?" Ty demanded.

Immediately, she reached behind her and unfastened

her bra, then pulled the straps from her shoulders and peeled the cups away, then dropped the lacy garment to the floor.

As she tucked her thumbs under the elastic of her thong, Ty said, "Wait."

She stopped.

"Turn around and face Zeke. Stroke your breasts, then hold them up."

She turned to face Zeke. As she stroked over her round mounds, his olive eyes remained fixed on her hard nipples. She tucked her hands underneath and lifted her breasts, as instructed.

"Good. Now take off your panties."

She rolled the tiny garment down her legs, bending forward, knowing she was giving Ty a great view of her backside. When she stood up, Zeke's hot gaze lingered on her patch of heart-shaped pubic hair.

"Turn around," Ty commanded.

She turned around to face Ty again.

"Now, you need to be punished."

Her eyes widened. "But why? I—"

He raised his hand and she stopped talking immediately.

"Because you are still learning, I will explain," Ty said. "Do not expect the same leniency next time. First, you stopped in the middle of doing something I told you to do. Second, you spoke other than to say 'yes, Master' or answer a question."

What would her punishment be? Would he bend her over his knee and spank her?

"Go to Zeke and do as he says."

"Yes, Master." She turned and walked toward Zeke and stood in front of him.

Zeke grinned and held out his hand. She took it and he drew her closer.

"Drape yourself over my knee so I can see that sweet little ass of yours," Zeke said.

She knelt on the floor, then positioned herself across his lap. His knees pressed against her belly and chest, below her breasts, and her head hung downward, her hair draping across the sides of her face. Zeke's hand lightly stroked over her ass, sending goose bumps quivering along her flesh. His hand slipped away, then smacked across her ass. It smarted, then tingled as he lightly stroked it with his fingertips. Then he smacked again. She moaned softly at the erotic sensation as he once again stroked her heated flesh.

He helped her to her feet.

"Now come here," Ty said.

Now Ty sat on the couch. She walked across the room and stood about two feet in front of him.

"Closer."

She stepped forward.

"Turn around."

She turned and his hand stroked over her heated ass. It was probably red. He stroked, then she felt his lips glide over her skin.

Ty stared at the flushed skin of her perfect, round ass. When she'd moaned as Zeke stroked her after smacking her bottom, Ty's cock had inflated painfully. He dragged his fingers over the silky skin—still hot. He pressed his lips to her delightful ass and kissed across the warm skin.

He reached around and stroked her belly, then upward until his hands reached the undersides of her breasts. So soft. He cupped her delicious mounds and stroked the nipples with his fingertips.

"Do you like that, slave?" he asked softly.

"Yes, Master."

The tremor in her voice sent his cock twitching.

"Turn around and face me."

She turned and he stared at her gorgeous round breasts. He stroked one, then grasped the nipple between his fingertips.

"I think this would look quite pretty with a ring piercing. What do you think?"

Eighteen

Ty grinned at Marie's look of panic. The only thing he'd told her she was allowed to say was "yes, Master" and clearly the idea of having a piece of metal shot through her sensitive nub was not on her short list of fun things to do.

"Um . . . yes, Master. I mean . . . no, Master. It was a question, right? So I can answer?"

He continued smiling. "You think it would hurt, right?"

He wrapped his hands around her waist and drew her forward. Sliding one arm around her waist, he stroked her breast with his other hand, then leaned forward to take the nipple into his mouth. The feel of the hard nub against his tongue, the pebbly aureola against his lips, sent heat thrumming through him. He swirled his tongue around her nipple, then sucked lightly. As she relaxed in his arms, he gripped her nub between his teeth and closed gently. She stiffened, but he held her close and sucked, then nipped again. She moaned.

"It wouldn't hurt any more than nipple clamps. You'd

like to try those, wouldn't you?" He teased her nipple with his teeth and nipped again.

"Um . . . yes, Master." Although she seemed to enjoy his teasing, she didn't look convinced.

"Bring my black bag," Ty said. "It's by the door."

She walked to the door and lifted his black duffel bag and carried it to him. He unzipped the top and pulled out a gift-wrapped box and handed it to her. She smiled and pulled off the black metallic bow, then unwrapped the crimson paper. She opened the gift box and stared at the leather collar sitting nestled in red tissue paper. From the D-ring on the front of the collar hung two chains, each with a tweezer-style nipple clamp with black rubber tips.

He held out his hand and she gave him the box.

"Turn around and lift your hair."

"Yes, Master."

She turned her back to him, then lifted her silky, shoulder-length hair out of the way so he could fasten the collar around her neck.

"Now face me."

"Yes, Master."

He admired the thick collar around her neck, the clamps dangling on the ends of the chains. He lifted one clip, which was about two inches long, and positioned the curved, rubber-tipped end around her nipple, then slid the small ring along the clip toward the nipple to force the arms together to hold the clip in place. Later, if he wanted to increase the pressure, he could simply slide the ring closer to the nipple. Right now he set it at such a light pressure she could keep them on indefinitely. Tighter and he'd have to take them off within twenty minutes or so.

Seeing the long, slender metal clip with the black rubber

tips gripping her erect nipple sent blood flooding to his groin. He attached the other nipple clip, then sat back and smiled. The clips hung straight down from her nipples, the chains draping below her breasts then curving back up to meet at the ring on her collar.

Delightful.

"Are they tight enough?" he asked.

Her eyes widened slightly.

"Yes, Master."

"Good. Now, go get two beers from the kitchen and bring them back to us."

Ty watched her walk toward the kitchen, her lovely, naked ass swaying as she moved. He glanced at Zeke, who also watched her. A moment later, she returned with two frosty glass mugs full of beer. She handed one to Zeke then crossed the room toward Ty and handed him the second one.

He dipped his finger in the cool liquid and stroked his finger over her distended nipple, then he leaned forward and licked it.

"Mmm. Delicious. Zeke, bring over the other gift."

Zeke pulled a shoe box from his bag and opened the top, then walked to the couch where Ty sat, Marie facing him. Ty took the box and held it toward Marie.

"Put these on."

She took one shoe out and stared at the five-inch heel dubiously, then leaned over and slipped her foot into it. Zeke admired her backside as she fastened the strap around her ankle. She took the other shoe and slipped it on, too. When she stood up again, a little wobbly, she stood a lot taller, her legs looking incredibly long and sexy.

"Zeke, grab the stool by the wall."

Zeke nodded and retrieved the wooden stool Ty pointed

to, then brought it to Marie. When she sat down on it, facing Zeke, the high heels forced her knees higher than her hips. Zeke grabbed four leather straps with metal rings from his bag and set them on the couch beside him. He leaned down and wrapped one around her ankle, then grabbed the clip on the end of the short chain attached to one leg of the stool and attached it to the ring. He did the same with the other ankle, forcing her legs apart, giving him a lovely view of her pussy.

"Hold out your arms."

"Yes, Master."

She held out her wrists to him and he fastened a strap around each one. Zeke grabbed the longer chain attached to the back leg of the stool and Ty clipped it to the ring on her wrist, then the other, so her arms were held at her sides. She could move them behind her, but not forward.

"Great. Zeke, grab your beer and turn on the TV."

Zeke retrieved the TV remote and his beer, then settled on the other side of the couch, Marie facing them. Sound filled the room as he turned the TV on, then Zeke flipped the channels until he found some adventure movie.

Marie sat still, listening to the movie playing behind her, wondering what would happen next. Her nipples ached a little. The pressure from the clamps was very light, but she wasn't used to it so it kept her attention. After sitting for a few moments, Ty rested his hand on her knee, then slowly stroked along her inner thigh. He stopped halfway and she drew in a slow breath. A couple minutes later, he slid a little higher, getting closer to her aching opening. Her insides quivered.

Zeke took a sip of his beer, gazing at her exposed pussy. Heat melted through her. She wanted to be touched. Ty stroked his finger along the chain draped from her nipple, and tugged lightly, then he fiddled with the clamp, tightening it a little, the slightly painful sensation exhilarating her. He tightened the other nipple clamp, too. Then he took a sip of beer, leaned forward, and took the tip of her nipple in his mouth. She gasped at the feel of the cold liquid he held in his mouth washing against her hot nipple. The liquid heated, then his tongue lapped against her hard nub.

He released it, then smeared beer on her other nipple.

"Try one, Zeke."

Zeke leaned forward and licked her dripping nipple. She arched toward him and he sucked lightly, then sat back.

The two men watched TV a while longer, sipping their beer, mostly ignoring her. Several times, they glanced at her, their gazes caressing her naked breasts—the clamps and chains hanging from her nipples—or gliding along her open thighs to her naked wet opening.

Finally, Ty's hand shifted to her thigh again and he stroked slowly upward as he took a sip of beer. She arched toward his hand, and he immediately stopped moving.

"Sit still," he said.

He began moving his hand again . . . slowly approaching her aching vagina. She tried to sit still, but he stopped within an inch of her opening and she wanted him to touch her so much . . . she wiggled forward.

He pulled his hand away.

"Because you were disobedient, you must be punished."

He leaned forward and fiddled with the nipple clamp and the pressure increased. She gasped at the intensity, then it loosened, but her nipples still ached.

Oh God, she wanted him to do it again. Then to lick her hot nipples until she groaned with pleasure.

His hand stroked along her thigh again . . . closer and closer to her now dripping slit. His finger hovered close to her opening for what seemed like forever. She chewed her lower lip, fighting the impulse to push her pelvis forward to feel his hand on her. He watched and smiled, then his hand moved again and pressed against her damp folds. She sighed, forcing herself not to move as he dragged his finger the length of her slit.

"She's very wet," Ty said. "Zeke, would you like to taste that delicious pussy of hers?"

"You're damn right I would."

"Slave, my friend is going to lick your pussy. Sit perfectly still."

"Yes, Master."

Zeke knelt in front of her and stroked along her thighs. He kissed her inner thighs, moving closer to her heat. When he finally reached the top of her thighs, and his tongue brushed her clit, she moaned. She had to concentrate fully to stop herself from shifting forward against his hot mouth. He licked her clit again, then nuzzled her slit. His tongue glided inside, lapping against the inside of her opening, then he licked her length. His mouth returned to her clit and he sucked. She moaned, arching against him.

Immediately, his mouth moved away from her. Her eyes widened and she sat upright.

Ty tightened the clamps again and she almost cried out at the exquisite pressure. Again, he released them, then licked each of her nipples. They were so sensitive the brush of his tongue felt incredibly intense.

"My friend is going to taste your pussy again. I can tell you like it and I think you want to come, but that is forbidden. Do you understand?"

"No . . . I mean, yes, Master."

He didn't want her to come?

Zeke positioned himself in front of her again and his tongue found her sensitized clit. He licked and sucked until she wanted to arch against him . . . but didn't. Pleasure blossomed through her and she knew if she just let go, she'd be swept away. But Ty had ordered her not to come.

Zeke licked again, then his fingers slipped inside. He stroked her insides and . . . oh man, he'd found her G-spot. He stroked as he licked and the pleasure thrummed through her until . . .

"Oh . . . yes . . ."

She arched and moaned as the orgasm rocketed through her. She moaned again, allowing the intense sensations to plummet her over the edge. When the ride was finally over, she sat up and gazed at Ty.

"You really aren't very obedient, are you?"

"No, Master. I'm sorry, Master."

He nodded. "Lean forward."

She obeyed and he reached for the clamps. Would he tighten them even more? But he surprised her and removed one clamp. Instantly, a painful sensation rushed through the freed nipple.

"When I remove the clamps, the blood flow returns. That's the pain you're feeling." He unfastened the other clamp and pain filled that nipple, too. "Are you enjoying it?"

"Yes, Master." And she did. It was exciting. Stimulating. *Wicked.*

"Zeke, go ahead."

Zeke grinned then leaned forward and took one aching nipple in his mouth and began to suck. She cried out at the agonizing pleasure. Ty captured the other nipple in his mouth and began to suck. She moaned at the incredible sensation.

Both men settled into a gentle suckling. Finally, they drew back again. Ty released the clips from her wrists.

"Since you like coming so much, I want you to show us how you make yourself come."

She hesitated, then stroked a finger over one nipple, still wet from Zeke's mouth. She stroked the other, too. Both men watched her every move with great interest. It made her feel hot and sexy. She stroked down her belly and into her wet folds, still stroking a nipple with her other hand. She slipped inside and stroked, then teased her clit.

"God, she's so fucking hot," Zeke said as he released his zipper and pulled out his giant cock.

She watched him stroke it and she flicked her clit faster. She wanted to lean forward and grab that cock of his and suck it deep into her mouth. She thought about her lips gliding over it, then sucking it inside her mouth, as she stroked her clit faster. She abandoned her breast and slid her other hand to her wet slit and glided two fingers into her vagina. She thrust inside as she pinched her clit. Pleasure blossomed through her and she arched backward as another orgasm washed through her.

Once the pleasure subsided, she drew her slick hands aside and glanced at Zeke. He stroked his stiff cock, his eyes glazed. If only he'd drive that huge shaft into her right now. She licked her lips and gazed at Ty.

He reached down to her ankles and unlatched the chains.

"Stand up."

She stood up, unsteady on those spectacularly high-heeled shoes, not to mention her highly aroused state.

"And now I want several of my friends to fuck you. Would that be okay?"

Nineteen

Excitement quivered down her spine. Was the idea of other men joining them for real or just a fantasy scenario? She remembered when Ty had blindfolded her and pretended that Zeke was in the room with them.

"Yes, Master."

"Good. Follow Zeke."

Zeke led her and Ty to a door, then opened it to reveal stairs down to the basement. She followed him down the enclosed stairway, being careful of her footing in the heels, and when she reached the bottom, her eyes widened. The place was set up as some kind of elaborate dungeon. And a rather elegant one. Deep gold walls set off the furniture made of black-painted wood quite nicely. Thick black beams adorned the white ceiling. A huge bed dominated the room. It had four square posts and crossbeams forming the headboard and footboard, all with a series of embedded rings, which she imagined would be quite handy for attaching chains.

Along one wall stood a large X formed from two dark planks of wood, with chains hanging from the top of each. At the end of the room was a large barred jail door, beyond which she could see the walls were made of large concrete blocks.

There were various padded contraptions around the room that she wasn't too sure about. Zeke led her to a narrow padded bench about hip height. He positioned her so the top pressed against her stomach, her back to Ty, then eased her legs apart and clipped each ankle ring to a short chain connected to the slanted leg of the bench.

"Lean over," Zeke instructed.

She did and the padding pressed against her stomach as Zeke attached her wrists to rings on the other side of the bench. This held her tightly stretched over the top with her torso parallel to the floor and her hands held below her knees.

"What a lovely sight," Ty said, and she realized he had a stunning view of her most intimate parts.

Zeke pushed against the bench and she felt herself turning slowly. She glanced down and realized she was standing on a big circle that turned like some huge lazy Susan. Once she was facing Ty, Zeke stopped turning the device. A moment later, Ty gathered her hair together and clipped it loosely behind her head, then blindfolded her.

Then she felt hands stroking over her naked skin. One. Two. Three. Four. Along her back and over her ass. One hand cupped her breast while another stroked along her shoulder. The hands behind her stroked along her inner thighs, then brushed past her aching slit without touching it, then continued along her stomach. Then the hands moved away from her.

Ty's face moved close to hers and he murmured against her ear, "In a few minutes, my friends are going to thrust their cocks into you and fuck you until you scream . . . but first, you will suck my cock."

She waited in the darkness of the blindfold. Suddenly, she felt a sharp smack across her ass.

"I want you to respond to every one of my commands with 'Yes, Master.' Mine or anyone else's. You are a slave to every man in the room. Do you understand?"

"Yes, Master."

Every man in the room. That would be Ty and Zeke . . . and the imaginary friends who would also have their way with her. Tingles danced along her skin.

She heard a zipper, then the sound of stiff cloth as she presumed Ty removed his jeans. A moment later, hot hard flesh pressed against her lips. She opened and Ty's large cockhead slipped into her mouth. She widened to take him, then licked around and around. He pushed deeper and she opened her throat to take him as deep as she could. He glided in and out in short strokes. She licked, then began to suck. He groaned as she sucked hard, her cheeks hollowing.

He drew out, then stroked the tip of his cock against her lips. She licked it, then swirled her tongue around the tip. She dabbed at the little hole in the end. He wrapped his hand around her head and pressed himself to her lips and eased inside again. He filled her mouth with the bulbous crown. She squeezed and sucked. If she could have raised her arms, she would have reached for his balls and cradled them in her hands.

He drew his cock from her mouth again and it glided along her cheek. As if reading her mind, he lifted his balls to her lips. They were still clean-shaven. She kissed them, then licked. She curled her tongue underneath and drew one into her mouth. He groaned.

After a few moments, she released his soft flesh, then licked his shaft, then nibbled with her lips. He slid his finger into her mouth and she sucked on it, drawing it deep inside.

"That's enough." He pulled free of her mouth.

"Yes, Master."

She jumped as she felt something moist against her ass. It moved, then she realized it was Zeke's mouth. He was kissing her. Along the curve of one cheek. His hand stroked across her other cheek. Heat thrummed through her. She could feel the moisture pooling between her legs. Waiting for the first thrust of a big, hard cock.

Ty stroked her breasts, then tweaked her hard nipples as Zeke's fingers glided closer to her waiting heat. She wiggled her ass, hoping to coax him closer to the target, but he slapped her behind, sending tingling excitement dancing through her. Finally, his fingers glided along her slit and she moaned.

His fingers slid inside her. One. Then two. A third slipped inside and he stroked her insides. She dripped with need.

"She's incredibly wet," Zeke said.

"Let me see," Ty said.

A second later, she felt a second hand gliding along her ass. Zeke's hands slipped away and Ty stroked her opening, then hooked a finger and slid it inside. He stroked her inner passage, along the front. Intense pleasure built steadily with each stroke. More . . . and more. The pleasure built fast and furious. Closer . . . and closer.

Just as she felt she'd go over the edge, he slipped away. She groaned.

"Did you like that, slave?" he asked, now in front of her again.

"Oh God, yes, Master."

Suddenly, she felt a hot mouth close over her nipple and suck hard. She moaned at the intense sensation. Then another mouth captured her other nipple and she cried out in pleasure. The two men suckled firmly on her breasts, not touching any other part of her body.

Her core ached with need. Finally, the mouths released and she heard sounds of cloth rustling. Zeke must be undressing.

"My friends are going to fuck you now, slave."

"Yes, Master." Oh God, finally.

Then she felt it. A hot, hard cockhead pressing against her. It pushed into her, steadily, until it filled her. Yes, now he was going to thrust into her . . . give her that orgasm. But he just stayed deep inside her, not moving. She squeezed his cock lovingly inside her, as if she could suck it in deeper. Then she felt it pulling away. Gliding against her tight, squeezing passage. Then it was gone.

"Each man gets one thrust at a time," Ty said.

A cockhead pushed against her again, then drove inside in a quick stroke, then disappeared. Another cockhead pressed into her. Bigger this time. Stretching her.

Ty.

He pushed in slowly, gliding in . . . and in . . . until he fully impaled her. Painfully slowly, he eased back. She gripped him tightly, as if she could keep him inside by squeezing him alone. She couldn't stop his exit, but the blissful stroking of his massive erection as it pulled out sent pleasure streaming through her.

Once he was gone, another cock pushed into her. Zeke again.

This exquisite torture went on for long excruciating moments. One cock gliding in, then out. Then the other. One did a little spiral, then the other shifted the angle of entry.

She moaned, her body trembling in need. Ty pushed into her and stayed inside for a few seconds, twitching. Ah, he was close, too.

"Oh God, Master, please fuck me and make me come."

He smacked her bottom, which nearly sent her over the edge, then he pulled back and thrust into her. She moaned as she felt her pleasure leap to heaven. With his hands gripping the bench on each side of her, he drew back then thrust deep into her again. An orgasm exploded inside her, bursting along every nerve ending as Ty thrust in and out, filling her with his tremendous cock. Faster and faster. Until he exploded inside her.

He collapsed on top of her, pressing her tight to the padded bench. After a few moments, he took a deep breath and eased his weight from her, but still held her enveloped by his big masculine body. His hand stroked her hair, which had escaped from the clip, with exquisite gentleness.

Finally, he murmured against her ear, "You naughty girl. You tempted me to distraction." He drew away and his cock slid from inside her, leaving her feeling empty.

Ty untied the blindfold over her eyes and tossed it aside. Marie blinked as he walked to one of the chairs facing her and sat down. She noticed that as his gaze glided along her body stretched over the bench, his wilted cock tightened again.

"Now it's time for my friend to fuck you." He'd dropped the pretense of several friends. Clearly, it had served its purpose to kick her excitement up a notch. And, boy, had it worked.

Zeke stepped forward and placed his hands on her hips, stroking lightly.

"Ready for me, sweet thing?"

"Yes, Master."

Zeke's cock pressed against her. The wall beside the bench was totally mirrored, so she knew Ty could see Zeke's erection push forward and glide inside her. She tightened around him, still quivery from the orgasm she'd shared with Ty. Zeke drew back and thrust forward again. Her eyelids fell closed as pleasure stormed through her again, rising to orgasm. He thrust and thrust, then groaned as he erupted inside her. At his heat, she moaned, flying off to heaven one more time.

When Zeke finally drew away, then unfastened her straps, she stood up on wobbly feet, but she wanted more. She couldn't believe it. After all the pleasure she'd already experienced, it still wasn't enough.

Zeke slumped on the edge of the bed and she dropped to her knees in front of Ty, then licked his semi-erect shaft. It rose under her attention.

"Master, I want you to watch while your friend fucks my ass. Then I want you to drive your huge cock into me, too."

His eyebrows arched and he smiled. "Really? Show me."

She stood up and approached Zeke, then knelt in front of him and wrapped her hand around his drooping cock, then wrapped her lips around it and drew it into her mouth. He grew immediately. She sucked and licked until he was hard as a rock, then she stood up and turned her back to him. He held his cock straight as she lowered herself onto his lap. His cockhead pushed against her opening, then she pushed down on it, taking it inside slowly. Finally, she sat all the way down, his cock deep inside her. He wrapped his hands around her waist as she toyed with her nipples. His finger stroked along her slit.

"I'm ready for you, Master."

Ty's eyes darkened and he stood up and walked toward her. Her Master. Hot and masculine. About to possess her. He knelt in front of her and pressed his cock to her sex, then drove into her in one quick thrust. She moaned and wrapped her arms around him. He drew back and thrust into her again.

She squeezed him inside her, both cocks embedded so deep. He began to move and she moaned at the exquisite pleasure of their cocks moving inside her in unison. Stroking her inner walls. Pleasure built . . . pulsing though her . . . building to a staggering crescendo . . . then exploded in a shattering climax as she catapulted into ecstasy.

She collapsed between them, then Ty shifted back, taking her with him. He held her in his embrace, tight against his big muscular body, and she sighed against his shoulder. A moment later, he laid her on the bed and she snuggled against him. Zeke moved behind her and she fell asleep between them.

Marie woke up snuggled between her two men, feeling warm and protected. She opened her eyes and gazed at Ty's face, asleep on the pillow beside her.

What a surprise it had been when Ty had taken the lead and dominated her so thoroughly. She hadn't believed him capable of being so . . . commanding. Her blood heated at the memory of his authoritative voice . . . his masculine presence . . . his sure touch when he stroked her body.

His eyelids opened. She smiled as he gazed at her. He leaned forward and brushed his lips against hers in a light kiss. Soft and tender. She stroked her hand along his rough cheek and met his lips again. He cupped her head and drew her close, deepening the kiss, his warm sensual lips moving on hers.

Their lips parted and she drew in a deep breath. He smiled and stroked her hair behind her ear. Her hand wandered down his shoulder to his broad chest and stroked over the muscular ridges, down to his sculpted abs. She could feel his cock twitch against her stomach and she wrapped her hand around his hard shaft and stroked. Earlier had been sexy and fun, but his tender kisses and loving touch made her want something more. She wanted to be close to him.

To make love with him.

She arched her breasts against his solid chest, her nipples hardening. He caressed her soft mound gently with one hand, then stroked her hip with the other. She rocked her hips forward as his hand nudged between her legs. His fingers slipped between her folds and glided along her sex. She could feel the slickness as he stroked her wet opening, then slid inside. She murmured her approval as she leaned forward and kissed him. Her lips clung to his as he pressed himself to her opening, then slipped into her, filling her.

She moaned softly, loving the exquisite caress of his huge member inside her. She arched her hips forward, taking him deeper. His hand slid around her waist, pulling her closer still. Then he drew back and glided into her again.

Another pair of male hands wrapped around her and

cupped her breasts. Oh God, she'd totally forgotten about Zeke. And . . . she felt guilty. Making love to Ty right beside him.

Zeke kissed her neck. "You two seem to be enjoying yourselves." He stroked her breasts, his thumbs grazing the nipples as Ty's cock glided deep, then drew back . . . then glided deep again. Ty captured her lips as Zeke kissed her neck while stroking her breasts.

Pleasure pulsed through her as Zeke tweaked her nipples and Ty drove deep. She moaned and grasped Ty's shoulders, pulling him closer, crushing Zeke's hands between them. Ty thrust into her, faster now, filling her with burning need. Ty cupped her ass and she wrapped her legs around his waist. She could feel Zeke's swollen cock pressing against her back as he moved with them.

Ty's slick cock stroked her insides, stoking her need and driving it higher until the intense sensations erupted into a cataclysm of pleasure. She wailed as bliss pulsed through her, carrying her to a mind-shattering orgasm.

Ty groaned and twitched inside her, claiming her lips as he joined her in ecstasy.

After a moment, his cock slipped from her. Before she could catch her breath, Zeke's cock slid inside her from behind. He wrapped his hands around her hips and drew her back against him, filling her sex with his hard cock. Ty slid down and caressed her breasts, then captured one of her nipples in his mouth as Zeke began to thrust. Barely finished with one orgasm, she felt another blazing through her. She gasped and squeezed Zeke as he thrust again and again. She moaned as the pleasure erupted inside her again. Zeke kissed her neck, then groaned as he filled her with liquid heat.

Ty rested his head on the pillow again and smiled. He leaned forward and kissed her. Zeke's cock still filled her. Zeke nuzzled the back of her neck, then kissed her cheek. His cock slipped free and he draped a hand around her waist.

Within moments, she heard a soft snoring behind her. She glanced at Ty and realized he'd fallen asleep, too.

She gazed at his sleeping face, felt Zeke's breath on her back, and thought about the guilt she'd felt making love with Ty a few moments ago. They were in a threesome. Why would she suddenly feel guilty?

But she knew the answer. She was in love with Ty. In fact, she had been in love with him all along, she'd simply convinced herself it wasn't true. She hadn't wanted to chance losing him as a friend, and convincing herself he couldn't dominate her the way she wanted . . . the way Zeke could . . . had allowed her to keep a distance. When he'd completely and unequivocally dominated her last night . . . she'd lost that last excuse. And the tender way he'd made love to her just now . . .

Her heart ached. She really did love Ty.

And she loved Zeke, too. And now she really did feel that she'd cheated on Zeke. Because she could no longer treat Ty as a casual addition to their relationship.

She would have to choose between the two men. Someone was going to be hurt.

Her stomach clenched. What a mess.

She disengaged herself from Zeke's arm, being careful not to wake him, then she slipped from the bed.

Twenty

Ty awoke to a warm body pressed against him.

Firm. Hard. And solid.

It wasn't Marie.

Ty's arm was loosely draped around Zeke's waist as Zeke's muscular back pressed against Ty's chest. Ty's cock was hard and pressed against Zeke's backside.

Ty knew he should pull away . . . but it felt . . . cozy. He liked being close to Zeke.

Deep down inside, he *wanted* to be close to Zeke.

Zeke shifted and Ty's cock expanded a little more. Was Zeke awake?

Zeke drew in a deep breath . . . then snored a little.

Ty relaxed, allowing himself to enjoy the experience of Zeke's body pressed close to his. Marie must have slipped away and he'd simply grabbed on to Zeke in his sleep. Nothing wrong with that.

Zeke murmured something in his sleep, then shifted back a little, pressing his backside closer against Ty's cock.

"You two look pretty comfortable."

At Marie's voice, Ty snatched his arm away from Zeke and rolled to a sitting position, careful to hide his erection.

Beside him, Zeke shifted, then rolled onto his back. "Morning."

"Where did you go?" Ty asked Marie.

"I wanted to get a little air. It's a beautiful morning. Sunny. And warm for September."

Marie hadn't missed the fact that Ty had a huge erection . . . or the fact that he was trying to hide it. When she'd walked into the room, the two men had been spooning cozily. She had noticed lingering looks between them during their three-way sexual adventures. Was there more to their relationship than friendship?

Judging from Ty's discomfort with the situation, she could tell he was struggling with some kind of attraction to Zeke.

Could it be that Ty was in this three-way more to be with Zeke than with her?

But she and Ty had been close before Zeke came into the picture.

Close . . . but he'd never asked her out. Or showed any kind of romantic interest.

Aw, damn, was she really in love with a man who was in love with another man? And what about Zeke? Did he return Ty's interest?

If the three of them continued as they'd been going, would the two men finally embrace their attraction for each other and she'd find herself out on her butt?

She would rather find out sooner than later.

If the two men were unsure of their feelings for each

other . . . or outright ignoring them . . . maybe it was time she gave them a push.

"I put on a pot of coffee. I'm going to go take a shower, but I thought maybe you two could be the slaves and make breakfast for me. What do you say?"

Zeke grinned. "I say, yes, Mistress." He pushed the covers aside and stood up, totally naked, his big cock semi-erect.

She cupped her hand around her ear. "What was that you said?"

Zeke's grin widened. "I said, 'yes, Mistress.'"

She grinned. "I like that." She gazed at Ty. "And what about you?"

Ty smiled, too. "Yes, Mistress."

He stood up and his cock stood fully erect. Her insides tingled at the thought of dropping to the floor and feasting on that. Better yet, at him pushing her down on the bed and impaling her with it.

"I'd like eggs, bacon, and toast with honey." She turned toward the door and strolled out, then entered the bathroom. She hung her robe on a hook outside the shower and turned on the water.

When she opened the door after her shower, she could smell the bacon cooking. She returned to the bedroom. Actually, the only bed in the cottage was in the basement dungeon. Only a kitchen, living room, and another bathroom were upstairs, plus a spectacular deck around two sides of the building overlooking the lake.

She sat down at a round wrought-iron table in the corner and opened a folder on the table. Inside, she found some information sheets that listed the various equipment included in the cottage. Specifically, in the dungeon. She glanced at the wall to see several chains and leather straps hanging there. According to the lists, the large dresser along the wall and the big armoire held several toys, like vibrators, floggers, et cetera. Even costumes and props. The information sheets also gave instructions on how to use the items, along with some creative suggestions for playful scenarios. Also included was a collection of stories to further spur the guests' imaginations.

Ty buttered the last piece of toast and placed it on top of the others on the plate, then sliced through the stack. He turned at the clicking sound of heels on the wooden floor.

When he saw Marie standing in the doorway, he nearly dropped the butter knife. She stood in shiny black patent leather from neck to toe. The tight catsuit clung to her slim, well-proportioned body. Silver laces crisscrossed the torso, pulling the outfit snug around her waist, accentuating her full breasts, and the spike heels made her legs look exceptionally long and slender.

Although her body was almost totally covered, her breasts were pushed up high, and the plunging neckline showed off the swell of her round creamy breasts. Round cutouts totally exposed her nipples, which were hardening under his gaze.

"Wow," Zeke replied, gaping at her with a wide smile.

"Is breakfast ready yet?" Marie asked.

"Yes, Mistress," Ty replied.

"Good. Serve it to me in the dining room."

She turned and walked away. Ty couldn't drag his gaze from her delightfully swaying ass.

Zeke spooned scrambled eggs from the frying pan to a large bowl as Ty retrieved the tray of bacon from the oven where he'd put it to stay warm. He placed the bacon onto a platter and handed it to Zeke, then grabbed the honey and the plate of toast and followed Zeke into the dining room where Marie sat at the table sipping orange juice. Ty had set one place only—for the Mistress. Zeke set down the plates, then refilled her glass from the pitcher of juice sitting on the table. Ty and Zeke both took a position on either side of the table, standing behind the chairs. Both he and Zeke wore only their boxers, assuming their mistress would appreciate the view of their naked torsos. Ty glanced at the dragon tattooed across Zeke's sculpted chest and down one muscular arm. Ty certainly appreciated it.

Zeke dropped his gaze, as a good sub should, and so did Ty.

Marie ate in silence, then when she was done, she sat back.

"More coffee."

Zeke reached for the white insulated coffee jug on the table and filled her mug. Ty added a spoonful of sugar and poured in a little cream, just as she liked it.

"Good. Now take away the rest. Both of you eat quickly. I have plans."

Ty and Zeke cleared the table, then stood in the kitchen and ate the leftover eggs and bacon. About ten minutes later, Marie strolled into the kitchen and smiled.

"It's such a lovely day, I think I'd like to go for a ride."

Did she mean on the Harley? Or could she mean . . . ?

She grinned wickedly. "After all, I have two such studly stallions at my disposal." She turned. "Follow me."

Ty glanced at Zeke, who grinned broadly.

"Yes, Mistress," Ty said at the same time as Zeke.

When they walked into the living room, she picked up a leather harness from a chair and handed it to Zeke.

"I want you to prepare my other stallion. Put on Ty's harness." She turned to Ty. "Take off your boxers."

Ty dropped his shorts. Zeke took the harness, then walked toward Ty. Zeke draped the straps over Ty's shoulders, then wrapped a strap around his chest and buckled it, then wrapped one around his waist and buckled it. The touch of Zeke's fingertips playing along Ty's skin as he adjusted the straps and fastened the buckles sent tingles flashing across his skin. His cock hardened as Zeke grabbed the strap hanging from his waist and slid the metal cock ring over Ty's cockhead, the cold metal brushing his sensitive skin. Zeke tucked his fingers under Ty's balls and drew them through the ring, then drew the leather strap under his crotch and up behind him, then attached it to the waist strap.

"Lovely." Marie's gaze wandered over him.

His cock swelled within the grip of the cock ring.

"Now I want you to brush him down." Marie handed Zeke an oval wooden brush with white bristles.

"Yes, Mistress."

Zeke took the brush and slipped his fingers through the black leather strap on the back and pressed it against Ty's chest, then began rubbing the soft bristles over Ty's skin in a circular motion. Round and round across his chest. Zeke's other hand trailed over the newly stimulated skin as the brush moved on. Over Ty's shoulders . . . down his back. Then lower. The soft bristles circled over his butt, then down his thighs.

Ty's cock rose at the stimulating sensations spiraling through him.

"Good." Marie walked toward Ty as Zeke stopped brushing and stepped back. She stroked her hand along Ty's heavily shadowed cheek. "My stallion looks quite handsome." She took the brush from Zeke and handed it to Ty. "Now you prepare my other stallion."

Oh God, the thought of touching Zeke like he'd just touched Ty heated his insides . . . and sent panic skittering through him. But his skin still tingled from Zeke's thorough attention. And Ty didn't want to disobey his Mistress.

He took the brush and walked to the chair where the other harness lay in a heap and picked it up.

Marie turned to Zeke. "Take off your boxers."

"Yes, Mistress."

As Zeke dropped his boxers to the floor, Ty noticed Zeke's cock was fully erect, too. He was just as turned on as Ty.

Ty attached the harness around Zeke's broad chest. His fingers brushed across Zeke's well-defined muscles as he attached the buckle. He fastened all the other body straps and buckled them, then lifted the lower strap with trepidation. Gingerly, he placed the metal cock ring over Zeke's cockhead and slid it down the shaft. Zeke's cock twitched. As a result, it bounced against Ty's fingertips. He reached the bottom, then pushed his fingers through the ring and tucked them under Zeke's balls, then gently pulled them through the ring.

Ty stepped behind Zeke and grasped the strap dangling from the cock ring and drew it behind him and up to the waistband, then buckled it into place. He tried to ignore how the strap enhanced the sexy view of Zeke's tight butt . . . and his desire to stroke his hand along those muscled cheeks.

He picked up the brush and began to rub it in circular

strokes over Zeke's back, just as Zeke had done to Ty. Round and round over Zeke's dragon tattoo, then over his shoulders. He moved to face Zeke and brushed over his chest and toward the center, following the front dragon, his other hand following the brush in a soothing caress after the stimulation of the bristles. He moved down over Zeke's stomach, ignoring the hard erection below, then over his hips to his tight butt cheeks. Stroking the hard, tight flesh with his hand as he followed the brush sent heat through his groin. God, he couldn't believe how hard he was.

"Good. Now put the brush on the table." Marie stepped toward Zeke and stroked his cheek. "You're a beautiful stallion, too," she murmured to Zeke.

Ty tugged his gaze from Zeke's hard body and watched Marie, so incredibly sexy in her shiny skintight catsuit. His cock throbbed with need. She stepped to a bag sitting on the coffee table and pulled out some leather bands.

"Zeke, come here and kneel down."

"Yes, Mistress." Zeke knelt in front of her.

She placed a studded collar around his neck and fastened it with snaps.

"Hold out your hands."

Zeke extended his hands in front of her and she wrapped a leather strap around each wrist.

"Now, Ty."

"Yes, Mistress." Ty knelt beside Zeke.

Her warmth and the play of her fingertips on his neck as she attached the collar sent heat thrumming through him.

"Your hands."

He held them out and suffered the delightful torture of her fingers brushing against the inside of his wrist as she wrapped the leather around it and snapped the strap closed, then did the same to the other wrist.

"Now stand up, both of you."

"Yes, Mistress," Ty and Zeke said at the same time.

Once they stood up, Marie circled around them, admiring.

"Quite nice. I think there's one important thing my stallions are missing, however."

Twenty-one

Ty watched as Marie reached into her bag again and drew out two long black tails. Attached to red butt plugs. Ty's ass clenched at the sight of them. She wasn't really going to—

She smiled wickedly. "My stallions look naked without their tails." She pulled a bottle of lubricant from her bag and handed it to Zeke. "Help Ty with his tail."

Zeke glanced at Ty, who grimaced.

"Uh . . . yes, Mistress."

Zeke opened the bottle and slathered the red butt plug with gel, then walked behind Ty. Ty leaned forward, resting his hands on the back of the couch, readying himself for his new appendage. A second later, Ty felt Zeke's slick finger stroke between his cheeks, then press against his back opening. Slowly, the tip of his finger pressed inside, then he circled around. Then a second finger pushed inside.

Ty drew in a deep breath. God, it was weird, and yet wildly erotic, having Zeke touch him this way. And the heat in Marie's eyes made it clear she was getting intensely turned on. Zeke drew his fingers away and then pressed the rubber plug against Ty's opening. Slowly, it slid inside. Hard and slender, it pressed in deeper, until he felt the flared end of the plug against his cheeks, which would stop it from sliding in any farther. Hair draped down his ass and over the backs of his thighs. His tail.

He stood up, very conscious of the rubber device in his ass . . . and the hair whisking along his thighs.

Marie handed a tail to Ty. "Now you do Zeke."

Right now, Ty really wanted to *do* someone. Marie would be preferable, but Zeke was definitely a real possibility the way Ty was feeling right now.

He took the bottle of lube from Zeke and smeared the gel on the plug as Zeke leaned his hands on the couch. Ty moved behind him, smearing lube on his fingers. Just as Zeke had done, Ty dragged his index finger between Zeke's ass cheeks, then pressed against his anus. His finger slid inside the hot, tight passage. He circled around, getting Zeke used to his finger, then slid in a second finger. Zeke's ass held Ty's fingers in a tight grip. Ty swirled around, stretching him, then drew his fingers out and pressed the red plug against the puckered opening. Slowly, he eased the plug inside, watching it disappear inside Zeke's ass. Finally, it was fully inserted and the black tail hung down his backside. Damn, it looked sexy.

Zeke stood up. Marie stroked along his tight butt, then slapped lightly. She reached for Ty's ass and squeezed his cheek, then slapped him, too.

She sat on the couch. The men stood before her, awaiting instructions. She smiled at the intensely erotic situation. Two men at her beck and call. Ready to satisfy her every whim. And she had a very wicked whim right now.

"Unzip me," she commanded.

Ty leaned forward and unzipped the crotch of her suit.

She opened her legs wide, very conscious of the cool air on her hot mound.

"Kneel down, stallions, and show me how good you are at . . . nuzzling."

They both dropped to their knees. Ty leaned forward and kissed the inside of her thigh, a few inches above her knee. She could feel only the pressure of his lips through the fabric, but not the heat and moistness of his mouth. Zeke lifted her other calf and pressed his lips to the back of her knee.

"Mmm. That feels good . . . but I was thinking higher."

Ty kissed upward, then nuzzled his nose along the naked flesh at the top of her thigh, beside her mound. Then he shifted, and his mouth covered her fleshy folds and he licked. Zeke kissed upward and licked the other side of her folds, then sucked the soft flesh into his mouth. Ty licked inside her folds, his cheek brushing Zeke's, then he licked her clit and her head dropped back. He wiggled the tip of his tongue against her button, then glided along her slit. Zeke covered her clit and licked, then sucked it. She moaned, tossing her head from side to side at the exquisite pleasure. Her eyelids fell closed as she gave herself over to it.

Fingers glided along her slick opening, then slid inside. Mouths and fingers moved on her . . . in her . . . stroking . . . licking . . . sucking. Her insides tightened as fiercely pleasurable sensations exploded inside her. She moaned again and heat washed through her in waves. She gasped as intense pleasure pulsed along her nerve ends, catapulting her over the edge. Another flick on her clit . . . fingers stroked inside her . . . and hot liquid gushed from her insides. She moaned again.

Her head dropped back and she sucked in air as she regained a sense of time. The mouths and fingers moved away and she glanced up at the two men grinning at her.

"Well, you really are fine stallions." She reached out for their hard cocks and wrapped her hands around them. "You deserve a treat."

She tugged their cocks closer, then leaned forward and took Zeke's cockhead in her mouth, then swirled her tongue over the tip. She drew him from her mouth and covered Ty's bigger cockhead, stroking her tongue along the bottom ridge.

She stroked their hard shafts with her hands as she moved back and forth, taking one cock, then the other in her mouth. When Zeke seemed really close, she kept him in her mouth, bobbing up and down, then she tucked her hands under his balls, feeling the ring of steel around his cock, keeping him engorged longer than normal. Maybe she should have made use of the additional stamina the cock ring would give him in a better way, but it wouldn't be fair to stop now. She cradled his balls firmly in her hand and sucked hard and fast as she glided up and down his hard shaft. He erupted into her mouth, groaning.

She released him, then turned to Ty and gazed at his huge cock. The desire to feel that immense shaft inside her became too much. It was time for her to ride him again.

"Lay down on the floor," she commanded.

Ty lay back on the carpeted floor and Marie climbed over him, resting her knees on either side of his hips. She grasped his big erection and pressed the huge head to her slick opening.

Oh God, it was so big . . . and so hard! She pushed down on it. The bulbous head glided inside her, them up into her slick passage, stretching her. It felt like heaven.

"Oh God, that feels good." She ground her hips down on him, impaling herself completely.

He stroked her hard nipple, peeking from the cutout in her suit. Zeke knelt beside them and licked her other nipple, then took it in his mouth. She moaned at the dual pleasure of being filled by Ty's big cock and Zeke sucking on her nipple.

Ty wrapped his hands around her hips and she began to move. Up, then down, driving his cock inside her again. Up, then down. Blissful sensations burst through her as she rode the wave of pleasure, then cried out as a phenomenal orgasm burst through her, hurling her into ecstasy . . . and beyond.

He tightened below her, then liquid heat erupted into her.

Finally, she dropped onto his chest, completely sated. His arms wrapped around her and he held her close, stroking her hair from her eyes.

Love filled her as she snuggled against him, totally immersed in this wonderful man.

Twenty-two

"The reservation is for two o'clock?" Marie asked as Zeke opened the front door of the car for her.

"That's right." Zeke got in the backseat behind her.

Ty put the car in gear and drove down the winding path back to the road.

"A steam engine?" Marie asked.

"It's a tourist thing," Ty said. "It takes us on a scenic tour of Garrett Hills to see the fall foliage. Then we'll stop in the village of Wakefield for an hour or so, then head back."

"Sounds like fun." She gazed out the window, watching the scenery pass by.

After they parked the car at the small train station, they approached the old train. A big black engine with three dark green and white passenger cars. Zeke took Marie's hand and helped her step up into the train, then followed her through the car. She selected a seat near the middle of the car and he sat beside her. Ty sat facing her, a table between them.

The green seats were comfortable and the table made the

arrangement feel cozy. People continued to board the train and, about twenty minutes later, the train whistle sounded, then the train chugged into motion. Soon the clickety-clack of the train on the tracks combined with the gentle swaying motion, providing a relaxing atmosphere.

Marie leaned back in her chair and enjoyed the delightful view of blazing red, orange, and yellow foliage beyond the lake, the calm water reflecting the fluffy white clouds in the blue sky.

Zeke and Ty talked about some of the cars Zeke had done custom paint jobs for recently at his shop while Marie watched a couple in a red canoe gliding along the lake outside.

About forty minutes later, the train pulled into the Wake-field station.

Ty led the way off the train, then held Marie's hand as she stepped onto the pavement. The business district of the lovely village consisted of quaint colorful buildings over-looking the lake.

"The bakery here is great," Zeke said as he led them to a red building with yellow trim around the windows.

They followed him up the steps to the door, then went inside. Ty picked up a loaf of multigrain bread and Marie se-lected some chocolate croissants and pecan tarts. Next, they poked around in the general store, with quaint craft items alongside food staples for cottage-goers.

Finally, Zeke led them up some stairs at the side of the store to a wonderful restaurant on the upper floor, over-looking the water. With the sun shining brightly, the after-noon had warmed up quite nicely, so they selected a table on the outside deck.

The men ordered beers and Marie asked for a white wine.

Ty took a sip of his beer, then leaned back and smiled at Marie. "So, I didn't know you knew anything about pony play."

She swirled her glass of wine. "Well, I read some of the literature in a folder at the cottage. They described a number of . . . um . . . activities I've never heard of before . . . and equipment . . . and how to use it."

"To our good fortune," Zeke said, grinning.

"You seem very relaxed with each other, which is really refreshing." She watched Ty casually, noticing that he seemed to stiffen. "Is it okay that I . . . pushed you a little?"

"If it turns you on, I'm definitely okay with it," Zeke answered with a grin.

"Ty?"

"Sure," he said, but she noticed the tightness in his voice. "As Zeke said, if it turns you on."

She leaned forward, capturing Ty's reluctant gaze. "I don't mean to be pushy, but . . . it seems like you two have a bit of a connection." She hedged her words, noticing Ty shifting uncomfortably and not wanting him to shut down the topic. "Look, with the kind of relationship the three of us are sharing, I'm hoping you won't mind if I'm frank. I know there's a mutual attraction between me and each of you. I'd like to know if there's one between the two of you, too."

Zeke glanced at Ty. "I'd like to know that, too."

"Why can't you two just leave it the way it is?" Ty asked in a strained voice. "We do stuff. We enjoy it. We don't have to talk about it."

"If that's what you want," Zeke answered, then leaned forward a little. "But if it makes you feel any better, I've noticed that I have certain . . . feelings toward you. More than a friendship. It confused me at first, especially since I don't have these feelings for other men . . . and I definitely enjoy women."

"Amen," Ty said.

"But . . . that doesn't change the . . . I don't know . . . attraction I feel for you. Maybe it's just because we're with Marie. She sees you as sexy, so . . ." Zeke shrugged. "It somehow feels natural to want to . . . share more with you when we're in that situation."

"Maybe exploring things a little more between you would be a good idea," Marie suggested.

Ty leaned back in his chair, his fingers gripping the wooden armrests. "How about we change the subject?"

"All right." Zeke turned to Marie. "So what do you think of Ty's dominant personality now that you've seen it put into action?"

She smiled and gazed at Ty. "Very impressive, actually. Ty, I never knew you could be so . . . authoritative and . . . sexy." She rested her hand on his arm and stroked. "Well, I knew you were sexy, but last night was sensational." Her insides quivered at the memory of him commanding her to take off her clothes. Of being chained to the chair, her legs wide, and Ty stroking her. Then when they'd taken her to the dungeon and fucked her silly.

Zeke watched the two of them, a sick feeling in his stomach. The way Marie gazed at Ty, her blue eyes soft and dewy. The heat in Ty's gaze that Zeke knew was more than lust. The guy was in love with her . . . had been from day one. Now, Zeke was pretty sure Marie loved him back. Which is what Zeke knew would happen, but . . . now that it had, he didn't want it to be so.

He wanted Marie. He *loved* Marie. How the hell could he just give her up to Ty?

After the train trip back, Marie sat in the car as Ty drove back to the cottage, and wondered what would happen with the three of them after the weekend.

She shifted uncomfortably in her seat. Just sitting in the car with the two of them, her senses totally aware of their masculine presence at all times, kept her in a constant state of yearning. Which was exciting, but it also threw her for a loop. It was no longer her and Zeke as a couple and Ty along for the ride. Ty was no longer just her friend . . . with benefits or not. He was much more to her than that.

The whole train trip, she could sense Zeke watching her, trying to figure out if her feelings had changed toward Ty . . . and toward him.

How could she find a balance? She wanted both men, but at some point, she'd have to choose just one. But the longer she spent with both of them as her lovers, the more difficult it would be to give up one of them. Or both of them, since the attraction between the two of them seemed to be building. Maybe they would eventually come to the conclusion that they didn't actually need her at all, and would choose each other.

Any way she sliced it, someone was going to be hurt.

Marie pushed aside her tumultuous thoughts as Ty parked the car next to the cottage, right beside Zeke's big Harley. Zeke opened Marie's door and she stepped out of the vehicle. She walked toward the powerful machine and stroked her hand along the black seat, remembering how it felt vibrating between her legs when she'd ridden it panty-less . . . the day Zeke had taken her to the movies, teasing her constantly. She'd been so turned on when they'd finally made love, she'd nearly exploded with pleasure.

She stroked her hand along the handlebars, the metal cold under her fingertips. Then she turned around, leaning back against the bike.

"You know, when I see this powerful motorcycle, I think of what might happen to me if I were here all alone and some powerful bikers were to come along."

Zeke stepped toward her and stroked his hands along her hips. Ty came up behind her and curled his arms around her waist, then cupped her breasts.

"You mean, if they were to . . . take advantage of you?" Ty murmured in her ear.

Zeke slid his hands around her, cupping her behind, then drew her close to his body. His lips captured hers and his tongue plunged into her mouth.

"So you want to be used and," he squeezed her behind, pulling her tight to his groin, "*abused* by a couple of bikers?"

She laid her hand on his chest. "Of course, I would resist."

"Of course," Ty said, sliding his hands from her breasts and moving over her shoulder, then nuzzling her ear. "That's what makes it fun."

Zeke lifted her onto the bike. She squirmed against the leather seat.

"You wait here. We'll be right back." Zeke nudged Ty's arm, then led him into the cottage.

A few moments later, they both came out in black leather jackets and torn jeans—Zeke's usual attire but a new look for Ty. They both had chains swinging from their belt loops and . . . *handcuffs*. Her insides flooded with heat.

"Well, look what we have here," Zeke said as he approached her with a devilish grin on his face.

She shifted on the bike in a mock nervous fashion, then lifted her leg over the seat to sit sideways. Zeke stepped in front of her and Ty behind, both dragging their gazes up and down her body in a suggestive manner.

"I think this little lady wants . . . a ride," Zeke said.

"I think you're right," Ty agreed.

Marie stared up at Zeke, an ominous figure in his black leather, with his studded eyebrows. If this were the first time she'd ever seen Zeke . . . if she didn't know what a wonderful, caring man he was . . . she might almost be nervous.

Ty grasped her waist and pivoted her around while Zeke caught her leg behind the knee and lifted it over the bike so she straddled it again. Ty threw his leg over the bike and sat behind her, then grasped her hips and drew her tight against his body, his swelling cock pressing against her behind. Zeke stroked along her thighs, then up her ribs and cupped her breasts, molding his hands over them and kneading them. She sucked in air at the heated sensations pulsing through her.

"Very nice," Zeke murmured.

Zeke began to unfasten the buttons of her shirt, exposing her breasts to the cool air. Ty grasped the fabric and drew it apart, then stroked her left breast while Zeke explored the right. Zeke ran his hand downward, past her waist and over the crotch of her jeans, then rubbed up and down over her heated mound. Ty hooked his hands around her arms, pinning them, as Zeke unfastened her belt, then unzipped her jeans. A moment later, his hand dove underneath her panties and he stroked between her folds. Oh man, she'd soaked her panties already.

Zeke stepped back and unzipped his jeans, then drew out his cock. Ty dismounted the bike and lifted Marie from the seat, then draped her over it, her stomach across the seat, her ass in the air. He held her arms behind her.

Zeke stepped toward her, his cock waving in her face. Red. Swollen. Hard. Ty drew her hair back from her face as Zeke bumped his cockhead against her mouth and she opened, then he pushed his cock inside. She wrapped her lips around him and licked.

Damn, she should be resisting, but she couldn't find it in her. And Zeke certainly seemed to be happy. He glided forward, filling her with his cock, the shaft sliding along her lips.

As Zeke's cock glided in and out of her mouth, and she sucked, Ty released her arms. She hooked her hands around the side of the seat to hold herself steady as Ty tugged off her slip-on shoes, then pulled off her jeans, dragging them from her legs and tossing them aside. His hands stroked over her naked ass, then he tucked his finger under the elastic of her thong and tugged, pulling the elastic tighter between her cheeks. The crotch pulled on her sensitive heated flesh. Ty ran his finger along the elastic, from her waist, between her cheeks, to the soaking wet crotch. When he stroked over her wet folds, only the thin silk between his fingers and her naked slit, she moaned. Zeke's cock fell from her mouth, so he grasped it and put it back in.

She concentrated on sucking Zeke while Ty disappeared briefly, returning to press against the back of her thighs and . . . oh, his big cockhead nudged against her wet core. He pulled aside the scrap of fabric covering her crotch and pushed against her, then slipped inside her vagina. She squeezed him, as she sucked Zeke harder. Zeke moaned, then thrust slowly into her mouth. Ty pushed in deeper, slowly, stroking her ass. She opened her throat and tipped her head back, taking Zeke deeper. He pulsed in short strokes, his balls tightening.

Ty caught her hips and pushed deeper inside her, impaling her completely. She reached for Zeke's balls and stroked them. They were tight and hard. Zeke groaned. Hot liquid pulsed into her mouth.

He drew out and stepped back, then watched as Ty drew back and thrust forward again. Back then forward . . . filling her with his awesome length. Zeke cupped her breasts as Ty thrust into her again and again. She moaned, then gripped Zeke's arms as an orgasm flashed through her. Intense. Explosive. Ty thrust deep again, erupting inside her, sending her pleasure higher. Then he tweaked her clit. She wailed as she plunged into absolute ecstasy.

Finally, she flopped onto the bike, hanging over it like a rag doll.

"I think we wore her out," Zeke said.

"Mmm. Too bad, because I had things I still wanted to do to her."

She drew in a deep breath. "No, you mustn't," she murmured in mock horror.

Ty chuckled out loud. Zeke wrapped his hands around her waist and lifted her onto the bike again, facing her backward. She rested her left foot on the chrome exhaust pipe, but couldn't find any purchase on the other side, so just let her right leg hang over the side. Zeke pulled her shirt off her arms, then quickly disposed of her bra. The cool air washed across her bare breasts and her nipples hardened into tight nubs.

Ty removed the handcuffs from his jeans and snapped them around her left wrist. The cold steel against her skin sent goose bumps racing along her arm.

Zeke held up a leather leash and smiled. "Don't want to scratch the Harley."

He coiled it around the handlebars as Ty pressed a hand on her chest, forcing her to lie back. Her behind settled comfortably against the rising slope of the contoured seat, which curved upward toward the back of the bike. He drew her hand behind her head and attached the other bracelet of the handcuff to one end of the leash.

Zeke retrieved his handcuffs from his discarded jeans and snapped a cuff onto her other wrist, then attached it to the other end of the leash. Now she lay sprawled across the top of the bike, her back arching upward with the curve of the gas tank. She rested her head on the handlebars, ignoring the gauges pressed against her upper back and neck.

Zeke picked up his jeans and rolled them loosely then slid his hand under her neck and eased her forward, then laid his jeans over the gauges as an impromptu cushion. When she leaned back, it felt much more comfortable.

Ty tucked his fingers under the waistband of her thong and drew it down her legs and off. She stretched her right leg the length of the bike and set her left foot back down on the exhaust pipe.

Naked and sprawled across the top of Zeke's motorcycle, her wrists handcuffed to the handlebars. This was getting interesting. What would they do now?

"I feel like a beer. What about you?" Ty glanced toward Zeke.

"Yeah, great idea."

They both turned around and walked away.

"Hey, you can't just leave me here," she cried.

Twenty-three

Marie's jaw dropped as Ty and Zeke just chuckled and kept walking toward the cottage, then went inside.

She lay there, totally naked in the great outdoors. Vulnerable. A light breeze caressed her body, sending her nipples tightening even harder.

This place was pretty isolated. The brochure assured visitors that they could play freely outside with no worry about passersby.

She flopped her head back and stared at the tree above her, the leaves rustling in the breeze. The sun neared the horizon, staining the clouds a rich orange, laced with purple.

She was a captive of two bikers. In real life. Zeke was a real biker and, judging from their history and what she'd seen of Ty yesterday, Ty probably had been a biker once, too. Soon they would come out of the cottage and have their way with her. Again. She was bound and helpless to their whims.

God, how sexy was that?

She heard the cottage door close and she glanced around. Zeke and Ty headed her way. Zeke had pulled on a different pair of jeans, since she still used his previous pair as a pillow. Both still wore their black leather jackets and T-shirts, looking badass all the way.

"That's what I like to see," Zeke said. "A naked woman handcuffed to my bike, all laid out and ready for me."

"For us," Ty added.

Something flashed in Zeke's eyes before he stepped beside her, then he grinned. He touched her cheek lightly, stroked down her neck, then over her breast. His big warm hand encompassed her breast and she stopped herself from arching against it.

Ty stepped to the other side of the bike and leaned down, sucking her nipple into his mouth.

Zeke leaned down and slid his hand under her head and captured her lips with his, then plundered her mouth with his tongue. He tasted of cold beer and hot male. His mouth left hers and roamed down her throat, pausing briefly at the base of her neck, lapping at her pulse point, then roaming farther down. His mouth covered her other nipple and she moaned with pleasure, both her nipples covered with hot man mouth.

Zeke's hand roamed along her side, from underarm to hip as he raised his head.

"That beer has made me hungry." He kissed downward, over her belly, then he moved lower down the bike and leaned toward her until his breath brushed across her thighs.

Ty, still lapping and sucking her nipple, stroked over her other nipple and toyed with the hard nub. Zeke's mouth brushed her inner thigh, right below her mound, and she jerked a little in surprise. His hands stroked either side of her naked folds, then his tongue brushed her sensitive flesh and licked along her slit. She arched a little and he wrapped his hand around her hips, holding her still. He settled over her clit and flicked his tongue. She moaned.

Ty sucked her breast as his hand flicked and teased her other nipple. She arched her chest toward him. The chains of the handcuffs clinked as she pulled against the cold metal surrounding her wrists. Zeke lifted her leg and rested it over his shoulder, then stroked her slit with his fingers. Tingles quivered through her. His fingers glided inside her, stroking her inner passage. Ty sucked harder.

"Oh God." She tossed her head from side to side.

Ty stroked up her body and caressed her cheek. She turned her head and licked his fingertips. He pressed his index finger to her mouth and she wrapped her lips around it and drew it inside, then sucked deeply.

He grinned. "Okay. Let's put that gorgeous mouth to good use."

He stood up and unfastened his jeans, then dropped them to the ground and stepped out of them. Zeke's stroking sent wild tingles dancing through her womb. Ty wrapped his hand around his erection and stroked, as he stepped closer, then pressed the tip toward her face. Zeke sucked on her clit and she moaned, then gulped Ty into her mouth and began to suck.

"Oh baby." Ty fed more of his cock into her mouth.

She lapped and sucked as Zeke stroked her inner walls with his fingers and flicked her clit mercilessly with his tongue.

Pleasure built within her like steam in a pressure cooker. She arched against Zeke's mouth and sucked on Ty with enthusiasm. Zeke's fingers stoked her pleasure higher and higher. His tongue sent bursting sparks of sensation fluttering wildly through her. Suddenly, she exploded in a mindshattering orgasm. Hot liquid flooded from her core and down her leg.

"Well, you certainly enjoyed yourself." Zeke grinned widely.

Ty plunged in and out of her mouth. She squeezed and sucked. He groaned, pulling away before he came.

Zeke climbed onto the passenger seat and pulled Marie toward him. Her arms pulled against the handcuffs, outstretched above her head, rather than bent as before. Her bottom sloped upward with the seat and he pressed his hard cock against her opening, then slid inside. A long, even stroke. Deep into her.

She dropped her head back and moaned. "Ohhh . . ."

He drew back and glided deep again.

"Oh God, I want both of you," she murmured.

"What was that our little captive said?" Ty teased.

"I want both of you hot bikers inside me. Please, fuck me now."

Zeke pulled out. As he stood up, Ty unfastened the handcuffs holding her down. Zeke took her hands and helped her off the bike, steadying her when her rubbery legs threatened to buckle. Ty climbed onto the bike backward and lay down on it, just as she had been, his stiff cock standing straight up.

"Time for your ride, sweet thing." Zeke grasped her around the waist and lifted her onto the bike, straddling Ty. She grasped the handlebars and settled her feet on the footrests. Ty held his cock and slid it along her slit. Her insides quivered with need. He pressed himself to her opening and she lowered herself onto him. His enormous cock impaled her, penetrating deeply. She gasped.

"Oh . . . God . . . That feels so—" She whimpered in pleasure.

Zeke climbed on the bike behind her and stroked her ass, then his slick cockhead glided up and down between her cheeks. He pressed against her opening and pushed slowly, stretching her as he slipped inside. She squeezed Ty's big cock inside her as Zeke slowly eased inside her ass.

Finally, Zeke was fully embedded in her, too. His hands found her breasts and drew her back toward him. There she sat, as if riding the bike, but with two big cocks impaling her. She began to move, gliding up and down on Ty. Zeke followed her lead, sliding his cock in and out of her backside. Thrilling sensations quivered through her. Ty grasped her hips and helped her move up and down. Zeke thrust faster and more deeply. Both cocks penetrated her deep and hard. Thrusting her higher and higher . . . blasting toward heaven. Her nerve endings burst with sensation and . . . She gasped as thunderous pleasure tore through her, catapulting her to an explosion of pure bliss.

She wailed, joined rapidly by Zeke, then Ty, all three of them groaning at once. She clung to the handlebars, squeezing the cocks lovingly within her. Then she collapsed on top of Ty. Zeke leaned over her, then kissed the back of her neck. Ty captured her lips and stroked the inside of her mouth.

She drew away and smiled down at Ty. "Man, you two really do know how to ride!"

Ty stood beside Marie on the wooden deck overlooking the moonlit lake. Zeke had volunteered to make dinner—his infamous soup-or-stew, which involved a myriad of ingredients that seemed to change every time—and was busy in the kitchen.

Ty leaned against the railing.

"Look, a shooting star." Marie pointed upward.

Ty glanced up in time to see the thin streak of light across the sky. Another meteor shot across the black sky in a streak of light.

"Must be a meteor shower."

"They're beautiful." Marie's face filled with awe as she gazed at the stars.

He cupped her shoulders and drew her close to him. "Not as beautiful as you."

She gazed up at him as he leaned toward her. She tipped up her face, her lips parting, ready for his kiss. He brushed his lips against hers—so sweet and delicate—then tightened his arms around her and deepened the kiss. He drew back and gazed at her, knowing he had to tell her how he felt about her. Needing to know if she shared his feelings.

"Marie . . ." He stroked her hair from her face. "I have loved you ever since I first met you. I've wanted to tell you so many times, but you were in a relationship . . . then after that . . ."

Damn, he didn't want to mention Zeke. Not right now. He stroked her cheek. "I love you with all my heart."

He kissed her again, his heart pulsing with the need to know that she returned his feelings. He eased back and their lips parted.

She gazed at him, her eyes shining brightly. "Oh, Ty. I love you, too."

He smiled broadly, then captured her lips again, plunging his tongue into her mouth.

Zeke watched through the sliding door as Ty kissed Marie in triumph, and his heart sank.

All along, he'd believed if Ty showed his true dominant nature that Marie would fall head over heels for him. Ever since Friday night, Zeke had sensed that love in her, but he had only been guessing. Now he knew for sure.

Zeke turned and walked back to the kitchen, aching inside. Now he would have to give her up. God damn it, he had sensed this would happen. But he hadn't known it would hurt so bad.

Twenty-four

Zeke took a bite of his stew, then washed it down with a swig of beer.

Marie set down her spoon in the empty soup bowl in front of her. "Zeke, that really was delicious."

He nodded as he chewed another bite. During the whole meal he hadn't participated in the small talk. All he could think about was his aching heart and the fact Marie loved another man.

"You're pretty quiet tonight," Ty said.

Zeke shrugged, then pushed aside his empty bowl.

"He's being the strong, silent type," Marie said, but she sent him a questioning gaze.

Ty pushed his chair back and stood up, then picked up the bowls and stacked them. "Since Zeke cooked, I'll clean up."

Marie stood up and picked up the serving bowl. "You want my help?"

"No, I can handle it." Ty placed the cutlery in the serving

bowl and took the bowl from her hand, then disappeared into the kitchen.

Marie walked toward the living room and Zeke followed her.

"So you and Ty were out star-gazing earlier?" he asked.

"Yes, it's a beautiful night. Very clear."

He nodded, thinking about the two of them on the deck, proclaiming their love for each other. Kissing each other. The thought made his gut clench.

He wanted to remind her just how much *he* loved her. To show her. He wanted to ask her if she still loved him. To ask her to stay with him forever, and forget about Ty.

His insides ached with the need to pull her into his arms and convince her to stay with him. And him alone.

"Is there something wrong, Zeke?"

He couldn't answer her. Couldn't tell her he didn't want her kissing Ty . . . or loving Ty. Couldn't tell her he wanted her all for himself.

But he could show her.

He cupped her cheek and gazed lovingly into her eyes, then he lifted her face and met her lips with his, brushing lightly. At her sigh, he deepened the kiss, pulling her soft, feminine body close, his arms tightening around her.

Holding her in his arms was a special type of heaven for him. He cherished the feeling, moving his lips on hers in a gentle persuasion. Telling her with his kiss what he couldn't tell her in words. That he wanted her always. In his arms. In his world. In his life.

Her arms glided over his shoulders and she tightened her embrace, her lips responding to his. He felt her nipples harden against him and she pressed her body tighter against him. His cock expanded, pushing against his jeans.

"Hey, I see you two got started without me." Ty stepped behind Marie and stroked his hands across her shoulders.

She released Zeke's lips and she smiled at him before turning to Ty. Zeke watched helplessly as Ty took his turn kissing her.

Not yet. I'm not ready to give her up yet.

As soon as Ty released her lips, Zeke turned her back to him and kissed her again, wrapping his arms around her tightly. Ty slid his hands around her body and cupped her breasts, his hands gliding between their bodies. Zeke could feel the backs of Ty's hands as he stroked over Marie's breasts. As he moved, his hand brushed against Zeke's nipples, too, sending tingles through him.

Ty lifted the hem of Marie's top and glided it upward. Marie's lips parted from Zeke's as Ty lifted her top over her head.

"Well, you two certainly make a girl feel wanted."

Oh God, she had no idea.

She shed her jeans and socks, now standing before them in only a skimpy lace thong and semi-sheer lace bra. Both crimson. She stroked her hands over her breasts and Zeke's cock shot to attention. He could see her erect nipples pushing against the thin lacy fabric of her bra.

"Sweetheart, you are so damned hot!" Ty slid his hands around her waist and drew her back against him. She leaned against his broad chest and hooked one arm around his neck while she stroked her breasts with her other hand, all the while gazing directly at Zeke.

"Should we go down into the dungeon?" she asked.

Zeke shook his head and reached for her, pulling her from Ty's grasp and into his own arms, then kissed her passionately, his tongue delving deep into her mouth.

"I don't need anything but you," he murmured against her ear.

Behind her, Ty unfastened her bra. Marie dropped the straps off her shoulders then eased back and slid the garment from her body. Zeke's gaze locked on her beautiful round breasts, the dusky rose nipples pebbled and hard. Her nipples thrust forward, erect and hard. He pressed his hand over one soft breast and stroked. Her hard nub pushed into his palm. He leaned over and took it in his mouth, licking and swirling his tongue around it. She sighed as she dropped her head back against Ty's chest again. Ty stroked her other breast.

Zeke wanted her. Bad. He wanted to sink his cock into her. To claim her as his own. To show her just how much he needed her. And loved her.

He sank down to his knees and drew her panties down her hips, watching as the fabric slipped away, revealing her lovely pussy. He dragged the panties down her legs to the floor, then tossed them aside. He stroked his thumbs along the sides of her pussy, then separated the folds to find her little button. He licked it, listening to her moan with satisfaction. He dragged his fingers along her damp sex as he pressed his tongue against her clitoris, then swirled around it. He slid two fingers inside her slick opening and she moaned again. Her hands clung to his head as he worked on her clit.

Ty stepped back and shed his clothes. Judging from her gasps, Marie was getting close. Zeke stood up and dropped his pants and boxers to the floor, then shed his shirt. He tugged Marie into his arms and kissed her, then guided her toward the couch, never releasing her mouth. He sat her down then knelt in front of her.

Ty sat beside her, his enormous cock standing straight up. Zeke couldn't help himself. He reached out and wrapped his hand around Ty's huge shaft and stroked while he sucked Marie's nipple into his mouth.

Ty looked a little surprised, but didn't pull away. Encouraged, Zeke licked Marie's nipple, then leaned over and licked the tip of Ty's cock, then took it in his mouth. He sucked a little, then went back to Marie's breast, his hand still wrapped around Ty's cock. Marie reached for Ty's cock, too, her hand resting over the bulbous head, as Zeke's hand stroked up and down. Ty cupped Marie's other breast and Zeke released his cock. Marie began to stroke Ty's shaft as Zeke pressed his cockhead to Marie's wet opening, then pushed inside.

Oh God, she was so hot and wet. Her tight pussy gripped him as she squeezed him inside. He drove deep inside, then drew back. Sheer heaven.

He thrust deep again. In and out.

Marie slipped her hand from Ty's cock to Zeke's shoulder. Ty stroked his own cock while he watched Zeke thrust into Marie. She moaned and he reached down and flicked her clit with his fingers. She clung tight to his shoulders, her breathing fast and hard. He drove into her. Deeper. Harder. Enveloped by her hot silky-smooth canal.

She gasped, then wailed as she exploded in orgasm. He plunged into her several more times, then erupted inside her.

He held her tight against his body, reluctant to let her go. Finally, he released her and she flopped back on the couch, smiling at him.

"Hey, man." Ty nudged him.

Usually, Zeke would move away to give Ty his turn,

but Zeke didn't want to. But he had no real choice. He pushed away and sat on the couch beside her as Ty positioned himself in front of her. Zeke watched in fascination as Ty's huge cockhead pressed against her pussy, then stretched her as it slid inside. Once her body swallowed that huge bulbous head, Ty leaned forward and kissed her, then he slowly pressed the rest of his shaft inside her. The smile on her face and the sheer look of rapture on Ty's reminded Zeke that they loved each other. Zeke was a mere accessory, as Ty had called the second man position not too long ago.

Ty drove deep into Marie and she moaned. That huge cock must feel amazing inside her. Ty began to move. Deep, long thrusts. She clung to him and within moments, moaned her pleasure. She tightened her arms around him and her moans turned to a long, trailing wail. Ty pounded into her, driving her pleasure higher. Then Ty groaned his own climax.

God, Zeke realized what Marie and Ty shared was magnificent. Ty gave her such pleasure with that huge cock of his. That paired with the love they shared . . . God, how could Zeke compete with that?

God damn it, what was wrong with him? He wasn't supposed to be competing with it. Marie belonged with Ty, not Zeke. It was time for Zeke to walk away gracefully.

Zeke awoke to the feel of Marie's soft warm body snuggled against him, her cheek pressed against his chest, her delicate breath fluttering against his skin. He stroked her hair, loving the softness of it against his fingers, then wrapped his arms a little tighter around her.

Moonlight washed across her features, so relaxed in sleep. His heart ached for her. He wanted her in his life. Just the two of them. His gaze shifted to the pillow behind her . . . and Ty's sleeping face.

Ty lay on the other side of Marie, his sandy hair tousled, his cheeks shadowed with whiskers. While Zeke stared at Ty, he had to fight the urge to reach out and stroke Ty's whisker-roughened cheek. This crazy attraction he had toward Ty still threw him off balance, but Zeke couldn't deny how incredibly sexy Ty looked lying there, his square jaw resting against the black pillowcase, his handsome face relaxed in sleep. No wonder Marie found him so attractive.

His gut clenched. God damn it, he should hate the guy for stealing his woman . . . but he couldn't hate Ty—his best friend since childhood. Ty had always seen the positive in Zeke when others labeled him as bad news. That's why, as much as Zeke loved Marie, he wouldn't challenge Ty for her.

Even if Zeke stood a chance—which he didn't—he wouldn't steal away Ty's happiness.

Anyway, Ty was the better man for Marie. He would fit better in her life.

But right now, he couldn't stand to be here. In the same bed with them. Knowing they loved each other. That he was just an extra complication in the relationship now, rather than Marie's true love.

Zeke carefully eased away from Marie's warmth and slipped off the side of the bed. He strolled to his duffel bag in the corner and grabbed some boxers and pulled them on, then tugged a T-shirt over his head. His jeans and jacket were still upstairs in the living room where he'd discarded them earlier. He grabbed a pair of socks and turned toward the door.

"Where are you going?"

Ty stood in front of him, a softly illuminated shadow between Zeke and the door.

Zeke glanced at Marie, still sound asleep. He jerked his head toward the stairs and Ty nodded, then turned and walked upstairs. Zeke followed him. Once in the living room, Ty crossed his arms.

"So what's up?"

Zeke shrugged. "I thought I'd leave you two to it."

"You were just going to take off in the middle of the night?"

"Why not? It seems pretty clear Marie has chosen you . . . or is going to." He shrugged again. "And that's the way it should be. You saw her first."

Ty leaned back against the desk and crossed his arms. "Are you doing this to make up for what happened with Ashley? Because you don't have to do that. You didn't do anything wrong."

Zeke glanced at him warily. He'd wanted so much to convince Ty of that years ago, but Ty wouldn't listen.

"I know it was Ashley who caused the problem. *She* pursued *you*. I chose not to believe it at the time because . . ." He sighed. "There was something else that was really bothering me."

Zeke nodded. So Ty had felt this thing between them even back then.

Ty uncrossed his arms. "You know, we really should figure out what's going on between you and me. Especially if we want to keep our friendship alive. Otherwise it'll just get in the way."

Zeke's gut clenched. He paced across the room, then turned back to face Ty. "As much as I want our friendship to work, I don't know how it can with this situation with

Marie. I overheard you tell her you're in love with her. And she said she loves you, too."

Ty's eyebrows quirked. "What about you? You're in love with her, too, aren't you?"

"Of course, I am."

"Did you tell her?"

Zeke banged his fist on his thigh. "Damn it, I tried not to fall in love with her, because I knew you were. But . . . damn, when she told me she loved me . . . I couldn't help but tell her back."

Ty raised an eyebrow. "Now that you know she loves me, you figure she'll choose me?"

"Of course she will."

Ty smiled at him. "My question is, why does she have to choose?"

Twenty-five

Marie opened her eyes to see Ty place a tray beside the bed.

"Good morning," he said.

"Mm. Breakfast in bed."

Marie sat up and he placed the tray over her lap. He fluffed her pillow, then tucked a second behind her. She smiled, then took a forkful of the herb omelette.

"It's delicious." She took another bite.

He poured cream into the full coffee mug on the tray, then added a spoonful of sugar and stirred. She took a sip. He turned and walked toward the door.

"You're not joining me?" she asked.

He smiled. "You enjoy. I'll be back in a few minutes."

Once she finished her omelette, she leaned back against the pillows and relaxed while she drank her coffee. Ty returned a few moments later.

"Where's Zeke?" she asked.

"Well, I have bad news for you."

Her gaze darted to him, her heart stammering, as he

took the tray from her lap and placed it on a table by the door.

"What is it?"

"Zeke's in jail."

Her eyes widened. "Why? What happened?"

"I caught him trying to escape, so I locked him up."

Oh, a role-playing game. She sighed in relief. But she wasn't sure of her role. Was she supposed to be a guard? Or a policewoman? Or was she supposed to try and escape, too? Then he could capture her and lock her up. Or use *handcuffs* again. Her heart stammered. Or hang her from the ceiling by her wrists.

She licked her lips. "Are you going to throw me in jail, too?"

He sat down beside her and pulled her into his arms, capturing her lips with a fervor. His hands roamed up and down her back as his tongue dove between her lips and undulated against her tongue. Then he sucked until it pulsed into his mouth. Her heart thundered in her chest at the passion of his kiss. Finally, he released her, leaving her breathless.

"Do you want to escape?" he asked, his voice husky.

With wide eyes, she shook her head, and drew in a deep lungful of air.

He smiled. "You don't seem too sure. Maybe I will have to lock you up."

"Yes, Master."

He chuckled. "Very well. Let's go." He stood up, waiting for her to follow.

She grasped the covers to throw them aside, then paused. "But, Master, I'm totally naked."

He tugged at the covers playfully, grinning as they drew away from her breasts. Her nipples puckered, as much from his heated gaze as from the cool air. He pulled more firmly, dragging the covers from the rest of her.

"There's only one way I like to see my sub rather than naked."

He walked to the big wooden wardrobe, opened the door, and pulled out leather straps and chains. "Come here."

She walked toward him, totally conscious of her nudity as his gaze roamed over her. Her nipples ached as they hardened even more.

The leather straps and chains he held turned out to be an outfit of sorts.

He attached a collar around her neck with three leather straps dangling from it. He adjusted one to lie down the center of her torso, to just below her breasts, and the other two went alongside each breast and around to the back. He turned her around and fastened them behind her. Between the center strap and each side strap hung a series of cascading chains, some draping over her breasts and several below, leaving her breasts totally visible.

"Turn this way. Let me see you."

"Yes, Master." She turned to face him.

He tugged one of the chains so the cold metal links brushed across her nipple. Tingles danced through her, straight to her crotch.

"Lovely." He admired her straining nipples.

He turned to the wardrobe again, then dangled a patch of leather and chains in front of her with a grin and she realized it was her . . . thong. He swirled his finger around, indicating she should turn her back to him again. She turned and he wrapped the leather strap around her hips, then buckled it behind her.

"Open your legs."

She shivered at his words. "Yes, Master."

She positioned her feet wider apart. The back of his hand brushed against her inner thigh as he reached between her legs to catch the leather strap dangling from the patch covering her crotch. He lifted the thin strip, pressing it between her cheeks, then attached it to the hip strap.

He pulled some shiny black boots from the wardrobe, peered at the soles, then handed them to her.

"I think these are your size. Put them on."

She pulled on the boots and zipped them up. They fit perfectly. Each had a tall spike heel and a ring attached to each side of the ankle with short chains that draped down the back of the heel.

He reached into the wardrobe again, then wrapped heavy, black leather cuffs lined with a thick, almost furry, fleece around her wrists. The leather extended along her hands, attached to heavy-duty steel D-rings.

"Good. Now you're ready."

He grabbed a leash from the cupboard and hooked it onto her collar, then held it a few inches from her neck as he led her to the jail door with the concrete walls behind. He unlocked the barred door then opened it with a metallic creak. He stepped inside, drawing her behind him.

She glanced first to the cot, which was empty. She'd expected to find Zeke lying on it, but she glanced around the large space and saw him against the wall, with a studded leather collar around his neck and thick leather straps around his wrists, attached to hooks on the wall with thick chains, holding his muscular arms above his head. They hung from the chains, his elbows bent. All he wore, besides the wrist straps, were black leather briefs. The rest of his fine body was totally naked.

Her gaze glided over his broad, sculpted chest, with the sexy dragon across one side, down his stomach, then over the zipper that ran down the front of the leather briefs.

"Zeke wanted to leave because he believes you are going to choose between the two of us," Ty said.

Her gaze darted to Ty. Of course she'd have to choose between them, but she was hoping to wait until after the weekend. The truth was, she had no idea which one she would pick. Both men had told her they loved her. And she loved both men. Zeke was extremely sexy and had attracted her right from the beginning because of his overpowering masculine aura. Ty had come off as a Mr.-Nice-Guy type, but after being dominated by him, she knew that was just a façade. Now, his authoritative manner sent her insides quivering. That, added to the deep connection they'd developed as friends, made a powerful combination.

Maybe that meant that she should pick Ty. Her gaze fell on Zeke's semi-naked form. But she wanted Zeke, too.

Ty led Marie to the bed, then attached the leash handle to a hook on the wall, essentially tying her to the bed like a pet.

Ty strolled over to Zeke. "Zeke believes you'll pick me, but I'm not so sure about that." He ran his hand along the tattoo on Zeke's arm, then over his shoulder and down his chest.

Heat streamed through Marie at the sight of Ty caressing Zeke's naked flesh. Ty's hand rested below the dragon, his fingertips lightly brushing against Zeke's tight nipple.

"This tattoo is pretty sexy. Does it turn you on?" Ty glanced at Marie expectantly.

"Yes, Master."

"Show me."

She stroked her breasts, then dragged her fingertips over her hard nipples. Ty smiled.

"Very good. You're turning Zeke on." Ty's hand stroked over Zeke's tight abs. "Push your fingers inside your panties and stroke."

She slid one hand down her stomach, then under the leather, while she squeezed her nipple with her fingers. She stroked over her bare folds, then along her slick slit.

"I'm sure Zeke is finding this leather quite confining right about now. Maybe I should help him out." Ty pulled the zipper down and the leather parted.

Zeke's big cock pushed out of its restraint. Tall and proud. Marie licked her lips. Then Ty wrapped his fingers around Zeke. Marie sucked in a breath, her fingers gliding over her sex more rapidly. Oh God, it was totally erotic watching Ty touch Zeke. He stroked up and down with one hand as his other hand stroked over Zeke's chest. Ty's fingers toyed with Zeke's nipple as he continued to stroke Zeke's erection.

"Is your pussy wet, Marie?" Ty asked.

"Oh yes, Master."

"Take off your panties. Let us see it."

She grabbed the sides of the leather-and-chain garment and wiggled out of it, then dropped it to the floor. She pushed herself back on the cot, until she leaned against the wall, her knees pulled against her, then she dropped them wide, exposing her opening to their gazes. Both men stared at her. Or rather, her fingers as she pushed them in and out of her opening.

Ty squeezed Zeke's cock, then released it and walked toward Marie. He unfastened the leash from the end of the bed.

"Kneel on the floor."

"Yes, Master."

She knelt on the smooth concrete floor. Ty tugged on the leash and she followed him, on her knees, across the room, then stopped in front of Zeke. Ty held the leash close to her collar and led her forward until her knees brushed against Zeke's feet.

"Now take him in your hands and stroke him."

Zeke's cock spiked forward only inches from her face. She reached for his big shaft and wrapped her hands around it. Hot and hard. She stroked, loving the feel of his intimate skin, kid-leather soft, in her hands.

"Suck it," Ty commanded.

She wrapped her lips around Zeke's cockhead, then glided forward, sucking him into her mouth. Ty wrapped his hands around her hair, then coiled it around his fingers. He guided her face back, then forward, then back again, setting her into a steady motion. Zeke groaned as she sucked and licked.

"Pull down his briefs," Ty commanded.

As she bobbed forward and back on Zeke's cock, she drew down the leather, dropping it to his ankles. Ty's free hand tucked under Zeke's crotch to cup his balls. Marie covered Ty's hand, enjoying touching Ty while he touched Zeke in such an intimate manner.

Zeke stiffened, his balls pulling tighter.

"Stop." Ty's hold on Marie's hair stopped her from continuing her forward stroke on Zeke's cock. Ty drew her head away and Zeke's cock popped from her mouth and bounced.

Ty drew Marie to her feet, then dragged her against his

chest. His tongue drove into her mouth with a vengeance. "God, you're sexy."

He led her across the room and sat on the small bed, then released his cock.

"Do you want to suck my cock, Marie?"

She stared at his huge cock standing straight up.

"Yes, Master."

"Do it. Now." His voice sounded almost desperate with need.

She dropped to her knees in front of him, careful to position herself so Zeke could watch her, and wrapped her hands around Ty's gigantic cock. She stroked several times, then pressed her lips to the tip of his cock. She licked it then dragged her tongue around the bottom of the corona. He stroked her hair as she wrapped her lips around him and swallowed his big cockhead. She sucked and licked, spurred on by his increasingly rapid breathing.

She dove down, squeezing him inside her mouth. When she rose again, she released his cock and glided down the front of the shaft, then licked his clean-shaven balls. She nibbled with her lips, then took one into her mouth, then the other, as she wrapped both hands around his huge shaft and stroked.

"Damn, you are so fucking hot." He groaned, pulling himself from her mouth. "Enough. I've had enough of you for now."

He turned to Zeke. The poor man hung on the wall, his cock hard and twitching.

"Attend to my other slave, Marie, but you're not to fuck him," said Ty.

She grinned, then stood up and strolled toward Zeke.

First, she ran her hands across Zeke's broad chest, then licked his nipple.

"Please let me fuck her," Zeke begged, clearly in pain. "I'll do anything."

"Shhh." Ty pressed a finger to Zeke's lips, then knelt down and grabbed Zeke's erect cock. Ty crouched lower and . . .

Oh God, Marie's insides quivered as she watched Ty take Zeke's cockhead in his mouth. Fascinated, Marie watched as Zeke's shaft disappeared into Ty's mouth. Within seconds, Ty's head bobbed up and down on Zeke. Zeke's head fell back against the wall and he groaned. Marie stroked Ty's moving cheek, then ran her fingers along Zeke's tight balls.

Ty released Zeke's cock and stepped back.

"Fuck him."

She wrapped her hand around Zeke's slick cock and moved closer, pressing his cockhead to her opening. She pressed forward. Zeke's cock glided into her. She rested her hands flat against the cold wall on either side of his body and pivoted her hips forward and back, driving him in and out. She squeezed and he groaned. Her breasts pressed against his chest with every inward thrust.

Pleasure rose within her, her body still quivering from her last orgasm. Zeke stiffened and groaned. She felt hot liquid pulse into her, which triggered another orgasm. She kept pumping his cock into her, squeezing him, feeling her pleasure rise even more. Ty reached between their bodies and found her clit, then tweaked. Intense pleasure exploded through her. Finally, she collapsed against Zeke. Ty leaned against her back, cocooning her between the two men.

A heavenly place to be.

Finally, Ty drew away, then snapped a clip onto one of

Marie's wristbands and attached it to one of the links of the chain attaching Zeke to the wall, then he attached her other wrist to the other chain. Marie stood facing Zeke, his cock still inside her, chained to him.

"I'll be back to check on you two in a little while," Ty said.

Twenty-six

Marie heard the jail door clang closed and glanced around to see Ty walking away from the door on the other side of the bars.

She stared up at Zeke. "I guess we're stuck here."

He pivoted his pelvis forward. His cock, which had been deflating, had cranked up a notch. "I'm not complaining."

Her breasts pressed tight against his chest. He drew his hips back, then pushed forward again. His movement caused the chains on her top to press against her skin, and roll . . . over her nipples. They hardened into nubs again. Zeke continued to push in . . . and out. It wasn't a serious thrusting. Just an extremely pleasant gliding.

She smiled and nuzzled his collarbone, then rested her head against his chest, his dragon staring her in the eye. She closed her eyes and snuggled. His cock continued to glide inside her. She squeezed him, knowing if this went on long enough, she would orgasm again. But for now, she enjoyed the gentle glow of being so close and intimate.

He kept moving inside her. Slow and gentle. She squeezed him, moving with him. Feeling the mellow pleasure building. He lowered his head to hers and nuzzled her hair. She tipped her chin up and he captured her lips. She felt so close to him.

"Zeke, what Ty said about me choosing him over you . . ." She gazed up at him. "It's not true."

"Really?"

Ty's voice caught her off guard. She heard the barred door creak open. Seconds later, she felt Ty's presence behind her.

"So does that mean you've decided to choose Zeke over me?" Ty asked.

"I didn't say that."

His hands slid around her body and cupped her breasts.

"So I still have a chance."

Ty caressed her nipples, then pressed the chains against them and stroked the metal over her hard nubs. She whimpered at the intense sensation.

He pressed his hot naked body close to her back, his hard cock pressing between her buttocks and along her lower back. He eased back and pressed forward, essentially pushing Zeke's cock into her. He pivoted his hips so his cock glided up and down between her butt cheeks while he pressed her forward and back against Zeke, all the while his fingers stimulating her nipples with the hard steel links. In fact, as he dragged the chain links up and down, they caught against Zeke's nipples, too.

Ty cupped her breasts and stroked, then released her wrists from Zeke's chains. He drew her back and kissed her, then took her hand and led her a few paces along the wall.

"Chain me to the wall." Ty handed her two carabiner

clips, then held his fisted hands in front of her. He wore thick black leather wristbands. And nothing else.

"Yes, Master."

She took the clips and attached them to the rings on the bands. He lifted his arms to within reach of another set of chains attached to the walls. Pushing herself on her tiptoes, she grabbed the end of one of the chains and clipped his wrist to it. Then the other. She stepped back and stared at him.

Now what?

"Unchain Zeke and use him as your slave."

She raised her eyebrows. "So I am the Mistress now?"

"To Zeke. I am still your Master."

"But you're chained up. Helpless to my will."

"Come here and suck my cock."

Without even thinking, she dropped to her knees in front of him and wrapped her fingers around his big cock, then took it in her mouth and sucked on his hard flesh.

His commands were irresistible.

She tightened her hand around the base of his cock, then released him from her mouth and licked down the shaft. He was right. He was her Master no matter what the situation. Cupping his balls, she lifted them, then drew one into her mouth and swirled her tongue over it. She was vulnerable to his authority.

Pumping up and down on his shaft, she kept his cock warm and stimulated while she drew his other ball into her mouth. Of course, he was just as vulnerable to her sub-mission. She licked him and then squeezed, smiling at his moan of pleasure.

"Oh yeah, sweetheart."

As long as she followed his commands, she owned him. She released his balls and sucked his cock into her mouth again and bobbed up and down. He arched his hips forward, his breathing accelerating.

"Stop."

She hesitated, then ignored his command and squeezed, enjoying her small rebellion. He groaned, then sucked in a breath.

"I said, stop!" he commanded through gritted teeth.

This time she stopped, then stood up.

"Unchain Zeke and use him as your slave."

She smiled. "Yes, Master."

Zeke watched as she walked toward him. As soon as she freed his arms, he tugged her against his hard body and kissed her, his tongue undulating inside her mouth.

Finally, he released her. She sucked in air.

"Um . . . you are my slave now."

"Yes, Mistress. What may I do to please you?"

She grinned and glanced toward Ty, chained against the wall.

"Show Ty how much you like my breasts."

"Yes, Mistress."

He knelt in front of her and stroked her breasts. Her nipples pushed forward. His lips brushed against one as his fingertips stroked over the other. She moaned as he licked her nipple, then took it into his hot mouth. When he sucked on her, she moaned. Delightful sensations danced through her.

"Okay, now stand up."

"Yes, Mistress."

She glanced toward Ty. It had been an extreme turn-on watching Ty touch Zeke. And it showed that Ty was coming to terms with his attraction to Zeke. Was Zeke, too? This was a good opportunity to find out.

"I . . . want you to go and touch Ty."

"Yes, Mistress."

He walked toward Ty and Marie expected him to touch Ty's shoulder or something innocuous like that. But he didn't. He stroked his fingertips over Ty's nipples. Lightly over each tight bud. Then he leaned down and took one in his mouth and began to suck. Ty moaned, his eyelids falling closed.

"Are . . . uh . . . are you enjoying that, Zeke?" she asked. Her fingers trailed over her own hard nipples. She certainly was.

He lifted his mouth from Ty's nipple. "Yes, Mistress."

He pushed out his tongue and dragged the tip down Ty's tight abs, then wrapped his hand around Ty's cock and licked the tip. She felt moisture pool between her legs as she watched Zeke licking Ty's huge cockhead. He began to stroke the shaft.

Marie stepped beside him and touched the hard shaft, too, then she leaned in and began to lick the enormous tip at the same time as Zeke. Their tongues touched and Zeke kissed her, then both their mouths returned to Ty's cock, each sucking half his cockhead between their lips.

Marie kissed down the shaft as Zeke covered Ty's big cockhead with his mouth. She licked upward as Zeke sucked. She wrapped her lips around the side of Ty's shaft and glided up and down. Zeke pivoted his mouth from Ty's cockhead and wrapped his lips around Ty's shaft, just as she'd done, then followed her up and down. Caressing Ty's cock with their mouths and tongues.

Then their lips continued past Ty's cockhead and met in a kiss. Ty's cock bounced against her breasts. Zeke drew back and smiled, then grabbed the big cock and pressed it between her breasts. She squeezed her soft mounds of flesh around Ty's shaft and moved up and down, loving the feel of his hard cock between her breasts. Zeke captured the cockhead in his mouth as she moved.

As Zeke sucked Ty's cock, his hand stroked down her belly and slipped between her legs. His fingers slipped over her slick slit, then glided inside her, heightening her arousal. She squeezed his fingers, then drew away.

She glanced around the dungeon to the wooden bench a few feet away. It had two horizontal surfaces, both padded, the lower one about the right height to kneel on while bending over the higher one.

"Unchain Ty and bring him here," she said.

Zeke unchained Ty's arms and led him to the bench. Ty knelt on the lower surface and bent over, his stomach resting on the higher surface as Zeke fastened Ty's wrists to rings on the other side of the bench.

She stood in front of Ty. "Good height." She stepped forward, her slit close to his face. "Now lick me."

Ty pushed out his tongue and dragged it across her slit. She opened her legs wider and he licked again. The tip of his tongue pressed against her clit and he wiggled it, sending glorious sensations thrumming through her.

"Lovely." She sighed as he continued to lick and cajole her clit.

Zeke stepped up behind her and cupped her breasts, stroking her nipples with his thumbs. She leaned against him as pleasure swirled through her at the gentle nudging of Ty's tongue and Zeke's caresses.

But she didn't want to come yet. She wanted to watch the men some more.

"Okay. That's enough."

Ty's tongue slipped away and Zeke released her. She walked around behind Ty and caressed his butt. So tight and muscular.

"Zeke, stand in front of Ty and put your cock in his mouth."

Zeke stepped toward Ty and held out his cock. Ty took it in his mouth. Marie stroked Ty's solid butt cheeks as she watched Zeke's cock disappear in and out of Ty's mouth. *So hot!*

She moved to the side wall and selected a flogger from a number of whips, riding crops, and other punishment devices hanging there. Made of hot pink suede, the lovely flogger had multiple tails, all soft to the touch. She returned to stand behind Ty and she flicked the flogger against his ass in a soft caress. Ty mumbled an encouraging sound as he sucked on Zeke's cock. She dragged the soft tails along his back, then down over his ass, then she flicked again. He arched his back, pushing his ass upward. She flicked a little harder. Then again.

Zeke moaned, his hand stroking through Ty's sandy hair. She flicked the flogger against his ass again, noticing the redness flushing his skin.

She drew back, her gaze locked on his reddening skin. "Oh, I'm hurting him."

"Don't worry. He likes it," Zeke said in a husky voice.

Her gaze flashed to Zeke. "How do you know?"

"Because . . . oh . . . every time you whip him, he sucks harder. Mm . . ." He bit his lower lip. "So, please, keep doing it."

She brushed the suede against Ty's skin, then flicked again. Zeke moaned. She began to flick again and again, a little harder each time. Soon Ty's ass was flushed red and

Zeke groaned in pleasure, then his pelvis twitched forward and he grunted. Coming in Ty's mouth, she was sure.

She ran her hand over Ty's hot ass, then slid it between his legs and cupped his balls. She stroked them as he continued to suck Zeke. Finally, Zeke drew away and sighed deeply.

"God, that was good," Zeke said.

Marie leaned down and wrapped her hand around Ty's hard shaft and stroked. She kissed his hot ass cheeks. Zeke joined her and stroked Ty's other ass cheek.

"Zeke, chain Ty to the wall."

"Yes, Mistress."

Zeke unfastened Ty from the bench and fastened his wrists to the chains on the wall again.

"Now hold his cock." She watched Zeke wrap his hand around Ty's cock. She stepped in front of Ty, her back to him. "Now slide it into me." She leaned forward and felt Zeke part her folds, then press Ty's big member against her slit. She pressed back, taking the giant cock inside her.

"Oh yes." She stood up and leaned against Ty, loving the feel of his solid chest against her back. "Now caress me."

Zeke ran his hands over her breasts as she moved her body to pump Ty's cock inside her, flinging her arm up to hook around Ty's head. Ty nuzzled his cheek against hers as she moved. Pleasure built in her as Ty's big cock thrust into her and Zeke stroked her hard nipples. Ty's cock drove deeper and Zeke stroked down her stomach, then his fingertip glided over her clit. She moaned.

Zeke knelt in front of her, one of his hands still caressing her breast, and she jumped as his tongue lapped across her clit.

"Oh God, yes."

Tumultuous sensations bombarded her and her insides pulsed with need. Ty's cock drove deep and Zeke flicked her sensitive bud. Her fingers raked through Zeke's dark wavy hair as she gasped, then plunged into ecstasy. Her body seemed to contract, then explode into pure joy.

She collapsed against Ty, then sucked in a deep breath.

"You two are incredible." She groaned as Ty continued to plunge in and out of her.

With great effort, she pulled away, Ty's engorged cock slipping from her sex.

"Zeke, go attach your wrist to the chain again," she said.

Obediently, he returned to where he'd been chained before and refastened one of his wrists. Marie followed him and fastened the other, then walked to the shelf beside the floggers and grabbed a bottle of lubricant. She returned to Zeke and slathered a generous amount onto his rising cock. She turned, glanced over her shoulder at him, and winked, knowing what both men expected her to do now.

She returned to Ty and dragged her hand down his hard-muscled chest.

"Will you grant me a request?" she asked Ty.

He nodded. She released his wrists and took his hand, then led him to Zeke.

"Stand in front of Zeke."

He stepped in front of Zeke, facing him.

"The other way around," she said.

He raised an eyebrow, but did as she requested.

She flattened her hand on his chest and pushed him back until his body touched Zeke's, then she lifted his arm and clipped his wrist to the chain holding Zeke's wrist, just as he'd done to her. Then she did the same with his other wrist.

"Good." She walked toward the door. "Now you two have fun. I'll be back later."

Twenty-seven

"Well, that was interesting," Zeke said.

He was extremely conscious of Ty's tight-muscled backside pressing against his cock. If his arms were free, he would be hard-pressed not to wrap them around Ty and hold him close.

He wasn't used to these feelings for another man, but being close to Ty . . . being in an intimate setting with him . . . did something to Zeke. And he liked it. A lot.

He gazed at Ty's muscled back. The eyes of the phoenix tattooed across Ty's back seemed to gaze back at him. He'd love to stroke those bright, colored feathers.

"How far are you willing to go to convince Marie she doesn't have to choose between us?" Zeke asked.

"How far are you willing to go to convince Marie that you and I will be happy in a long-term relationship together?"

"Why do you think it's just Marie I'm trying to convince?"

Ty leaned back a little, his whole body brushing against Zeke.

The clack of heels approached the door and Marie called out, "Yoo-hoo. You two decent in there?"

"We're naked and chained together, but . . . sure, we're decent," Ty answered.

Marie peered through the bars. "Ah, so you are." She opened the door and walked toward them.

Zeke peered past Ty to watch her semi-naked form walk toward them. What she did wear had all the benefits of leaving her totally naked. The chains draping over her breasts did nothing to cover them. The tall, spike-heeled boots accentuated her long, sexy legs . . . and emphasized the fact she was naked from the waist down. His gaze fell to her hairless pussy and his cock swelled harder, pushing against Ty's tight butt.

She stopped a few feet from them and stood with her feet apart and her hands on her hips. "You two look incredibly sexy chained up there together."

She stroked her hands up her sides, then under her breasts and lifted, as if offering them forward. Her thumbs flicked over her nipples, which jutted forward into hard buds. Zeke watched hungrily as one of her hands slid down her belly then slipped between her legs and stroked over the thick folds of skin. He licked his lips as her fingers glided inside, then moved in and out.

"I'm getting hot just thinking of your two hard bodies pressed together like that." She stepped closer.

She arched over Ty's erect cock, capturing it between her thighs. Was it inside her pussy? Zeke didn't think so, but couldn't be sure.

She lifted her breasts and Ty leaned forward and captured

one in his mouth. Zeke leaned sideways, around Ty, and Marie leaned so he could reach her other breast. He dragged the tip of his tongue over her nipple then swirled it around the pebbly aureola . . . then sucked. She moaned.

She drew back and crouched down, then wrapped her fingers around Ty's cock. Zeke watched as she captured Ty's cock in her mouth and took him deep. Zeke's cock pushed forward, jabbing against Ty's back. Marie reached under Ty and grabbed Zeke's cock and drew it forward. It brushed against Ty's balls as she stroked it.

Marie shivered as she stared at the two cocks in front of her. Ty's big cock in one hand and Zeke's pushing forward from under Ty's balls in the other. As if Ty had two cocks. Marie released Ty from her mouth and captured Zeke between her lips, stroking Ty in her hand. After a few moments, she returned to Ty. Back and forth. Licking them. Sucking them.

She drew Ty deep into her mouth, squeezing him, then she released him. She licked Ty's balls, then leaned back and stared up at her two sexy lovers.

"This is totally hot." She stood up. "But I think we all want more."

She kissed Ty, then stepped to his side and kissed Zeke. She reached behind Ty and guided Zeke's hips sideways, until his cock was accessible, then she stepped forward and pressed it to her slit, then slid it inside her slick passage. He groaned as she pivoted forward and back a couple of times, then she stepped back. His hard cock dropped free.

"That should be enough." She took his cock and pushed the tip against Ty's ass.

Would Ty protest? She glided Zeke's slick cock up and down Ty's ass, between his butt cheeks. No protest. She settled it against his opening and pressed a little. Still no protest.

She stepped back and smiled.

"I want to watch Zeke fuck you while I suck your cock."

She gazed at him, waiting. He drew in a deep breath . . . and nodded. She smiled broadly.

"Zeke?" She didn't know if Zeke would do it, but he pressed forward. Then his cock slipped away.

She grabbed it and placed it at Ty's opening again, and held while Zeke pushed forward. Slowly, Ty's opening widened as Zeke's cockhead pushed into him . . . stretching him. Ty groaned as Zeke's entire cockhead disappeared into his ass. Marie watched in fascination, feeling wetness dripping down her thighs.

Zeke pushed forward, slowly, and she watched as Ty's ass swallowed Zeke's entire cock. She dragged herself away and crouched in front of Ty.

Strange new sensations pulsed through Ty as he stood there with Zeke's cock buried deep in his ass. He felt full and . . . totally turned on. His cock had swollen tighter than he'd ever felt it before.

Marie crouched in front of him and took his cockhead in her mouth. He groaned at the insanely intense sensation. Marie's hot mouth on his cock. Zeke's hot cock in his ass.

Marie sucked on his cockhead and he arched toward her, driving his cock deeper into her mouth. She squeezed. He shifted back, pushing Zeke's cock deep into him. He arched forward again.

Marie wrapped her hand around Ty's hips, holding him still, while she drove down on his cock, then began to move up and down, squeezing him in her mouth. Zeke began to arch against him, thrusting into his ass.

The dual sensations—intensely pleasurable—rocketed through him, boiling his blood. Hot. Wet. Hard. Pulsing.

His wrists strained against the restraints as he struggled against the overwhelming need to find release. But he didn't want to. Not yet. It was too incredible. But the blissful sensations exploded through him and he groaned as his cock erupted inside Marie's mouth. Zeke grunted and . . . oh man, he could feel the hot liquid fill his ass.

He groaned again and . . . another climax. God, it had nothing to do with ejaculation. Just intense pleasure gripping his entire body. He gasped and collapsed back against Zeke.

Marie released Ty's cock from her mouth and stood up. She released Ty's wrists, then Zeke's. Overwhelmed by the intense experience he'd just enjoyed, Ty turned to Zeke and grasped his face firmly in his hands . . . then kissed him. Zeke's full lips met his hungrily. Ty's tongue darted forward, meeting Zeke's halfway. They tangled and danced, then Ty drove into Zeke's mouth. Finally, their lips parted and he hugged Zeke tightly to him.

"Maybe I should leave you two alone," Marie said softly.

Ty turned back to her.

"No way." He grabbed her and tugged her into a tight embrace, then slid her between Zeke and him. He hugged Zeke again, this time with Marie between them.

"Now it's time to torment you." Ty stepped back and tossed her over his shoulder and stroked her behind as he walked through the dungeon toward the far corner, then placed her on her feet again.

"Zeke, attach her wrists to the chains." Ty wrapped his

hands around her waist and lifted her feet from the floor. Zeke lifted her arm and she heard a clink. Then he lifted her other arm and . . . clink.

Ty released her waist. Her feet dangled below her, several inches above the floor. Her weight pulled on her wrists, protected by the padded wrist straps. She stared at the two men standing smiling at her. She stretched her toes, trying to reach the floor, but couldn't. She was totally helpless. Excitement tingled through her.

How sexy is this!

Ty and Zeke each grasped one of her legs and drew them apart. Zeke pressed his cock to her opening then glided inside. She gasped at the feel of his hard flesh pushing inside her. His hand tucked under her butt, easing the weight from her wrists.

After a few strokes, he drew out, then Ty pushed inside, his bigger cock stretching her more. After a few strokes, he drew out, too. Ty tugged the chains across her nipples as Zeke entered her again. The two of them continued sharing in this manner while teasing her nipples with the steel links.

Finally, Ty stopped gliding, but did not pull away. Zeke stepped in close beside him and pressed his cock against Ty's. She gazed down in fascination as Zeke pushed against her opening, tight against Ty's shaft. To her amazement, Zeke's cockhead eased into her . . . stretching her . . . then he slid all the way inside. Oh God, she felt incredibly full. The two men began to move in unison, gliding their two cocks forward and back, pushing deep into her, then dragging back along her stretched passage.

She threw her head back and moaned at the intense pleasure. As they pushed forward again, heat washed through her, every nerve ending tingling.

Zeke captured her lips as they drew back and pushed forward again. "Marie, I thought you'd have to choose between us, but . . ."

"We decided," Ty said as they both continued to move inside her, "to prove to you that we can work together and make you happy."

Zeke tucked his hand behind Ty's head and said, "As well as each other." He pulled Ty's lips to his in a kiss.

Marie's insides quivered, in physical pleasure as well as welling emotions at the sight of her two men kissing with such passion.

Waves of pleasure flooded through her. She was so close.

Zeke drew back, easing the tightness in her vagina. He moved behind her and Ty lifted her legs around his hips as Zeke pressed his cockhead against her back opening. His cock slipped into her ass easily. Now the two men thrust into her . . . stroke after stroke . . . driving her pleasure higher.

She gasped and hurtled over the edge, soaring into ecstasy. The cocks continued thrusting . . . filling her . . . then both exploded inside her, catapulting her into a complete state of rapture.

She collapsed, dangling freely from the chains. Both men hugged her, then kissed each other over her shoulder.

Ty lifted her and Zeke released her wrists, then Ty settled her gently on the floor. Both men steadied her as her knees threatened to buckle. They guided her from the cell and all three of them collapsed in a heap on the big bed.

"Marie, we want to stay together, the three of us. We believe we can make it work. We don't want you to choose between us."

She grinned. "That's a good thing, because there's no

way I could." She stroked Ty's cheek and kissed him, then turned to Zeke and kissed him. "And even though it's clear that any of the two of us would make a great couple, we'd always know that we were missing so much by denying the third."

She couldn't believe how lucky she was. Now she had Zeke, *and* Ty.

She sighed, enjoying the heat of their bodies snuggled up beside her. She stroked her finger along Ty's chest, then along Zeke's dragon.

"So, what tattoo should I get?"

Keep reading . . . for a sneak peek of
Opal Carew's next novel

Total Abandon

Coming April 2011 from St. Martin's Griffin

"I can't believe you've gone an entire year without sex. And by choice."

Sandra grimaced at her friend's comment. She tightened her fingers around her champagne flute. Many times this past year she'd regretted telling Aimee about her resolution but, in fact, her confession to Aimee had forged a closer friendship between them. A friendship that had helped her through some tough times. Especially the loneliness.

Aimee held up her glass. "Happy anniversary." She grinned. "A year well behind you."

Sandra clinked her champagne glass against Aimee's, then sipped the bubbly wine. Not that a failed marriage was something to celebrate.

She glanced around Maelstrom's Bar, wondering when Devlin would arrive to join them. He'd called to say he'd be a little late because he'd had to attend an afternoon meeting in Kanata on the outskirts of the city. That meant he had to brave the Ottawa rush hour traffic, driving back downtown to meet them. Once he got here, he'd have some trouble finding parking, too, since the bar was in the Byward Market area.

Sandra pushed her long hair behind her ear as she shifted on the upholstered seat. It was Friday evening and the bar was filling up fast, but she and Aimee had walked here right after work and grabbed one of the cozy curved booths near the window.

"So, you're sticking with your story that your ex wasn't a stinker? Because I'm all ears if you want to diss him. It'll help get it out of your system."

"No, Eric was just the wrong guy for me."

Not that it hadn't hurt to find he no longer loved her. Or really, that he had *never* loved her. They'd dated since high school and only *believed* they'd been in love. But neither of them had wanted the marriage to fail—to admit *they* had failed—so it had taken ten years for them to finally realize that divorce was the only answer. Because they simply weren't happy together.

Aimee pursed her lips. "Okay then. Moving on."

She leaned toward Sandra and her lips turned up in a crooked smile. Sandra could tell Aimee had had a little too much to drink. And Sandra probably had, too. Champagne tended to affect her a little too much.

Aimee sipped her glass, then giggled. "I have an idea. Let's make a list."

She opened her purse and pulled out a pen, then grabbed one of the small square cocktail napkins the waitress had left on the table with the appetizer platter. Aimee wrote down the numeral 1 followed by a period.

"Okay, I want you to think about,"—she giggled—"you know . . . men . . . and what you'd really like."

"What I'd like? I guess I'd like a guy who's really sensitive, with a good sense of humor and . . . well, a sense of adventure."

Aimee pointed at her and winked. "That's what I'm talking about. Adventure." She sipped her drink again, then set down her glass. "Forget that Mr. Sensitive stuff. Think about Mr. Muscle-Bound-Hunk meets Mr. Sexy-Bad-Boy and how he,"—she winked—"or, better yet, *they* could make your dreams come true."

Sandra knew exactly what Aimee was talking about. Sandra had made the mistake of telling Aimee about one of her ultra sexy dreams, which had been a frequent occurrence over the past few months. Fantasies brought to life in steamy erotic detail in the middle of the night, leaving her hot and frustrated in the morning.

"I don't see the point in making a list." Sandra really didn't want her fantasies written out in black and white. That seemed too . . . sordid.

"Ah, come on. If you can dream about them, you can talk about them."

Sandra's cheeks flushed. "I don't think so."

Aimee patted Sandra's hand. "Honey, there's nothing wrong with having fantasies. And it's good to examine them. It'll help you know what really turns you on. Which is good since you're going to start dating again. Look, I'll get us started. You told me about that one where you were captured by pirates and carried off to their ship, so. . . ."

Sandra watched as Aimee wrote *Be held captive* beside the numeral 1.

"Now you," Aimee said, pen poised.

Sandra shrugged. "I don't know. I can't think of anything."

"What about that book you were reading a couple of weeks ago? It had bondage, didn't it?"

"Um . . . Dominance and submission, actually."

Aimee smiled. "You'd like to try that?"

Sandra shrugged again. Aimee nudged her shoulder.

"Come on. Get into the spirit of it. I'm just trying to help."

Sandra took a sip of her champagne and gazed at Aimee's deep blue eyes. She did want to help. Sandra sighed.

"Okay. Well, I'm not sure about the bondage and domination stuff. I'd have to know the guy pretty well."

"Well, yeah." Aimee nibbled on one of the chicken wings, then picked up the pen again. "Okay, let's leave that one a little open."

She wrote down item number two as *Experiment with bondage.*

"What else? Think about some fantasy that has really intrigued you that you know you'll never try, but wish you could." She grinned. "And don't be shy."

One fantasy immediately popped into Sandra's head. She'd caught part of a show on sexual fantasies and she'd been intrigued by one woman's fantasy about being with a stranger. To her surprise, that had turned Sandra on immensely. Which was just crazy, especially since the only man she'd ever been with was her ex-husband, Eric.

"You've got one. I can see it in your eyes. Spill it."

Sandra pursed her lips. "Well . . ."

"If you go, I'll go."

Sandra nodded. "It's . . . well, being with a stranger."

"You mean a one-night stand?"

"No, more like making love with someone and not knowing who it is."

"So, like, some sexy guy is making out with you and you can't see who it is? That's pretty intense."

Aimee wrote *Make love to a sexy stranger while I'm blindfolded* as the third item.

"Now yours," Sandra said.

Aimee wrote the numeral 4 on the napkin, then turned it toward Sandra so she could see.

Sex with two men at the same time (maybe more)

Sandra felt her cheeks heat. "That's some list we have there."

Aimee laughed. "It's only four items. We're not done yet."

"I think I am."

"Okay, then I'll just put some down for your consideration."

Aimee jotted several more items on the napkin as Sandra watched. Finally, she turned it so Sandra could read it.

1. *Be held captive*
2. *Experiment with bondage*
3. *Make love to a sexy stranger while blindfolded*
4. *Sex with two men at the same time (maybe more)*
5. *Be a love slave*
6. *Have a love slave*
7. *Voyeurism*
8. *Exhibitionism*

"Want anything else?"

Sandra nearly jumped at the waitress' voice. She wanted

to snatch the list from Aimee and stuff it in her purse, but the young woman didn't even glance at it.

"Yes. How about a couple of Piña Coladas?" Aimee said.

Sandra smiled and nodded. She loved Piña Coladas.

The waitress picked up the empty bottle from the table and placed it on her round tray, then grabbed the two empty flutes. She disappeared into the crowd.

Sandra picked up a piece of zucchini from the appetizer tray and dipped it in the dressing, then took a bite. The waitress returned a few moments later with their drinks. Sandra took a sip.

It's about time." Aimee looked over Sandra's shoulder.

Sandra glanced around to see Devlin approaching their table. His glittering gaze locked on her as he walked toward them in his usual relaxed gait, a charming half-smile curling his lips.

Although she couldn't see the color of his eyes in this light, she knew they were as blue as the sky at dusk, dusted with golden specks, and surrounded by a midnight blue ring. The raspy shadow across his jaw gave him a definite masculine allure and he'd tied back his medium brown shoulder-length hair, which was typical on a workday. His relaxed casual Friday outfit consisted of worn jeans with a brown tweed blazer over a shirt of varying width stripes in earth tones, ranging from beige to chocolate brown. A narrow stripe of burnt orange in the shirt exactly matched the round-necked T-shirt visible underneath.

Sandra slid further into the booth to make room for him and he sat down beside her.

His gaze fell to the table. "What's this?"

Oh, damn. Sandra tried to grab the cocktail napkin as

he plucked it from the table—the napkin with The List scribbled on it—but he snatched it out of reach and began to read.

His grin broadened to a smile, revealing his strong white teeth. "Well, this is quite the menu."

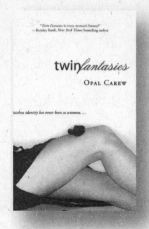

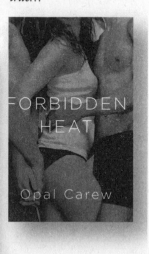